THE DRAGON'S TREASURE

A SEVEN KINGDOMS TALE 1

S.E. SMITH

CONTENTS

Acknowledgments — iv
In the Beginning… — vii
Prologue: The End of the Great Battle — ix

Chapter 1	1
Chapter 2	12
Chapter 3	18
Chapter 4	24
Chapter 5	29
Chapter 6	34
Chapter 7	41
Chapter 8	46
Chapter 9	51
Chapter 10	57
Chapter 11	64
Chapter 12	70
Chapter 13	73
Chapter 14	79
Chapter 15	83
Chapter 16	93
Chapter 17	100
Chapter 18	105
Chapter 19	112
Chapter 20	119
Chapter 21	126
Chapter 22	132
Chapter 23	139
Chapter 24	147
Epilogue	154

The Sea King's Lady	159
Read on for more samples!	183
Alexandru's Kiss	184
Destin's Hold	199
Taking on Tory	216
Additional Books and Information	221
About the Author	227

ACKNOWLEDGMENTS

I would like to thank my husband Steve for believing in me and being proud enough of me to give me the courage to follow my dream. I would also like to give a special thank you to my sister and best friend, Linda, who not only encouraged me to write but who also read the manuscript. Also to my other friends who believe in me: Julie, Debbie, Christel, Sally, Jolanda, Lisa, Laurelle, and Narelle. The girls that keep me going!

—S.E. Smith

Paranormal Romance
The Dragon's Treasure: Seven Kingdoms Tale 1
Copyright © 2017 by S.E. Smith
First E-Book Published July 2017
Cover Design by Melody Simmons

ALL RIGHTS RESERVED: This literary work may not be reproduced or transmitted in any form or by any means, including electronic or photographic reproduction, in whole or in part, without express written permission from the author.

All characters, places, and events in this book are fictitious or have been used fictitiously and are not to be construed as real. Any resemblance to actual persons living or dead, actual events, locales, or organizations are strictly coincidental and not intended by the author.

Summary: A young woman seeking shelter from a storm finds herself in a magical realm where dragons live, leading to a series of events that will affect all of the Seven Kingdoms.

ISBN (paperback) 978-1-944125-11-0
ISBN (createspace paperback) 978-1985580442
ISBN: (eBook) 978-1-944125-09-7

Published in the United States by Montana Publishing.
{1. FIC027030 Fantasy Romance
2. FIC009120 Fantasy Dragons & Mythical Creatures
3. FIC027120 Paranormal Romance
4. FIC002000 Action/Adventure }

www.montanapublishinghouse.com

SYNOPSIS

Internationally acclaimed, New York Times and USA TODAY Bestselling author of Science Fiction, Urban Fantasy, and Paranormal Romance brings another action, adventure, and suspense-filled story to transport readers out of this world.

Choose your treasure carefully, thief...

Drago, King of the Isle of Dragons, is the last of the magnificent dragons of the Seven Kingdoms. Bitter and alone, he abandons the emptiness of his realm and retreats to the caverns beneath the palace. In the form of his dragon, he remains hidden from the world, protecting the Dragon's Heart, the last legacy of his people – until he is disturbed by a most unlikely thief.

Carly Tate's trip to Yachats State Park takes an unexpected turn when she is caught in a sudden storm. Seeking shelter, she stumbles through a magical doorway into a cavern filled with treasure! Yet, as incredible as the piles of glittering gold and jewels are, her gaze is transfixed by the slumbering form of a magnificent dragon.

Carly's appearance begins a series of events that will not only change Drago's life, but will affect all of the Seven Kingdoms. Can a centuries old dragon protect his most valuable treasure, or will the evil that destroyed his race take Carly from him as well?

IN THE BEGINNING...

Long, long ago, peace reigned over the Isles of the Seven Kingdoms. Each kingdom: the Isles of the Dragon, Sea Serpent, Magic, Giants, Elements, Pirates, and Monsters were ruled by seven powerful leaders who watched over their realms. Each ruler was given a gift by the Goddess who created their world; a gift that promised harmony among the kingdoms as long as these gifts were kept safe and not used against each other. The rulers were fair and just, and understood their kingdoms needed each other to flourish.

Alas, the peace was not to last. One night a strange and brilliant light fell from the sky and landed in the ocean. Those who saw the meteor streak through the dark skies made lighthearted wishes. One young sea witch saw the falling star and swam out to sea to catch it. She was unaware that something dark and evil lived within its core – a darkness that would slowly overpower her and threaten the very fabric of the Seven Kingdoms.

PROLOGUE: THE END OF THE GREAT BATTLE

"Return to the isle, I will join you soon," Drago ordered.

"Drago, do you think it safe?" Theron asked, glancing across the waves at the man who had emerged from the inky blackness.

Drago released a growl of warning. His second-in-command tilted his wings and fell back, increasing the distance between them. Five dragons, all members of his elite guard, hovered close by. The three males and two females kept a wary eye on the water below them. Even with a dragon's eyesight, they could see nothing within the growing darkness of the storm clouds around them or through the turbulence of the waves.

"Return now," Drago ordered.

"Yes, my king," Theron reluctantly agreed, rising higher and issuing a sharp order to the other guards.

Drago kept his gaze locked on Orion. The Sea King gazed back at him with the same intense expression on his face. The large sea dragon that Orion rode shook its head, feeling the tension between the two men.

"Orion," Drago growled.

"I come asking for a truce, dragon. You are the last of the kingdoms. The others agreed to peace," Orion stated.

Drago snorted, small puffs of smoke swirled from his nostrils and blew away in the gathering wind, floating toward Orion. The sea dragon jerked in alarm. A smile of satisfaction curved Drago's lips when he saw Orion fight for control of the huge sea dragon. The sharp, angry glare Orion shot him told Drago that the Sea King was well aware that he had frightened the sea dragon on purpose.

"What brings on this sudden desire for peace?" Drago asked in a mocking tone.

Orion's mouth tightened in irritation. "It was all lies," he replied.

"What were lies?" Drago demanded.

"I had no desire for your treasure nor to steal the Dragon's Heart, Drago. The Isle of the Sea Serpent has its own treasures. We do not need the enchanted gold and jewels of the dragons and I know better than to try to steal the gift of the Goddess," Orion said.

Drago snapped his teeth. "You claim that, yet I've captured your men who swear just the opposite. You also blamed the dragons for scorching your fields above the sea. None of my people attacked your kingdom and still they lie at the bottom of the ocean while their mates and children cry in sorrow," he retorted.

"I know, but I swear on the Trident that those who you captured are under a curse of dark magic, forced to do deeds they would never have done otherwise. I also swear that it was not my people who struck the dragons from the sky. They… Drago, they lay as statues, turned to stone by a spell I have never seen before," Orion replied, his voice barely audible above the sound of the wind and waves.

"You swear? Then who did such dark magic? The only ones with such power are those from the Isle of Magic," Drago demanded.

Orion hesitated and looked out over the sea before returning his gaze to Drago. Drago could see the regret in the other king's eyes. He could also see the sincerity.

"Nay, it was not the Isle of Magic, it was my cousin Magna," Orion finally said.

"The Sea Witch?" Drago asked.

"Yes, something has happened to her. I have banished her, but I fear that is not enough. Her magic grows more powerful and must be stopped once and for all. It was her lies and treachery that started the wars between the kingdoms. She cast a spell – there is a darkness within her unlike anything I have ever seen before, Drago. It is unnatural. The more we fight each other, the stronger it grows. The only way to defeat the spell is to work together," Orion said.

"I sensed the darkness in her when she came to me for asylum. I should have killed her then, but instead gave my word to protect her from you when she said you had gone mad. Know this, Orion, if I find her first, all the water in the ocean and her black magic will not save her from the fire of my dragon," Drago swore.

"I hope it will not come to that. Do you accept the truce, Drago? I pledge to do everything I can to bring justice for the hideous deeds Magna has done," Orion said in a solemn tone.

"Yes, Sea King, I have no desire to continue the battle – especially one that fuels the dark magic of the Sea Witch. There has been enough death and destruction. I accept your truce, Sea King, but be warned – the Sea Witch will pay for her treachery if our paths ever cross," Drago said, tilting his wings so the winds could lift him higher.

"I understand. Go in peace, Dragon King," Orion replied.

Drago watched Orion pull on the reins of his sea dragon. The beast eagerly turned and dipped its head. Within seconds, all that was visible was the turbulent sea. Lightning flashed, cutting across the sky, followed by the rolling sound of thunder.

Turning, Drago thought about what Orion had said – a truce, the end of the Great Battle. Peace had finally come to the Seven Kingdoms again, but not before there had been great suffering caused by one woman's greed for power. Rage burned deep inside Drago. He had meant what he'd said to Orion – he would show no mercy to the Sea Witch.

As king of the Isle of the Dragon and ruler over all dragons, it was his duty to keep his people safe. When the Sea Witch had washed up on the shores of the Isle of the Dragon, he had believed her lies. Her body had been shrunken and pale. She had sworn to him that her cousin had gone mad. Her claims that Orion wanted to steal the dragon's hoard of treasure to finance his bid to take over the Isle of the Dragons had sounded foolish until raiders from the sea were captured. They had all said the same thing.

Next, had come the attacks against the dragons flying to other kingdoms. Many had disappeared, having fallen to their deaths into the deep abyss beneath the ocean that separated each kingdom, including his own parents. The Sea Witch, Magna, had whispered into Drago's ear that it wouldn't have happened if only he had the stones of the Trident. If he did, then not only would he control those beneath the waves, he would also have a treasure of unimaginable power.

Drago understood the dangers of controlling an artifact that was not from his realm – to do so could tear the delicate threads of magic holding the Seven Kingdoms together. There was a reason why dragons could not control the trident, just as there was a reason that the people of the sea could not steal the Dragon's Heart. The sacred stones controlled the very essence of each species – water and fire. Each kingdom had an ancient artifact.

His father had groomed him to always take into consideration the far-reaching consequences of his decisions. What good was it to have such a powerful treasure if the world no longer existed? Magna's quiet whispers finally became too much and he had threatened to drop her back into the sea and let Orion deal with her if she did not stop. She had disappeared the next day.

With a loud sigh, Drago soared along the water as fast as his wings could carry him. His body rose and fell with the building waves. Storm clouds swirled high above, and the rumble of thunder and the static feel of the electricity building in the atmosphere warned of the severe gale about to strike.

Drago and his guards had been conducting one last patrol of the waters surrounding the island before the storm hit when he had seen Orion. A quick scan of the sky warned him that the squall was likely to turn into a full-fledged cyclone. As if to confirm his thoughts, icy spears of driving rain began to fall in thick, blinding sheets.

Drago was several kilometers away when he heard the first cry for help from his people. Confusion swept through him when more and more cries of terror rang out. Fighting against the savage winds, an uncharacteristic fear drove him onward, pushing him at a reckless pace to reach his home. The fear wasn't for himself, but for his people.

The anguished cries of his people resonated inside his head. His confusion grew when the sounds of their piercing screams suddenly began to fade.

Drago's blood boiled inside him. He snapped his tail like a whip, shattering the sound barrier with its speed, and the crack echoed through the air like lightning. He had been betrayed – but, not by Orion. Something else was attacking his people – something alien to their world.

The cries of the other dragons pierced his soul, making his struggle to reach them seem painfully ineffective. As each voice grew silent, a sense of panic began to wash over him. When there was nothing but a black void where his connection to the other dragons had once been, the panic engulfed him completely.

"No!" Drago roared out, spying the Isle of the Dragon through the rain.

In the distance, he could see a figure on the rocky cliff turning to look at him in triumph – the Sea Witch! Her black hair swirled around her pale form. Dark threads of sorcery radiated outward from her fingers. Drago saw Theron and two other members of his elite guard flying toward her. The dark threads pierced them. Drago watched in disbelief as their bodies stiffened, turning to stone. As if in slow motion, each dragon fell from the sky. Two of the dragons tumbled into the sea and disappeared beneath the waves. Theron's form crashed to the ground, tumbling over before coming to a standstill – the fire from his dragon frozen for eternity just centimeters from the Sea Witch.

"They are gone, Drago. You are all alone. Give me the Dragon's Heart and I will give you back your weak, pathetic people," the Sea Witch whispered, her words carried to him on the wind by magic.

"Never! Die, Witch!" Drago roared.

"I will have it when you are gone. A dragon cannot survive alone for long. Not even your precious treasure will keep you alive," she retorted with a mocking smile.

Infuriated, Drago released a powerful ball of white dragon fire. The Sea Witch's mad laughter rose above the sound of the storm as she dove from the cliff into the waves below, disappearing into the dark depths surrounding the island. The dragon fire exploded against the cliff, sending an avalanche of super-heated rock into the sea below and scorching Theron's frozen form.

Drago scanned the edges of the cliffs. The still figures of his people stared back at him. Their faces forever etched in expressions of horror. All Drago could see was his failure to protect them.

He glided over the edge of the cliff. His powerful wings folded and he dropped down next to Theron and shifted to his two-legged form. He raised a trembling hand to touch his friend and comrade. Grief unlike anything he had ever known surged through him, encasing his heart as if in the same stone that had transformed his people. Tilting his head back, Drago released a roar of rage that spread across the Seven Kingdoms. Each ruler sensed the void and knew that while the Great Battle between them was over, a far deadlier war was about to begin. Fear reached out, wrapping its greedy hands around the hearts and souls of the other inhabitants, then the world stilled when the sound of Drago's roar faded to a deafening silence.

∽

Several days later, Drago stepped back to survey his work. He had all of his people that he could find inside their homes to protect them from the elements. Those that lived and worked in the castle, he had moved to inside the great hall.

He turned his gaze to the figure nearest him. Theron stared back at him. He raised his hand and ran it over the black streak along the side of the dragon's neck in remorse.

He paused and closed his eyes as the familiar, agonizing shaft of pain ripped through him again. For a moment, he wished it was powerful enough to strike him dead. The pain, emptiness, and feelings of helplessness and remorse were almost more than he could endure.

All of his attempts to locate the Sea Witch through magic had been fruitless. It was as if she no longer existed. Without knowing how she was able to transform his people to stone, there was no way of reversing it. There was nothing else that could be done. Not even the Dragon's Heart had the power to break such a spell – he knew because he had tried to use it. Drawing in a deep breath, he opened his eyes and stiffened his shoulders in determination. One day, the Sea Witch would resurface and when she did, he would be ready. Until then, he would protect those that could not protect themselves.

Drago turned and walked through the doorway of the great hall, shutting the massive doors behind him. He uttered a spell to lock the doors of the room before striding through the double doors leading outside. With a whisper, he cast a spell to enchant the castle. He would do the same for the entire Isle of the Dragon. No one would be able to set foot on the island – not even those of the magical realm. It was a spell no others knew. Those unlucky enough to make their way to the shores would perish, trapped between the high cliffs and the water.

Shifting, he launched himself up into the air. He circled the isle five times, re-enforcing the spell until the mists grew thick and heavy. Only when he was satisfied did he return to the castle. Landing on the top tower, he scanned the isle one last time. This would be the last time he would see it.

Drago blinked and turned his gaze to the ground. Pushing off of the turret, he swept downward. A moment before he impacted with the hard surface of the courtyard, the ground opened and he disappeared inside. The chasm was nearly thirty meters deep and as he shot through, the opening sealed behind him. He curved his body, swooping down the elaborate stone staircases and through the arched doorways to the massive cavern below. In the deepest chamber, he swept over the sea of treasure until he landed on a mountain of gold coins and jewels. His body slid down the avalanche of treasure to where a large platform towered.

Drago stepped up the stairs to the top. With a swipe of his tail, he brushed off the coins and jewels that had fallen onto the stone platform before turning in a circle and lying down. His gaze swept over the immense wealth of the dragons. In the distance, he could see the replicas of his father and mother. They had been the first to disappear, shortly before the Great Battle had begun. They had traveled to the Isle of the Monsters to see Nali. Their loss had hit him and the other dragons hard.

"I let you down, Father, but I will not give up," Drago vowed, gazing at the statue of his sire. "I have nothing left to protect but the Dragon's Heart that you hold. I will guard it until the very end."

Drago lowered his head, closed his eyes in grief, and as the silence grew, began the task of guarding the treasure of his people. Soon, hours passed into days, and days passed into weeks. The weeks blended into years, and the years faded into the chasm of emptiness that grew inside Drago. He eventually grew tired, sleeping more as his loneliness and the magic he needed to use to keep his body strong began to take its toll on him. He briefly woke when a slight disturbance shook the isle. The ground trembled beneath him, but he did not sense another's presence and he soon fell back to sleep.

The Dragon's Heart glowed brightly, shimmering as if the Goddess was aware that the last of the dragons was in danger of perishing. Drago was unaware of the huge blood-red diamond rising from its resting place between the claws of his father's statue. Lost in the realm of his dreams, he slept as a nearby passage slowly opened to another world.

CHAPTER 1

Carly Tate hummed to the music playing on the radio as she slowed to a stop at the front entrance to Yachats State Park. Today was the day! She was taking control of her life. In reality, today was actually the third day of 'Today was the Day'. She was going to start exercising, lose some weight, focus on getting a better job, and perhaps even think about moving out of Yachats, Oregon. Heck, she might even consider moving to Portland or Seattle.

"One baby step at a time," she said out loud, repeating her new mantra.

She just needed to concentrate on staying focused, which was not something that she was especially good at. Luckily, her roommate and best friend, since forever, loved her just the way she was – most of the time. Poor Jenny had the best shoulders to cry on, and only went a little nuts when Carly went to pieces after she chose to date the wrong kind of guys – like Ross Galloway.

"How many?" the ranger asked in a slightly bored tone.

"Just me," Carly replied, handing him her state park pass.

"Be careful along the trails; it looks like we have a storm coming. Park closes at sunset. Please park in designated areas only and don't feed any wildlife," the ranger said, handing back her pass, along with a map, and the parking pass for her car dash.

"Thank you," Carly responded.

She decided it was probably best not to tell the ranger that they had had this same conversation the last three days in a row. This would make her fourth trip in as many days. She now had a nice stack of maps littering her passenger seat.

Accelerating, she followed the winding road. The same old feelings started to choke her the farther she drove. She reached over and turned up the music just as she had done for the last three days, hoping it would kick her adrenaline into gear and not her imagination.

Tall redwoods and other evergreens lined the narrow, winding road. Green moss grew on the rocks, making them slippery, and lush ferns rose up past her hips. Carly knew exactly how slippery the moss was and how high the ferns were because yesterday when she'd reached the top of the path, she had stepped up on a rock for a "Rocky movie moment" and had promptly – and very inelegantly – landed on her ass in the middle of some ferns.

Carly was not a graceful athlete. In fact, just using the word athlete and her name in the same sentence was enough to qualify to go on the Comedy Central Standup Comedian circuit. She had decided the day before that she had a better chance of becoming a mega-star comedian than she did losing the weight she wanted and hiking the full length of the trail without killing herself in the process. Still, she had sworn to Jenny – her very athletic best friend – that she was going to do this even if it killed her.

"Unfortunately, it just might," Carly muttered when she shifted in the driver's seat of her dark red Ford Focus and felt the bruises and protesting muscles from her fall the day before.

She was still muttering under her breath when she pulled into the parking spot near the entrance to a hiking trail and turned off the ignition. She hadn't tried this trail yet. Picking up one of the maps from the pile, she glanced at it and wrinkled her nose before releasing a low groan.

"Four miles," she moaned, leaning her forehead against the steering wheel. "You can do this, Carly. It's only four miles. It will be a walk in the park." A snort escaped her at the pun. "Okay, you do this and you can treat yourself to a small ice cream at the Dairy Queen on the way home, how's that for a reward?"

Leaning back in the seat, she bent over and picked up the small backpack from the floorboard and shoved the map inside. Opening the door, she slid out with another loud groan before glancing around to make sure no one else could see or hear her. She turned, slammed the door shut, and pocketed her car keys.

"Ice cream. Remember the ice cream," she mumbled under her breath as she forced her aching muscles into motion.

She stepped onto the trail and pulled the denim and leather backpack onto her shoulders. Gripping the straps, she started down the uneven path. "Ice cream…" she muttered with each of the first two hundred and seventy-one steps before she started focusing on other more important things – like hungry bears, mountain lions, and Big Foot.

∽

Nearly two and a half miles later and barely half way into her hike, Carly was in a foul temper. She had fallen – again – when the large iced coffee she'd drunk earlier flooded her bladder and made stopping for a pit stop an urgent priority. Since there were no restrooms along the trail, she had been forced to find a bush to water.

Of course, there was no flat ground to be found. The only options available were a rock wall to climb up or a steep slope to climb down. Her protesting muscles and lack of coordination, plus the fact there was nothing to hide behind if she climbed up, meant she was left with no alternative but to navigate the steep drop off. She had made it but not without a few slips and slides. The seat of her jeans and her knees were covered in damp, cold mud which added to the misery of her aching body.

Fortunately, she had discovered a small stream of water coming out of the rocks a little further up the trail to clean up a little. The icy water had given her an opportunity to wash the dirt off of her hands and refresh herself. Of course, now her fingers were frozen.

Think positive, Carly. At least you're not still completely filthy, she thought ruefully as she continued to trudge up the trail.

Carly couldn't help but think that if all of her earlier misadventures hadn't been enough to convince her that she should have just gone to the gym, the unpredictable Oregon weather should have been the final decision maker. The dropping temperature and the rolling, thick clouds told her that she was an idiot for being a miser and letting her embarrassment get the best of her. Those two concerns had kept her from going to the local gym – money and Ross – and not necessarily in that order.

She had been reluctant to purchase the annual membership until she knew she was going to stick with her exercise plan. She had bought the membership once a couple of years ago – and never went. Of course, she was older and more mature now which should have meant she was more disciplined – only Carly knew herself well enough when it came to exercise to know that she wasn't. If she had thought more about it, she should have just purchased the monthly contract, but it would have cost her five dollars more each month, which in a year would have been a whopping sixty dollars more than the yearly membership.

The real reason she didn't go to the gym, though, was because of her reluctance to run into Ross Galloway. Ross put the bad in 'bad boy'. Jenny had warned her, but Carly had been all goo-goo eyed when Ross had shown up in his faded jeans, ratty t-shirt, black leather jacket, and his devil-may-care attitude down at the local bar near the waterfront. She really knew better than to date a guy she met at the bar. She had known better than to date Ross Galloway – hell, he had been bad in high school! Still, she had been feeling pretty mellow after her first beer when he had asked her out – not something that happened all that often. He also went to the gym – the only one in town.

By the fourth date, Carly had realized her mistake and called Jenny to come pick her up. Granted, it hadn't all been Ross's fault. She hadn't meant to release the fishing net on his boat. It had been an accident. Also, he had been the one who had wanted a smoke! It wasn't like she had dropped the match on purpose. You'd think if the guy owned a boat, he'd know if there were flammable items on board.

Carly looked up when a fat raindrop landed on her cheek. Almost in tears, she focused on the trail in front of her when another drop hit her on the end of her nose. Lightning flashed across the sky, followed by an earth-shaking roll of thunder.

"Really? You think I'm enjoying this so much you wanted to add to the fun? You could have waited, you know. I'm almost half way back. Just another hour… or two," Carly argued with the sky. She was rewarded with three more large drops and a heavy mist approaching at a rapid clip. "Great! Thank you so very much… not! I hope you are having fun because I have to tell you that this really sucks big time. I HATE EXERCISING!"

Of course, arguing with the sky wasn't something most sane people did, but it made Carly feel a little bit better. She cringed when a bolt of lightning struck close enough that she thought her hair was standing on end. Okay, maybe the sky gods were listening and they were not entertained by her yelling at them.

Picking up speed, Carly tried to half walk, half jog along the uneven trail. She smothered a cry when another bolt of lightning struck. Didn't the weather know that it was just supposed to rain, not have a full-fledged electrical storm? She should have checked the weather forecast before she got out of her car.

"Shouldn't the ranger have insisted that no one go hiking? He frigging knew there was a storm coming. Isn't it his duty to help protect idiots like me from themselves?" Carly cursed under her breath.

She jolted to a stop when a small group of rocks tumbled onto the trail ahead of her. Then the rain started coming down in thicker sheets, drenching her. She pulled the hood of her jacket up over her head, cursing again when it caught on her backpack. She needed to find a safe place to weather the storm. A loud cracking sound made her look up. Her eyes widened in horror when she saw a leaning tree sway dangerously toward her. Small rocks rained down around her, hitting her shoulders.

Carly jumped closer to the rock face and was surprised when she noticed a dark crevice running vertically from the ground to almost a half meter over her head that appeared to be a very narrow entrance to a cave. Perhaps her luck was changing. It might not be the local hotel, but it was better than getting struck by lightning or crushed by falling trees and rocks.

Carly squeezed into the narrow crack in the rock face and released a frustrated groan. Why couldn't the stupid opening be just a few centimeters wider? It wasn't until she was halfway in the crevice that the sudden image of horrible, scary bugs flared in her mind. She really hoped there weren't any spiders, snakes, or other creepy crawly things in the dark recesses.

A flash of lightning and the crackle in the air had her frantically sucking in her stomach so she could slip inside. Of course, she became stuck. Wiggling back and forth, she added a few loud curses to go with the new bruises she was adding to her collection before she popped through the opening into inky blackness.

She turned and grabbed a branch just outside the opening; then wildly waved the damp branch around, hoping against hope that it was enough to chase off any of the nasty gremlins and their sticky webs that might be lurking near the entrance. The rain picked up even more, pouring down the side of the mountain until the entrance looked more like the back of a waterfall. Carly hiccupped in the dark.

"This is why I hate to exercise," she groaned with a shiver.

Turning away from the wall of water, she absently waved the branch with her left hand while she reached for her cell phone with her right. She tried sliding it to unlock the screen and cursed loudly when it didn't work. She slid the thin branch between her dirty, jean-clad knees and used her right index finger to open the flashlight option on her cell phone. Slowly shining the light along the walls and floor, she looked around the narrow cave.

"I told Jenny this would be the death of me. Archaeologists are going to find my mummified body a thousand years from now and say 'Yep, this is a perfect example of Darwin in action'," she muttered in her best 'learned scientist' voice. She stared at the walls with growing dread, certain that she could see them moving with all kinds of deadly bugs determined to suck her dry. "Forget being mummified. I'm going to be picked clean to the bone!" She took a breath, then her lips quirked up. "I guess that is one way to lose some weight."

Jenny Ackerly, her best friend and roommate, had laughed earlier this morning when Carly had dramatically foretold her own death by exercise. Well, Jenny wouldn't be laughing when Carly went missing.

Carly vowed she would come back from the dead just to point out to Jenny that hiking was not for everyone. Of course, she would also have to admit that Jenny was right. After all, Jenny had been the one to point out that Carly sucked at exercising and would be better off – and much safer – to just buy the gym membership.

"Okay, it wasn't really a hike, so much as a stroll, but it still counts," Carly told the dark walls in defiance. "The state should have put up better signs and they need to hire rangers who tell you that you're stupid if you ignore them when they say a storm is coming."

Carly tilted her head when she thought she caught a glimpse of light coming from the back of the cave. Her mind swept through all the possibilities. What if there was a serial killer waiting for her, or a vampire, or a… she slammed the door shut on her wild, out of control imagination when the sudden vision of the walking dead appeared in her mind. Drawing in a shaky breath, she swore she would never attend Horror Night at the local college ever again.

"Or horror movies," Carly whispered, her hand beginning to shake. "No more Saturday night horror movie marathons. God! Why did I have to go on an alien binge this last weekend?"

Swallowing, Carly felt herself drawn to the warmth and light coming from the back of the cave like a bug to a bug zapper. Unable to resist, she stepped closer on trembling legs. The walls and floor of the cave were smoothing out the farther she walked.

Turning the corner, she stopped in surprise when she saw the light was coming from a glowing torch in a sconce attached to the wall. Further down the passage, she saw an arched doorway. It reminded her of old castles, like the one out of the Dracula movie she had watched the night before.

"Carly, you really, really need to get a better taste in movies!" she growled to herself in annoyance. "Romantic comedies are good. Animated cartoons are even better."

She released a long breath and glanced down at the phone in her hand. She didn't need the flashlight anymore. Swiping her finger across the screen, she turned it off. There was no sense in wasting the power on her phone now that she had the light of the torch. Plus, she needed to conserve the power so she could call the ranger and admit that she needed help – a lot of it.

Fascinated by the beauty of the elaborately carved stone that formed the walls and floor, she soon became lost in the twists and turns as she followed the passageway. A magnificently carved entrance held her spellbound. The pillars were carved into the shape of dragons.

"Oh, oh, oh! I love dragons!" Carly breathed, hurrying forward to run her hands over the beautiful sculptures.

Her mind swirled in awe. If there had been any way she could slip the huge dragons into her backpack, she would have done it in a heartbeat. Her bedroom was covered in dragon figurines and medieval castles. Carly lovingly ran her hands over the rough stone belly of one of the dragons.

"Wow! This is just… Wow! Who would have thought to put something like this here? I've never seen this part of the park before, that's for sure!" she breathed out in excitement.

Turning her head, she gazed through the entrance, expecting an amusement ride attendant to be greeting her. Since when did the state parks get into the theme park business? Hell, how could they have built this without her knowing anything about it? She worked at the bank, for crying out loud. If anything happened in town, the first place to learn about it was at Barb's Hair-n-Care; the second place was at the walk-in clinic; and the third was at Bank of the West where she worked. All gossip went through those three venues.

Carly's hand flew to her mouth to hide her gasp when she stepped through a curved archway into the massive chamber. Rivers and mountains of gold and jewels glimmered in the faint light. She didn't know if they were real or not. They looked like it, but she wasn't an expert.

Despite the beauty of the glittering treasure, the gold wasn't what caught and held her attention. No, her attention was caught by the truly magnificent form half buried at the bottom of the mountain of gold and jewels.

The statue of a brilliant, midnight black dragon lay curled up in sleep. The unbelievable detail of the creature held her mesmerized. If there was one major thing Carly had a weakness for, it was dragons. She absolutely adored the mythical creatures. She had collected them, painted them, and dreamed of them ever since she could remember. She was so bad about it that Jenny liked to tease her. Jenny often said that the only way she would ever find a man she could love was if he was part dragon. Carly completely agreed.

She swallowed and slowly descended the steps. Her feet slid and she wobbled, trying to keep her balance when the pile of gold shifted. In the back of her mind, she wondered if she was dreaming or had died and gone to her own version of heaven. If so, she was ready to move in.

"It sure beats the hell out of being mummified or gnawed on by bugs like a starving dog at a barbecue," she observed.

Halfway down, she fell. The pile of coins shifted under her and she was pulled down to the bottom of the mountain. Her eyes widened and she leaned back a little to try to keep from tumbling over. Digging in her heels, she braced them against the base of the half buried platform, stopping her descent. Carly lay stunned for a moment, staring up at the dragon curled in peaceful slumber.

He's so beautiful, she thought in awe.

Her eyes glowed with delight as she ran her gaze over the silky scales covering his head. His brow was high, with two large ridges curving around his eyes. Thick, long lashes lay against the smooth, black scales like twin crescent moons. A series of ridges ran down his face to the narrow tip that made up his nose.

He looked… real. She knew it was impossible, but he looked like he was warm and soft. Standing up, she bent forward and climbed up onto the steps. She had to use her hands to help steady herself against the loose debris scattered across the steps. Once she was at the top of the platform, she stood for a second, just staring at the creature in fascination.

Carly rubbed her right hand along her damp jeans before lifting it to run her fingers gently along one of the ridges of his brow. She gasped softly when she felt the warmth of the dragon's scales beneath her touch. Shock coursed through her when the dragon's eyelashes rose to reveal dark, sapphire blue eyes with a glitter of gold sparkling in them. She swayed when she felt more than heard a strangely accented voice whisper.

"Choose your treasure carefully, thief," the soft, honey-rich voice stated.

Her hand fell to her side and she stumbled back a step in shock when the dragon's mouth moved as he spoke. Carly decided she must have died in the storm after all. Her trembling legs refused to support her. She sank down onto the pile of coins. Her lips parted, her gaze lifting to maintain eye contact when the dragon raised his massive head.

Carly fell back when the dragon stretched his neck in her direction. She could feel his warm breath sweep over her. A soft moan escaped her, echoing in the large cavern. The warm air of his breath surrounded her, melting the bone-chilling cold that had encased her body from her rain-dampened clothing.

Carly raised her hand as the dark head drew nearer. She tenderly ran her fingers along one nostril, tracing the outline in gentle exploration. She didn't notice his long, sharp teeth. Her gaze was focused on where her fingers followed the vivid contours of a scale. The warmth of his breath heated her blood with strength and hope instead of fear.

Licking her suddenly dry lips, Carly slowly rose to her feet again. She lifted her head to gaze into the brilliant eyes of the dragon watching her with an intense expression. She didn't think, she just whispered the first words that came to her mind.

"Can I choose you?" she asked in a barely audible voice.

Her eyes fluttered and she shivered when the dragon shimmered. A startled gasp escaped her when his form disappeared and a man stood where the dragon had been. Her foot caught on the edge of the platform and she began to fall. She reached out and was captured in a pair of strong, warm arms.

Carly gaped at the man in shock. A strange darkness began to edge the corners of her vision and her trembling legs suddenly felt overwhelmingly heavy and uncooperative. Her last thought before darkness fogged her vision was that the man who was sweeping her into his arms was just as magnificent as the dragon. A part of her was aware that she was being lifted. Fighting against the darkness, she reached up to touch his chin in concern.

"I'm too heavy," she muttered as her head fell limply against his shoulder. "You'll get a hernia trying to carry me."

Her eyelashes fluttered shut when she felt his body shake with laughter. Maybe dragon men were stronger than the guys she had dated before. A slight smile curved her lips and she snuggled closer to the warmth of his body. Carly released a contented sigh. She decided it was nice to be carried as the heat of his touch lured her deeper into the darkness of unconsciousness.

"Sleep, little one," the deep voice rumbled. "We will speak later."

CHAPTER 2

*D*rago held the sleeping woman in his arms. He gazed down at her with a slightly bemused expression. This was no ordinary thief. He could count on one claw the number of times a thief had made it this far and only then because he had allowed it.

The spells and the maze of staircases that ended in drop offs or dead ends had prevented even the most savvy thief from achieving their quest. How this woman had made it all the way to his hoard tantalized his curiosity. But more than that, she had ignored all the treasure, including the Dragon's Heart which lay near her feet, choosing him above it all. Why had she come for him? What was it about him that had such an effect on her when she did find him?

Her presence had awakened him long before he had let her know that he was aware. After so many years of stillness, her presence had stirred the air and finally roused him from the slumber that had held him in its dark grasp. He had forced his eyes open just a crack to scan the room, irritated by the disturbance. There had only been the great mounds of treasure. Drawing in a deep breath, he had tried to determine what had awakened him. The soft sounds of her footsteps against the stone had echoed through the chamber. His ears had twitched and he had bit back the low growl that threatened to escape him at the intrusion.

He had felt the red hot lava of fury burn in his throat, and he felt it cool when the woman had reached out and caressed him. She wanted *him* as her treasure, and she certainly wasn't acting as if she meant to take him by force.

"Who are you?" he murmured with a frown.

The sound of her sigh and her snuggling closer caused an unexpected wave of emotion to wash through him. He bent and sniffed her hair. She smelled different – not like any of the other species from the Seven Kingdoms that he could remember.

His gaze ran down over her figure. She had a soft, full figure. His eyes twinkled when he saw the mud on the knees of her trousers and shoes. She had been carrying a bag on her back, but it had slipped off her shoulder when she slid down the mound of treasure. He would retrieve it later – after he locked her up so she couldn't escape.

She was now a part of his treasure. She piqued his interest, something that hadn't happened in centuries, even before the devastation to his people. She also made him feel less… empty. He looked forward to the fight they would have when she realized he was derailing whatever her agenda was. Perhaps he would even discover what abilities she had that allowed her to get past the spells, wards, and non-magical traps he had created to make his castle impenetrable and the treasure beneath it safe from all intruders.

Impatient to get her up to his living quarters, Drago shifted without releasing her. He murmured the spell that would open the passage to the surface. The ground groaned in response, as if the Isle was waking from a deep slumber, as well.

Drago glanced up as the first rays of sunlight streamed down, touching him with its warmth. For a moment, he was almost blinded by the bright light. It had been so long since he had felt the sun's warmth against his scales that a shiver of joy ran through him.

"Joy! Will wonders never cease? So many surprises today…" he marveled.

Launching upward, his powerful wings carried him and his precious cargo through the passage. He emerged and soared high above the Isle of the Dragons. His gaze swept over the terrain below him. Pride, sorrow, and regret warred within him. Pride for the magnificent castle, thick forests, and vast beauty of his kingdom. Sorrow came from the emptiness and neglect in a kingdom once thriving with joy and riches. But weighing heaviest on him was his regret that he had been unable to protect his people.

Drago quickly circled the isle to ensure that the spells protecting his kingdom were still strong. Satisfaction coursed through him when he saw nearly half a dozen ships – most from the Isle of Pirates – and the remains of the few who ignored the protective spells that should have warned them away. Not a single ship was intact. Was Carly's ship among the wrecked or had she come another way? He glanced down when the woman in his arms moved. His claws tightened around her when she arched backwards. At first he thought she was trying to escape, but he quickly realized that she was just stretching when her mouth opened wide in a loud yawn.

Once again, he chuckled when she lifted a hand and rubbed her nose. The chuckle grew to a deep, rumbling laugh when she opened her eyes, took one look at him, and released a squeak of surprise. He had to be careful not to squish her in his claws when the squeak turned to a blood-curdling scream after she glanced down.

"Holy shit!" she exclaimed in a trembling voice.

Drago shook his head, his ears still ringing from her scream. "You have a very loud scream for someone so small," he remarked.

"You haven't heard anything yet if you drop me – and thanks," she choked out, clutching her arms around his claws.

"Thanks?" Drago asked with a raised eyebrow.

The woman nodded her head. "For calling me small. I don't think that word and my name have been used in the same sentence since I was about ten," she replied with a rueful expression. "How can you talk? Heck… How can you be real? Am I dead? I didn't really mean it when I told Jenny that exercising was going to kill me."

Drago soared over the tall cliffs, keeping one eye on the ground far below and one on the woman in his arms. He was trying to process all of her questions. It dawned on him that she was the first person he had talked to since the Sea Witch's devastation of his isle.

"What is your name?" he asked with a sudden need to know.

"Carly... Carly Tate. What's yours? Didn't you change into a guy or was I dreaming that as well?" Carly asked.

"Carly... I like that name. I am Drago, King of the Dragons, ruler of the Isle of Dragons," Drago responded.

"King.... Wow.... I'm loving this dream," she grinned.

Drago glanced down at her again when she released his claw and wiggled. He loosened his claws just enough to allow her to move. She rolled over onto her stomach and gazed down at the isle below them.

He was beginning to consider the possibility that she hadn't come here for any devious reason at all, but how could it be that she had arrived here by accident, with no knowledge of where she was or who he was? Was that simply what she wanted him to believe until she stole the Dragon's Heart? Was she an unwitting pawn that someone else had sent? Had he been meant to kill her or keep her? Who was she?

"What makes you think this is a dream?" he asked in a voice that hid his all-consuming curiosity about what she would say next.

She released a sigh and laid her chin on his claw. "It has to be. There are no such things as dragons, not real ones anyway – especially talking, shape-shifting, magical ones. Even if there were, which there aren't, I hardly think they would be living undiscovered in Oregon," she replied.

"I have never heard of the Isle of Oregon before," Drago responded with a frown. "Which kingdom is it closest to?"

"What, Oregon? It's between Washington State and California. I guess there are some islands off of it, but I wouldn't call them kingdoms," she replied, glancing back over her shoulder before looking down again. "Hey, is that a shipwreck?"

"Yes, some fools came too close," he said, tilting his head trying to see her reaction to that statement, but she was turned away from him so he could not see her expression. "The spell I cast created a thick fog to protect the isle. None can penetrate it without striking the rocks," he said grimly.

"You can do magic, too? That's pretty cool. So, is this like hypnosis and illusions and stuff to make me think you're really a dragon and we are flying? I have to tell you, this is the best act ever if it is. Though, how on earth I could have been hiking a frigging death trail in Yachats and then end up in some kind of magic show is beyond me, unless...." Carly looked up at him again with horror in her eyes. "... I'm in a coma and I've recreated all of this from the dragons and stuff in my head. Damn it. I'm probably on the operating table with my brains spilling out everywhere," she groaned, dropping her forehead down to rest on his claw.

Drago's deep laughter echoed through the air. "Where do you come up with these ideas?" he asked in amusement. "Your brains are not spilling out of your head. I can create magic, but I am no illusion and neither are you."

"Well, if I was in a coma with my brains spilling out, I would probably be telling myself that all this is real," she reasoned, lifting her head to scowl at him before turning her attention back to the ground. "Where are we going?"

"If your leaking brains cannot tell you, surely that proves that you are not in this coma," he stated, turning inland.

"Maybe instead of spilling out, they got toasted by lightning and all of this is the result of an electrical shock to some recessive part of my brain," Carly argued. "It was raining and there was lightning. That is a good explanation."

Drago chuckled. "Your brain is not smoking," he assured her.

"I didn't say smoking. I said a shock," she grumpily pointed out.

"If you were struck by lightning, you would be smoking," Drago insisted.

"You are not helping. Are we going to the castle?" Carly asked, pushing up and staring in awe at the magnificent tower that was growing bigger and more defined the closer they flew.

"Yes," Drago replied.

It had been over a decade since Drago had been in the castle. Thick, lush vines grew up the sides of the ivory colored turrets and the outer walls. He would have to cut them back. The cobbled stone streets, traders' carts, and homes for the dragons wishing to live within the castle walls all stood empty. Pain filled Drago. The loneliness of the silenced voices still resonated inside him. He blinked and looked down when he felt something small and warm against his chest, near his heart. The woman had turned in his claws again and was rubbing her hand over his chest, as if she could feel his pain and was trying to soothe it.

"Where are all the other dragons?" she asked in a low, compassionate voice.

"Gone…. All of them gone," Drago replied, blinking away the memories and focusing on the large balcony.

His massive wings rose and fell as he slowed his descent. He landed on the stone balcony, balancing on his hind legs. Bending forward, he reluctantly placed Carly on her feet before he shifted into his two-legged form. She stumbled back, her eyes wide with awe and a touch of confusion before she shook her head at him.

"That is totally awesome, in case you didn't know," she stated before walking by him to gaze down at the city. "This place looks like no one has lived here in years."

"No one has," Drago admitted, stepping up to stand beside her.

Carly turned and looked at him with a bemused expression. "Are you sure I'm not in a coma or dead?" she asked with a crooked, skeptical smile.

Drago returned her gaze. "There is one way to prove it," he murmured.

"How? By pinching me?" she retorted with a roll of her eyes.

Drago's lips curled upward in a wicked grin. "No, by kissing you," he replied, reaching for her and pulling her into his arms.

"Holy shi…."

The rest of her words were cut off when he lowered his head and captured her lips. Drago felt the swift connection between them. He had heard tales of such a thing – a dragon knowing when he had found his mate by the threads of his magic reaching out to wrap around the female. He could feel Carly's threads connecting with his, sealing both of their fates. For the first time in years, Drago felt the warmth of another's touch and he wasn't about to let it disappear.

CHAPTER 3

Carly held still in Drago's arms. Her mind raced in a million different directions before hitting a blank wall and coming to a full stop when he kissed her. Her arms automatically rose to wrap around his neck and her lips parted.

Several things flickered through Carly's brain: first, that this sure felt real; second, that he towered over her and was stronger than any guy she had ever met because he had lifted her off her feet to kiss her; and third, that he tasted really – and she meant really – good.

She whimpered softly when he started to end the kiss. Tangling her hands in his long hair, she kept him from pulling away. She could feel his surprise when she deepened the kiss, teasing his tongue with her own. It wasn't until she felt the shudder run through his body that she relaxed her hold on his hair.

Drawing in a deep breath, Carly gazed into his dark blue eyes. "Okay, I concede. I'm not dreaming, but I'm still not ruling out being dead," she replied with a stubborn pout and a mischievous glint in her eyes.

He returned her gaze. His eyes glittered with an emotion she wasn't sure how to interpret. Then he chuckled again and released her slowly to slide down his body. Her breath caught when she felt his obvious arousal. She now had an answer to the emotion in his eyes – somebody was horny and she was the reason for it.

"Trust me, you are not dead," Drago remarked.

"How can you be sure?" Carly asked.

"You smell of forest, rain, and dirt. Dead things don't smell – or taste – this good," Drago commented before releasing a chuckle when a large flock of birds swept by the balcony and startled Carly. "The birds will not harm you. They feast on the fruit that grows from the vines," Drago murmured when she backed into him.

Carly nodded and grabbed his arm to pull it around her. She wasn't completely convinced that these birds were fruit eaters. They had long, narrow beaks that looked more like spears. She swallowed and watched the birds fly off into the forest. Some of them had a wing span that made her think of the Pterodactyls from the picture books and movies she had seen.

A shiver ran through her body when Drago wrapped his right arm around her waist and pulled her against him. Carly didn't bother trying to contain the grin that lit her face. She was thankful he couldn't see her face, just in case she was misreading his actions. In the back of her mind she knew that she could really get used to this – having a hot sexy man who turned into a dragon, lived in a magical world, and loved full figured women – for the rest of eternity. Hell, who would have thought being dead could be so wonderful?

"This is… incredible," Carly whispered, looking down over the castle far below and out over the mist covered sea.

"This kingdom was once one of the most majestic of all the Seven Kingdoms. Now, I am the only inhabitant that remains," Drago stated.

Carly heard the grief in his voice. Compassion filled her. Something bad must have happened. Something had brought her here for whatever crazy reason. What she couldn't understand was how all of this was possible.

"What happened?" Carly asked.

Drago's arm slid from around her waist. She immediately felt the loss of his heat when he stepped away from her. She watched him walk over to the stone railing. The breeze coming off the ocean blew his hair back, revealing the steely line of his jaw. His fingers curved around the stone and he leaned forward.

"The Sea Witch."

His body shimmered and the powerful dragon was once again in front of her. Carly stumbled back against the double doors behind her when Drago released a terrifying roar and launched into the air. She watched in awe as the mythical creature she had somehow awakened swept down from the castle.

Carly hurried over to the balcony, trying to keep Drago within sight. He released a fine stream of blue flames that burned large sections of the tangled vines from along the castle walls. It had to be close to an hour later before he disappeared into the vast forest.

Swallowing, Carly finally pushed away from the balcony and turned. She walked to the double doors, and paused just outside the doorway, trying to see in. The glass was covered with a thick layer of grime.

She reached for the door handle and slowly turned it. Pushing the door open, Carly discovered a beautiful but very dark and dusty living room on the other side. She turned and pulled the other door open so the brilliant early morning light could stream inside.

"Jumping bullfrogs! I've fallen into a fairy tale!" Carly whispered, turning back to gaze around the room.

∼

Hours later, Drago turned back toward the palace. He had searched every corner of the isle for other intruders. The only things he had found were the long ago bleached white bones of those unfortunate enough to have been shipwrecked along the Isle's treacherous shores. There was nothing else but the animals that made the Isle of the Dragon their home.

"How did she come to be in the treasure room?" he growled out loud.

There were no entrances to the cavern except through the castle. He had checked that first and the door was sealed. The only other way to enter would have required a very powerful magic. The wards he had placed throughout the passageway would have killed even the most skilled thief, and Carly did not strike him as being very skilled.

Drago shook his massive head and snapped at several birds that flew too close. They quickly scattered. Folding his wings, he plunged down into the forest, swerving back and forth through the thick branches and snapping those that got in his way. He grimaced and snarled with impatience when a branch cut a long, thin line across his shoulder.

He broke through the forest just east of the wide road. There was a small, open meadow near the front gates of the castle. With a whisper, the magic sealing the great doors released, the drawbridge lowered and the gates opened. Drago landed with a ground-shaking thump.

He snapped his tail back and forth as he walked forward, gazing around him. In his mind, he could still see the sentinels standing on the platforms above the gates and hear the laughter of the young dragons learning to fly. The streets would have been filled with people going to the markets, entertaining, and visiting with each other.

Instead, the only sound he heard was the noise of his claws against the cobblestone street. He slowly walked along the winding roads until he reached the front steps of the palace. They were covered with a thick coating of dead leaves.

Drago bent his head and breathed a fine line of super-heated flames at the cover. The leaves caught fire. The flames were so intense that they quickly disintegrated. With a swipe of his tail, he scattered the ashes and walked up the staircase, transforming back into his two-legged form as he moved.

The massive doors opened with a wave of his hand. Dragons were not as powerful with their magic as the witches and wizards on the Isle of Magic, but they were still powerful enough to cast protective wards and spells. Drago was the most powerful of the dragons and could create a vast number of spells when needed.

Torches ignited as he climbed the long staircase off the great hall. He grimaced when he saw cobwebs draping the tall statues. It shamed him to think of the years of neglect the castle had seen over the last decade.

Drago didn't understand why he cared if Carly saw his home in such a state of disrepair, but he did. He reached the top of the stairs and strode down the long corridor to the far end where a set of intricately carved wooden doors sealed his private living quarters.

His footsteps slowed as he drew closer. Stopping outside of the doors, Drago raised his hands and gripped the handles to the doors. He paused, trying to think of what he would say. It had been a long time since he'd had a conversation with another person.

"Perhaps I will just kiss her. That does not require talking," he muttered before drawing in a deep breath and pulling the doors open.

Drago stepped through the doors. He frowned when he saw the closed balcony doors and empty living quarters. He started forward, a low rumble escaping him as he glanced around the room. A faint sound caught his attention when he was halfway across the room.

Turning his head, he listened. The faint sound of a feminine voice singing could be heard coming from down the hallway where his bedroom was located. The frown on his face changed to a satisfied smile. His little thief had not disappeared.

Drago pivoted on his heel, changing his direction. He walked down the hall, listening to Carly. She was singing an unfamiliar tune. His eyebrows rose in surprise – she had a very pleasant voice.

Stepping into his bedroom, he saw the bed covers stripped off the bed, the balcony doors open, and a small pile of leaves. Drago followed the sound of Carly's voice to the large bathing chamber adjoining his bedroom.

Carly's voice rose. "It's a pirate's life for me…." she was saying.

"Pirates? You are a pirate?" Drago demanded.

Sudden, intense physical pain, unlike anything Drago had experienced in centuries, flooded him. His low, choked groan mixed with Carly's startled scream. His gaze dropped down at the same time as her eyes dropped to the broom in her hand that had made contact with his groin.

He stumbled back a step. Unfortunately, she stepped forward with him. Looking up, he saw her eyes were rounded and her lips parted into what would have been a delightful 'O' if he hadn't been in so much pain. He reached down and grabbed the end of the broom. She immediately released the handle.

"I... You startled me. Did that hurt?" she asked in a slightly squeaky tone.

"Yes.... It hurts," Drago responded, dropping the broom which made a loud clattering sound on the marble floors.

"Oh. I'm so sorry."

Drago would have responded that he was alright, but Carly had bent over to pick up the broom again. At the same time, a small rodent ran out of the bathing chamber. Her loud scream and the upward movement of the broom echoed through his brain even as the end connected once more with his groin. His knees buckled at the second assault and he dropped to the floor in agony. The frightened rodent scurried up his thigh. Carly swung the broom at the poor creature – and missed. The broom struck Drago instead.

Pain exploded along the right side of Drago's face. The rough bristles of the broom dragged a dirty path along his cheek, catching in the light beard covering his face, and depositing bits of dust, dirt, and leaves along the way. He fell to the side, his head connecting with a resounding thud against the marble floor.

Darkness colored his vision, and briefly he thought that at least if he was unconscious, the pain in his groin and now along his face wouldn't matter. The rodent, realizing that it still wasn't safe, abandoned him and scurried off with Carly, still squealing, chasing after it with the broom.

Who would have thought a broom could be such a dangerous weapon, he thought, watching Carly disappear out of the balcony doors before he closed his eyes.

CHAPTER 4

"I'm so sorry," Carly whispered about an hour later as they sat across from each other in the living area of his rooms.

Drago lowered the cold, damp cloth he was holding against his cheek and glared at her. She gazed back at him with wide, contrite eyes. Her bottom lip was slightly rosy from biting on it.

He had never lost consciousness. Instead, he had lain there breathing deeply and waited for the pain to subside. He had also been trying to keep as low a profile as he could from Carly.

After she scared the first rodent out of the room, she had searched the rest of the room to make sure there were no other creatures lying in wait to cause him grief. All the while, she had begged for his forgiveness and asked him continuously if he was 'okay'. He wasn't sure what the word meant, but he suspected from her tone that she was asking him if he would live.

He instinctively flinched when she lifted her hand to touch his face. With a loud sigh, she dropped it back to her lap, adding to his feelings of guilt. He shouldn't have growled at her. When he did, her bottom lip trembled and her eyes filled with unshed tears.

"You did not mean to hurt me – did you?" he responded.

"No, I didn't mean to hurt you. Now you are just being mean," she pouted, sitting back in the seat across from him and crossing her arms.

Drago's gaze immediately dropped to her cleavage. The scooped neck of her blouse combined with her movements lifted her breasts. He wrenched his gaze back to her face when she emitted a soft snort and uncrossed her arms.

"You never did answer my question," he said, lifting the damp cloth back to his cheek.

"What question?" she asked with a confused look.

"You were singing. You said it was a pirate's life for you. Are you a pirate?" Drago asked, tossing the damp cloth onto the table next to him.

"Pirate? Who me? Of course not! Do I look like a pirate to you?" Carly asked.

Drago studied Carly's incredulous expression. He studied her slightly rounded face, flushed cheeks, and curvy figure clothed in a low cut sweater with stained blue trousers.

"No, you don't," he finally replied.

No, she looked nothing like the pirates that he remembered, and she wore no weapons, though she didn't need anything more than a broom from what he'd seen and felt.

And the tears in her eyes, he couldn't help adding.

The tears had struck him more sharply than any blade. Normally, Drago would be the first to argue that a woman's tears did little to move him. Tears were not something that a dragon shed. Yet, seeing them in Carly's eyes had tugged at an emotion that he was unaware he possessed.

"Listen, I don't know what happened. I was hiking on the trail in Yachats State Park. I've lived there my whole life and never had anything this crazy happen. Granted, I've only been hiking the trails for three days, but I've been to the park hundreds of times over the years. Shoot, more than half the town has been all over this place including my best friend, Jenny. She's like this hiking-jogging-swimming guru from another planet. I don't know why she thinks any of this is fun or exciting. I practically killed myself just trying to go to the bathroom – and don't get me started on bugs and animals! I was terrified I'd get eaten by a bear or a mountain lion or Big Foot. When that rat-like creature came out from under the cabinet...."

Drago watched Carly shudder and draw her legs up off the floor. A wry smile curved his lips. He knew all too well what happened when a poor, defenseless animal met Carly – it escaped and he got beaten up.

"I will make sure that all such creatures are banned from the castle," Drago promised with dry amusement.

Carly's eyes widened and she leaned forward, almost falling out of her chair. "Can you do that? Sort of like the Pied Piper, only you'd be the Dragon Piper," she mused.

"I do not know who this Pied Piper is, but the answer to your question is yes, I can send away the creatures that have made their home here," Drago replied, wincing when his cheek protested his amused smile.

"Great! You can do that while I finish cleaning up in here. Do you have a washing machine? I swear there has to be an inch of dust on everything. With a little elbow grease and some water, we can have this place sparkling in no time," Carly said eagerly.

Drago watched Carly slide her legs back down to the floor and stand up. His hand automatically reached out when she started to tilt. He stood up to steady her when she hopped on one foot.

"What is wrong? You have hurt yourself?" he demanded.

Carly grimaced. "My foot went to sleep. Ugh... It tingles," she groaned, holding on to him and wiggling her right foot.

"You are dangerous even to yourself," Drago retorted in a low voice laced with exasperation when she almost fell.

She shot him a heated glare. "I can't help that I'm not very graceful. It's hereditary. My mom was always running into stuff. The Tate women were not made for sports," she informed him, carefully placing her foot on the floor again.

"I shudder to think of you playing any type of game," he agreed.

Carly stared at him with a suspicious look. Drago did his best to keep his expression neutral. It was much more difficult than he had expected when her eyes narrowed and her lips twisted. It wasn't until she glanced away that his lips twitched. He had to quickly press them together when she turned to glare at him again, as if she knew he was laughing at her.

"Why don't you go make sure all the mice and bugs are out of here while I finish cleaning?" she suggested.

"Are you trying to get rid of me?" Drago asked with a raised eyebrow.

Carly's gaze flashed over his bruised cheek and she nodded. "It might be safer for you," she admitted with a rueful expression. "I get kind-of wild when I'm cleaning. Jenny's learned to disappear when I get on a roll. Besides, I figure cleaning is exercise. I've got to be burning calories and exercising muscles when I'm doing that, right? It will cover the last two miles I missed on my hike."

Drago shook his head. "You are a very strange woman, Carly Tate. Do not try to escape. I have strengthened the wards and protection spells around the castle. If you try to escape, I will know," he warned.

"Escape? Are you kidding? This is like…." She paused, waved her hands, and glanced around the room with wide eyes.

"It is like what?" Drago asked.

Carly looked up at him again. He swore he could feel the threads of their connection pulling him toward her. He shook his head trying to stay focused on their conversation.

"This is magical," she whispered, gazing up at him with huge eyes. "I don't want to wake up yet."

"If it means you will stay, I hope you do not wake up either," Drago replied without thinking.

"Really?" Carly excitedly asked.

An exasperated sigh escaped Drago. "Yes, really," he growled before cupping her chin and pressing a hard kiss to her lips. "I will return shortly."

He turned before Carly could respond. A swift glance over his shoulder showed that Carly hadn't moved. Her eyes were closed, her head tilted back, and a bemused smile curved her lips. If she was here to steal from him, she was doing a pretty good job – she was quickly worming her way under the wall he had built around his heart.

With another shake of his head, he strode out of his living quarters. He would try his hand at a cleaning spell – something told him it would be safer to create one than to have Carly do the cleaning. His hand lifted to his cheek, the bruise would be healed in a few hours. Thank the Goddess, his other pain had also subsided, he thought with a shudder. He never wanted to feel that kind of agony again.

Another amused chuckle escaped him and he shook his head. He hadn't felt this alive in centuries! And it was all due to a mesmerizing woman named Carly.

CHAPTER 5

Later that evening, Drago stepped out onto the balcony as the sun was setting on the horizon. He silently stood watching it disappear into the sea. It had been over a decade since he'd seen it.

A wave of sorrow held him in its grasp. In his mind's eye, he could still see the majestic dragons of his people silhouetted against the brilliant, fiery sky as they flew and the sounds of their laughter rising up from the village below. Young dragons would be learning how to land on the cliffs while their watchful parents murmured encouragement. Music would fill the air as residents settled down for dinner and to share their day's adventures. Theron and the other guards would be jesting with each other and boasting of their exploits. Tonight, there was nothing but silence.

Well, except for the crashing of the surf against the rocks and the loud clatter of Carly dropping yet another item and muttering curses under her breath, he thought, turning to face the opened doors.

"I got it! Damn it, no I don't," she said in exasperation as another clatter struck the marble floor. "I need to get another set of silverware."

"Let me take this. The floors are exceptionally clean after your rigorous scrubbing. I'm sure the set can be used," Drago stated. He walked forward and took the tray of food from Carly and carried it out onto the balcony.

"I thought we could eat out here. I don't know where you found all this food. It is amazing that you did because I could have sworn this place looked like no one has lived here for at least a year," Carly exclaimed, bending to pick up the fork and knife that had fallen from the tray.

"Over a decade," Drago corrected, turning to the small table and chairs that Carly had dragged outside.

"A decade! Wow, that's like… a really long time. How come you are still here? Where did everybody else go?" she asked.

"Gone long ago," he replied.

Drago placed the tray on the table, focusing on the colorful array. The plates were laden with the fresh fruit and vegetables he had harvested from the forests and overgrown gardens. The vegetables were sautéed to perfection. On another platter, fresh fish that he had caught earlier lay perfectly grilled to a golden brown on a bed of fresh greens. It had been a long time since he'd eaten such a feast.

Carly had insisted that while she might not be good at exercising, she was a master in the kitchen. From the delicious smells teasing his nose, he would have to agree. He pulled out one of the chairs and waited for her to sit down before he walked around the table to sit down in the chair across from her.

"Tell me about the place you come from," he requested, picking up a spoon and adding some of the vegetables to his plate.

"Yachats? That conversation will take all of about two minutes. There isn't a lot to it," she responded with a wiggle of her nose.

"Then I look forward to an informative two minutes," Drago replied in a dry tone.

Carly stuck her tongue out at him. Drago's lips twitched. That had to be another first. He couldn't remember any woman ever sticking her tongue out at him. He liked that Carly appeared completely at ease with him – enough even to tease him. With a shake of his head, he slid a piece of fish onto his plate. He began eating, savoring the burst of flavors from the fish and vegetables.

"Yachats is a tiny town. There are less than seven hundred people within the city limits. I can't believe it was voted as one of the ten best vacation spots! There's hardly anything there. Still, I guess it is pretty and there are some beautiful homes, cool shops, and a marina. I wish the homes weren't so expensive. Jenny and I were thinking of going in together to buy a house, but what would we do if we fell in love with someone and got married? It would make it awkward, and there's no way I can afford one on my own," she added with a sigh before taking a bite of the vegetables.

"Where do you live then?" Drago asked, pouring the wine that he had retrieved from the cellar into their glasses before setting the bottle down and lifting his glass to sip from it.

"We're renting a little house along Main Street. It's really cute and we've got it decorated up. The landlord is a sweetheart and doesn't mind as long as we pay the rent on time. Jenny teaches at the local school and I work at the bank. We don't make tons of money, but we do alright," Carly replied with a shrug, lifting the glass of wine to her lips and taking a tentative sip. It was a light, white wine, dry instead of sweet and surprisingly good considering she didn't care for wine. She replaced the glass and pierced a piece of fruit with her fork before continuing. "The local Farmer's Market on Saturdays is about as exciting as it gets. They have all kinds of fresh produce, seafood, and crafts for sale. I have a booth there and sell the jewelry that I make. I do okay during the tourist season. It gives me a little extra money. I've been saving it toward the purchase of a house. Once a month, they also do a movie under the stars since we don't have a movie theater. Of course, they never show any of the newest releases. I told you, Yachats is about as exciting as watching grass grow. So, what's your story? How come you stayed behind after everyone left?"

Drago glanced down at his empty plate in surprise. Placing his fork on the plate, he sat back to stare out over the city. The sun had set, but the edge of the world still had the glow from it. He hadn't planned to tell Carly anything, so when the words slipped from his lips, he was surprised.

"Many years ago, the seven kingdoms were at war with each other. My guards and I were completing a last inspection of the isle before a storm arrived. The wind and sea had become turbulent, but in the distance I saw a familiar figure. It was Orion, the Sea King," Drago murmured, looking out at the ocean.

"You mean there are others like you?" Carly asked in a hushed voice.

Drago shook his head. "Not like me – not a dragon. Orion is king of the Isle of the Sea Serpent. They live in great cities under the ocean but have homes on the island above them as well. They are merfolk, sea dwellers who breathe under the water," he explained.

"Mermaids! Are you saying that mermaids are real?!" Carly exclaimed, pushing her chair back and standing up so she could stare out at the ocean in awe.

Drago pushed his chair back and stood up as well. He walked around the table to stand next to Carly. Together they stared out at the horizon for several moments. A cool breeze swirled up from the cliffs, and Carly shivered. Drago glanced down at her. He reached out an arm and pulled her against him. He raised an inquiring eyebrow when a grin curved her lips.

"If your mermaids are merfolk, then yes, mermaids are real – though, I don't think Orion would appreciate being called a maid," he chuckled, turning to stare out at the ocean again.

"Yeah, I guess a guy would take offense to that. So, you were doing a last inspection and you saw the merman," she encouraged.

"Yes," Drago replied. "Orion requested a truce between us. He told me the other kingdoms had agreed. The war had been instigated by his cousin. Magna was – is – a very powerful witch. She was much more powerful than Orion or I realized."

Carly turned to face him. "What happened to her?" she asked.

"I don't know what happened to her, only what she did to my people," Drago replied, staring out at the ocean and thinking of that fateful day. "I heard their cries first. I felt their horror. Mothers and fathers watching their children become cold and lifeless, yet helpless to stop the spell. Even as they reached for loved ones, the spell overtook them as well, encasing them in stone. The warriors had no enemy to fight. They could not see the magical threads. We had fought the people from the Isle of Magic before, but this was different – alien to us. Our own powers, in our dragon forms, give us some measure of protection, but nothing could stop this. Magna's magic was darker, stronger, and unlike anything we had ever encountered before. Many of my people fell into the ocean as they tried to escape. Others were frozen in their homes or as they were making their way along the streets. By the time I made it back to the isle, they were all gone. I could no longer hear their quiet murmurs or sense their presence." Drago turned his head to gaze down at Carly with glittering, rage-filled eyes. "Magna stood on the cliff. The sound of her insane laughter danced upon the winds of the storm, mocking my inability to stop her annihilation of my people. She disappeared into the ocean before I could kill her."

"Oh Drago, I'm so sorry," Carly whispered, her eyes filling with tears. "I can't imagine what it must have been like. What did you do? How could you survive such devastation?"

Drago lifted his hand and brushed it along Carly's cheek, capturing the tear that escaped. "I cast a spell to protect my kingdom, moved my people into a safe place, and found solitude in the caverns far below the castle. There I slept, daring any to try to take the last stronghold of the dragon," he murmured, gazing down into her liquid brown eyes.

She lifted a hand, brushing aside a lock of his hair that had fallen forward when he looked down at her. He liked the way she touched him. It was gentle, tender, yet hesitant. He slid his hand up to cup hers, raised her hand to his mouth, and pressed a warm kiss to the center of her palm.

"I wish there was something I could do to help you," she said.

"You already have. You have awakened me." His hand engulfed hers in a possessive hold and his eyes burned into hers. "I claim you as part of my treasure, Carly. I will never let you go," Drago stated, watching her eyes widen at his declaration.

Carly gazed back at him for a second before her lips curved up into a brilliant smile. "What girl in her right mind would turn down a seriously cute dragon when he says something like that? Does this mean you've forgiven me for the broom incident earlier?" she teased, a mischievous twinkle brightening her eyes.

CHAPTER 6

Carly bit her lip as she finished washing the dishes and placed the last one on a dish towel. Drago had disappeared shortly after he had told her what had happened. She had sensed that he needed to be alone. She wasn't going to argue about his leaving because she could use a few minutes to get her head straight.

"I can't be in a magical land, but I am. This is crazy, Carly. You need to find the way back home. Jenny has probably called out the National Guard by now. I can see it plastered all over the news – 'Assistant Branch Manager of small bank goes missing – foul play or stupidity? More at eleven,'" Carly muttered under her breath.

Wiping her hands, she glanced around the kitchen. It was obvious the room had not been used very much. Despite the layers of dust, there wasn't a speck of evidence that the cooking utensils, pots, or pans were ever used. With a sigh, Carly knew what she needed to do.

"Well, I know what I want to do. I want to stay here," she said, jutting out her chin. Then she took a breath and firmly shook her head. "I can't leave Jenny wondering what happened to me, and I can't leave poor Drago alone again. So, first thing is to tell Jenny what's happened so she doesn't worry. Once I've done that, I'll come back and see if I can help Drago."

She turned and bit her lip again. It was dark outside. There was no way she could find her way down the trail – if she even found her way back to it – in the dark. There was nothing else for her to do tonight. She would have to wait until morning.

Satisfied with her reasoning, she wiped her hands down her pants. She had discovered her backpack in the living room earlier. Walking into the other room, she picked it up and placed it on the couch. She opened it and rummaged inside.

There were three packages of peanut butter and honey crackers, a bottle of water, a flashlight, a small first aid kit – she'd learned the hard way that she needed to always carry one of those – and a pair of gloves. Nothing fantastic, but she was proud she had the essentials: food, water, light, and medicine – if you counted Band-Aids and aspirin as a first aid kit.

"Tomorrow I'll search for the passage back home," Carly said with a large yawn.

She rubbed her eyes. After all of her adventures today, she was exhausted. She glanced at the closed doors, worried because Drago was still out. Surely dragons could see better in the dark than humans....

Sinking down onto a long couch, she dropped her backpack onto the floor, pulled off her shoes, and stretched out. She would just lie down for a few minutes. Reaching up, she pulled her jacket off the back of the couch and spread it over her upper body before rolling onto her side.

"I'll just rest my eyes for a minute… or until Drago returns," Carly murmured, already more than half asleep.

∽

Drago pulled in his wings and stretched out his lower legs, landing on the railing of the balcony before jumping down. He shook his head and turned to look up at the waning crescent moons and the brilliant stars above. He sniffed the clean, fresh air blowing in from the ocean.

He had been gone longer than he'd planned. He had wanted to check over the isle one last time before he settled down for the night.

He wanted to be sure he hadn't missed anything. He had even returned to the cavern below to reassure himself that no one else had found a way in to the treasure.

All his wards and spells were still in place, as strong as ever. A thorough search had revealed no breaches. How Carly had found her way to the treasure room was still a mystery to him. He did not know of a single creature that had the powers to break through his magic. Not even Orion, the Sea King, or the King and Queen of the Isle of Magic possessed that type of magical power.

With a mere thought, his body shimmered and he shifted. He glanced up at the night sky before he turned and walked toward the closed doors. Soft lights glowed from the interior, but he didn't see any movement.

Pulling open the doors, he stood in the entrance gazing around. It had been a long, long time since he had felt warmth in his home. The room was spotless and the faint aroma of the meal Carly had prepared earlier still hung in the air. He had started a fire in the fireplace before he had left to rid the apartment of the chill that had crept into the very walls of the palace.

His gaze narrowed on the plush couch when he heard a soft sigh. Pulling the doors closed behind him, he quietly walked over to gaze down at Carly. His lips twitched. She was lying curled up on her side with her hands tucked under her cheek. She snored softly.

"If you are a thief, you are the strangest one I have ever met – and not a very good one either," he murmured with a rueful shake of his head. "A bed would be much more comfortable than this piece of furniture."

He bent and slid his arms under her. A fierce wave of possessiveness swept through him as he held her close. This soft, warm thief was now tied to him by the ancient creed of the dragon – what a dragon claimed, he kept – and Drago had claimed Carly. Whether she understood the implications of that or not did not concern him. She would understand it soon enough.

Drago chuckled when Carly snorted in her sleep and snuggled into his warm body. He turned and strode through the living room and down the long hallway to his bedroom. With a whisper, the covers magically drew back. The fresh scent of clean linen teased his senses. Carly had managed to get so much accomplished in one afternoon; it was no wonder that she was exhausted.

He laid her down gently. He sighed in exasperation when she immediately rolled onto her side. Reaching down, he carefully removed her jacket. Another soft chuckle escaped him when she blindly swatted his hand away.

"Go away, Jenny. Today's Saturday," she sleepily mumbled.

"I'm not this Jenny and I am not sure what day it is," Drago replied.

"Saturday… so's I don't have to go to work," Carly muttered in a slightly slurred voice filled with exhaustion before she started snoring again.

"A thief that works," Drago replied with a shake of his head. "You continue to amaze me, little one."

He ruefully reached down and gently removed her stained trousers. He chuckled again when she rose up enough for him to pull them off before blindly reaching out with one hand to search for the covers. Drago reached down and pulled the covers over her shivering form.

Straightening, he glanced around the room. The fire in the hearth had not been started so there was still a chill in the air. With a flick of his wrist, Drago sent a small fire ball to the logs. Blue, red, and yellowish-orange flames danced over the enchanted logs that would never burn down.

"If only I could have enchanted my people to protect them," Drago said, staring at the flames for several long seconds before he pushed the melancholy emotions away.

He slowly removed his long, black coat, bent and picked up Carly's jacket off the floor where he had dropped it, and carried them over to several pegs on the wall. After hanging them up, he removed his boots and socks and unbuttoned his soft, silk shirt.

It had been such a very long time since he had done the simplest tasks that even undressing felt odd. Drago carried his discarded clothing over to a woven basket inside the bathing chamber. He unfastened his trousers and pushed them off. Catching the soft, leathery trousers with one foot, he tossed them high enough to grab them and deposited them with his other clothing.

After crossing the smooth stone floor to a shower built into a corner of the room, he stepped inside and turned the tap. A smothered groan escaped Drago when a rain shower of warm water, supplied from deep beneath the castle, fell on him, caressing his broad shoulders and running down his body. It seemed like an eternity since he had felt anything remotely warm in his life. Bowing his head, he stood under the flow, losing himself in the enjoyment of the moment.

The water soaked his long hair. His hands rose to thread through it before running down along his face. He grimaced when he felt his beard. He would need to trim it.

He reached for the bar of soap Carly must have found and placed on the ledge. The soap lathered quickly between his hands, emitting a fresh rain scent that teased his nostrils. Running his hands over the light coating of dark hair that covered his chest, he drew in a deep breath. His body felt like it was awakening from a deep, eternal sleep. The palms of his hands slid down across his stomach before trailing downward.

A shudder ran through him. It had been a long, long time since he'd been this awake – and aware. He tilted his head back and closed his eyes. The image of Carly flared into vivid detail. He shivered when he pictured her standing in front of him, looking up at him with wide, startled eyes and a very sexy O-shaped mouth. That image had ingrained itself in his mind even as his body had exploded with pain after she had connected the broom with his groin.

Yes, that feeling was not something he was going to forget any time soon. Opening his eyes, he finished washing his hair and body and rinsed off the soapy residue. Several long minutes later, he shut off the water and reached for a towel. He dried his body, toweled the moisture from his hair, and walked over to the sink.

He grimaced and wrapped the towel around his waist, tucking it in securely before he leaned forward to stare at his reflection. His dark, sapphire blue eyes glimmered with fire. He raised a hand and ran it over his beard.

It had been a long time since he'd seen his own reflection. There were a few new lines near the corners of his eyes and around his mouth. The spell he had cast over the Isle had preserved most things. While dust and leaves had settled and the vines had grown, time for him had slowed until it remained as still as the statues of his people.

Several minutes passed while he stared at his reflection, lost in thought. A scowl crossed his face when he realized the only reason he was scrutinizing his appearance was because he wanted to impress Carly. With a snort of self-disgust, he made sure the bathing area was as spotless as before. He didn't want Carly to think poorly of him for messing up the room that she had worked so hard to clean.

"Since when did I have to try to impress a woman?" he asked his reflection with a raised eyebrow. "You are Drago, King of the Dragons! You do not have to impress women."

Pushing the unusual feelings aside, Drago stepped out of the room. The light behind him faded, casting the bedroom into a soft glow from the moons shining through the long bank of windows and doors. He walked over and pulled the doors open so the fresh, chilly breeze coming off the ocean would sweep through the room.

He turned when he heard a sigh come from his bed. Carly had rolled over so her back was to him. Her arms were wrapped around one of the plush pillows. She had stopped snoring, and from her slow, steady breathing, Drago knew that she had fallen into a deep sleep.

Removing the towel as he walked closer to the bed, he tossed it across the foot of the bed before waving his hand for the covers to fold back. He slid between the sheets and pulled them back up before rolling over to wrap his arm around Carly and hug her tightly against him.

Tilting his head, he brushed a light kiss along her pale throat before relaxing against the pillows. The wards and spells would keep them protected while they slept. His arm tightened around Carly, holding her firmly as if afraid she might disappear.

"Never," he said in a barely audible voice. "I bind you to me, Carly Tate. Thief, wanderer, unusual woman that you are – you are mine. I will always know where you are."

The spell he wove with his words wrapped around Carly's sleeping form. Drago could see the red fire threads of the dragon spell settling over Carly's body before fading. Satisfied that she was locked to him, Drago's eyelids slowly lowered, and he fell into the first deep, dreamless sleep he'd had in centuries.

CHAPTER 7

The first thing Carly realized when she woke the next morning was that she was not alone. Coarse, black hair that tickled her cheek and nose was her first clue. The second was the warm arm wrapped around her, holding her against a very hot – as in the smoking sexy, melt in your mouth kind of hot – body.

Correction, Carly thought, afraid to move. *A very hot, smoking sexy, melt in your mouth, bare-naked body.*

Carly cracked her eyelids open, curious to see if her assessment was correct. She carefully lifted her right hand from where it was resting over Drago's heart and moved it down to the covers that were draped across his stomach. She paused and glanced up to make sure he was still sleeping. Yes! His breathing hadn't changed and his eyes were still closed.

A delighted grin curved her lips. It wasn't like she had a lot of experience to fall back on, but he appeared to be sound asleep. Carly decided if she had to do a trial run, she couldn't have dreamed up a better guy to experience it with. Drago was built like 'The Rock' only with hair, not that TR wasn't fine just the way he was. Still, never in a million, bazillion years would she have thought getting lost would turn out like this.

Biting her lip, she glanced back down. Her fingers hovered over the covers for a brief second before she slowly lifted the soft material. Her gaze followed the trail of black curls lower… and lower… and….

"Holy macaroni!" Carly hissed under her breath when she caught her first sight of aroused manhood. "That's… wow!"

The sudden movement under her cheek told her that Drago had not only awakened but that he had heard her exclamation as well. Heat filled Carly's cheeks and she slowly lowered the covers then patted them for good measure. Her fingers played with the material of the sheets as her mind raced to figure out what she would say next.

"You're awake," she said, watching the sheet where his cock was raised up a little.

"Yes," Drago replied with another shake of his body which told Carly he was amused.

"You sure are big. Shut up, Carly. That is not what you meant to say. Brain before mouth. Jenny's always reminding you of that. Brain… wake up. Carly is doing it again," she commented, wincing when the words slipped from her mouth.

Drago's deep laughter echoed through the room. Carly closed her eyes and decided if she was going to die from embarrassment, at least this was a good way to go – Drago's laughter filling the air and his arm wrapped around her. Yes, she could think of a million other horrible ways to die.

"What is Carly doing again?" Drago asked after he quit laughing.

Carly released a long sigh. "Making a total fool of herself. She does that quite frequently. Jenny says it is one of the things that makes me – me. I think it is one of the things that drive people crazy. Mr. Kranz, my boss at the bank, is forever telling me I need to have a censor installed on my mouth," she rambled then released another sigh and turned her head to bury her face into his chest. "Just ignore me. I'm going to die of embarrassment now."

"Carly…," Drago said in a soft tone.

Carly felt his strong, firm fingers under her chin. She stubbornly kept her eyes closed and her mouth clamped shut in a tight line even as she willingly tilted her head back. Her mouth relaxed when she felt

Drago run his thumb across her bottom lip. His touch sure did feel good.

"Won't you open your eyes, little one?" Drago asked in a voice still rough from sleep.

"No," she replied.

"Why not?" he asked.

Carly's lips twitched in amusement. "Because I like the image in my brain," she admitted.

There was a moment of silence before Drago responded. "And what image is that?" he asked in a voice laced with curiosity.

"I like your curls," she finally said.

"My curls…?" Drago repeated in a slightly confused tone before his eyes widened in understanding and he began to laugh again.

Carly opened her eyes just in time to see comprehension dawn in his eyes. A muffled giggle escaped her. At least he was seeing the humor in the situation instead of thinking she was a total crackpot.

Her enjoyment of his amusement ended in a gasp when she suddenly found herself trapped beneath him. His laughter had faded and he was staring down at her with a very serious expression. Her hands rose automatically to splay across his chest. She couldn't resist squeezing her fingers just a little to see if he really was as solid as he looked. He was – with some to spare for half the guys back in Yachats.

"You… you are very muscular," she reflected in a slightly choked voice.

"I know," he replied. "I want to kiss you, Carly Tate."

Carly's eyes widened. She wanted to kiss him too, but there was one little problem – morning breath! She couldn't imagine kissing him without brushing her teeth. A sense of panic swept through her when he started to bend his head. She reacted without thinking, drawing her legs up to try to escape at the same time as she pushed against his chest. Two things registered the moment she moved. First, she hadn't taken into consideration the position of her left leg between his thighs; and second, the part of his anatomy that she connected with wasn't muscular, but very vulnerable.

Drago's loud, indrawn breath, followed by his eyes closing and his face tightening told her that she had reacted rather more strongly than she had intended. His arms trembled before he released a low, guttural groan and fell to the side. One good thing happened... he no longer was in the mood to kiss her. The bad thing was... he probably would never want to try again.

Carly rolled out of the bed and stared down at Drago lying there pale and obviously in a lot of pain. His eyes were closed and his hands were cupping his groin over the covers. Mortification swept through her. She had done it again – sabotaged any chance of keeping a guy interested in her. She cupped her hands and lifted them to her mouth.

"I'm sorry... I didn't mean... I.... Oh, hell. That must have hurt. I kneed you pretty good and you were probably still sore from the last time," Carly whispered.

"Yes, yes, it does and I did not need a reminder of how painful the first time was," he bit out.

Carly watched as Drago's eyes slowly opened and he gazed up at her. His eyes were dark with pain and an emotion she wasn't quite sure of. She hoped it wasn't the desire to kill her – slowly, tortuously by dragon fire. Just the thought had her taking a cautious step backwards.

"I... Yes, I guess... I'll just go brush my teeth. Then, if you still... but, I'm sure you don't... but, if you did... I don't have a toothbrush. I'll just go hide in the bathroom for a bit if you don't mind," Carly stammered before she turned and fled to the other room.

∼

Drago's gaze followed Carly as she quickly left the bedroom. Only when the door closed firmly behind her did he roll onto his side and released a smothered moan of pain into the pillow. Goddess, but that hurt!

It had taken everything inside of him not to roll into a ball and cry like a babe. A startled chuckle started to escape him, but he quickly swallowed it back when the movement caused another wave of pain to wash through him. Carly's stammered words, and the meaning of them, hit him hard.

"Teeth... She unwittingly strikes me down because she has to brush her teeth before I can kiss her," Drago reflected, breathing deeply through his nose and releasing the breath through his mouth. "Goddess, she would have killed me if I had tried to make love to her! I need to wear protection when I'm within a meter of her."

"I can hear you," Carly's muffled voice stated.

Drago glanced toward the door when it opened a tiny bit. He could see Carly's flushed face, bright eyes, and... tears?! Yes, it was tears. She impatiently raised her hand and brushed it across her cheek.

"Why are you crying?" Drago asked with a frown, forgetting his own agony for a moment in his confusion.

"Because I always screw things up," she sobbed with a loud sniff. "I wouldn't have killed you if you had tried to make love to me. I might have maimed you, but it wouldn't have been intentional. I just do things that always end up messing things up. Is it any wonder that I'm still a virgin? Who else do you know who accidentally sets their high school date's car on fire – on the first date? Or knocks their date off a cliff because of a mosquito? Okay, so maybe it was just the front porch, but still...! Or causes their boyfriend to have a concussion just because they were trying to throw the softball back over the fence – to the other team?! Even poor Ross wasn't immune to Carly's Curse. How many girls do you know who have their own curse named after them? Huh?"

Drago blinked, each one of her statements bringing up vivid images of total chaos. It took a minute for him to realize that she had asked him a question. But in all honesty, he was still stuck on 'virgin'.

"You're a virgin?" he asked.

Carly glared at him with wide eyes for a moment before firmly shutting the door again. Drago didn't realize his body had relaxed, the pain faded, until he lifted a hand to run it over his face. Rolling onto his back, he stared up at the ceiling, a grin curving his lips. His thief was a virgin?

"I wonder what will happen next?" he chuckled.

CHAPTER 8

*C*arly stared in dismay at the reflection of her red face in the mirror. If *that* spectacle hadn't been enough to nominate her for Biggest Fool in the Guinness Book of World Records, wearing makeup to go hiking should give her the extra points she needed. The image staring back at her looked like a red raccoon – if there was such a thing. She'd need to Google it when she got home. She looked like she had two black eyes thanks to the remains of her mascara creating dark patches around each eye. If that wasn't bad enough, her shoulder-length brown hair was a mass of tangles, sticking out in all different directions like a troll doll after a kid with sticky fingers had played with it.

"That's it… I need a shower. Even if it means wearing the same dirty clothes again, I really need a shower," she retorted in defiance at her reflection, before pointing at the mirror. "And if you dare smirk or say one nasty thing, I'll break you. I don't care how many years of bad luck it gives me. It isn't like I don't have enough on my own!"

Carly waited. When the mirror didn't react, she breathed in a sigh of relief. A least this magic land didn't appear to have an enchanted mirror. It was probably a fantastic thing considering she realized she needed to use the restroom and would have probably peed her pants if it had responded. It was then that she noticed she wasn't wearing any pants.

"How the heck could I lose those on top of everything else?" she groaned with a shake of her head.

Refusing to look at her reflection again, she turned her back to it and walked over to the toilet. After relieving herself, she glanced around the room. She pulled a towel out of a cupboard before opening another one near the sink. Thankfully, she knew where everything was after her cleaning spree yesterday. Some of the items had seemed strange, but it didn't take her long to figure out that the tin of powder next to the toothbrush was a type of toothpaste.

She wrinkled her nose at her lack of toothbrush. She glanced at the one on the shelf. She wasn't about to use Drago's. No matter how cute the guy was, there were some things that were personal and a toothbrush was one of them. Maybe if they had been together for a while, but using his toothbrush so soon after meeting him wasn't happening. On a side note, she couldn't help but be pleased that she had only found one when she was cleaning. If she had discovered a second one, well – that would have been a huge warning sign that Drago wasn't unattached.

Carly released a sigh and picked up the tin. It wouldn't be like she never had to use her finger as a toothbrush before. She popped the top on the long, thin can and was about to pour some onto her finger when the door behind her suddenly opened.

"What the...?" she exclaimed, almost dropping the can. "How the heck did you get in? I locked the door."

Drago leaned against the doorframe and grinned. "I am King of this Isle. No door can be locked against me," he retorted with a slight shrug.

"That's just wrong on too many levels to count," Carly replied with a shake of her head and placed the tin on the counter before her gaze caught on the items he was holding in his hands. "What are those?"

Drago glanced down at the articles of clothing he was holding. He straightened and walked toward her. He didn't hold them out to her; instead, he kept them just out of her reach. Carly's gaze moved over his bare chest. Her fingers itched to run over his smooth skin again. It took a few seconds for her brain to catch up with her eyes. Holy crud! His legs were bare! Her eyes shot up to his face.

"Please tell me you aren't – I mean – you are wearing clothes behind those in your hands," she asked in a strained voice.

Drago's eyebrow rose. "No. I thought you would like a change of clothing. These belong…." His lips pressed together in a straight line for a moment before they relaxed. "These belonged to my mother. I thought they might fit you."

Carly didn't miss the sorrow that flashed through Drago's eyes. Her hand lifted in response and she laid it against his cheek. She brushed her thumb across the coarse hair of his beard.

"Thank you," she said.

Drago's lips twitched. Carly should have known he was up to something. Her lips parted when he swiftly bent and pressed a kiss on them.

"You're welcome," he replied, gazing down into her eyes before pulling back and handing her the clothing. "I will prepare our meal."

"Okay," Carly replied.

She blinked, refocusing when he turned. The strangled gasp that escaped her drew an amused chuckle from him. Her eyes narrowed on his muscular back and firm buttocks.

"If you need help washing your… back, call me," he threw out over his shoulder.

Carly shook her head. "I'm locking the door," she called out when he pulled the door shut behind him. "But… I wouldn't be opposed to you coming in to wash my back. Wow, what a cute butt!" she whispered, staring at the door.

Her face flamed again when she heard his muffled laughter. Damn dragons! She needed to remember that Drago had super-power hearing.

Carly warily glanced at the door one more time before she placed the clothes Drago had given her on a small bench near the large, open shower. She blinked when she saw that on top of the clothing was a transparent cloth bag with a toothbrush in it. A smile curved her lips at the thoughtful gesture. Her fingers moved to her lips when she remembered his brief kiss.

"I so have to tell Jenny about this guy," she said, blinking back the tears. "I just hope I'm not dreaming all of this."

∽

Twenty minutes later, Carly peeked out from the bathroom. Her gaze swept over the neatly made bed with relief. She had a few more minutes to make sure she had a firm control over her emotions.

Running her hands over the soft tunic and pants, she couldn't help but admire the quality of the fabric. The tunic was a deep rose color with tiny mother-of-pearl buttons sewn along the bottom and the pants were an ivory color. Both were absolutely gorgeous and so soft she swore they felt like silk. She'd bought a silk blouse once at a fine boutique in Portland. The blouse was still one of her favorites.

She had washed her panties out and dried them on the body drier built into the floor. The device had scared the daylights out of her yesterday when she had stepped on the grate and felt a warm blast of air enveloping her. It reminded her of the Marilyn Monroe pose and it sure made drying off a lot faster!

Her toes curled against the polished floor as she padded barefoot over to the end of the bed. She noticed that Drago had brought her backpack into the room and placed it on the chair near the window. Walking over to it, she unzipped the back section and slid her dirty clothes inside. She zipped the bag closed again and set it on the floor. Sitting down, she pulled on the pair of socks that Drago had added to the pile of clothing and then pulled on her boots that he'd placed next to the chair. She wasn't used to having someone be so thoughtful – well, besides Jenny.

Carly glanced up when she heard a slight sound near the door. She straightened in the chair and gazed at Drago. His expression was thoughtful, as if he was contemplating some serious issue. Running her hands down her thighs, she nervously stood up and gave him a tentative smile.

"Thank you for the clothes. They are really nice," she said, trying to break the awkward silence that had descended between them.

Drago shrugged. "I hoped they would fit; you are plump like my mother. I have prepared food to break our fast. It is simple, but should be filling until I can secure more supplies," he replied.

A surge of anger and hurt washed through Carly. *Plump like his mother?* Wow! She had heard a lot of insults and put downs over the years, but this was the first time she had ever been compared to a guy's mother.

"No problem, I'm not that hungry," Carly stated in a deceptively calm voice as she walked by him.

She ignored the frown that creased Drago's brow at her frosty tone. She continued down the hall to the living room. Her gaze turned to the open French doors. On the balcony table, where they had dined last night, were several covered dishes. Carly turned toward the doors and proceeded out onto the balcony.

CHAPTER 9

Drago sensed a change in Carly's mood. He glanced out over the castle walls to the ocean. Something had struck the outer wards, searching for a way past them. Returning his attention to Carly, he pulled out her chair and waited for her to be seated before he moved to the one across from her. Sitting down, he uncovered the simple fare of fruit, nuts, and leftover grilled fish from the night before. He would need to travel to another Isle to gather provisions. With his people gone, he was limited to what he knew how to prepare and could obtain locally.

"It is not much. I do not have the skills you do," he admitted, gazing at the plates.

"I'm sure it will help me lose some weight eating like this. After all, I am on the plump side as you know," Carly couldn't resist retorting before she bit her lip and looked away.

Drago's gaze snapped to Carly's tight face. He was shocked when he saw the glimmer of tears and sensed the hurt in her voice. He watched her blink several times before she lowered her gaze to the table. His hand shot out and he covered the back of hers when she reached for the cloth napkin next to her plate.

"Tell me," he ordered.

Carly refused to look at him. Instead, she held her body stiff and straight. Her lower lip trembled before she pressed her lips firmly together.

"Carly…." Drago waited until she reluctantly looked up at him. Yes, there was definitely an expression of hurt in her gaze. "Tell me why you are upset."

Carly started to shake her head. She gazed at him for several long seconds before she lifted her chin. A hint of a smile tugged at the corner of Drago's mouth. A flash of stubbornness replaced the hurt. He could see his defiant little thief again.

"I know I'm on the… mature, womanly-figured side. That is why I was trying to exercise. I swear just thinking about exercising adds five pounds to my hips and don't ask me about ice cream or pasta! I'm not fat! I'm genetically built to be cute and cuddly," she said with a stubborn thrust to her jaw. "If you can't handle cute and cuddly, go find yourself someone who isn't. I don't care. I'm proud of who I am and I don't have to apologize to anyone for being me."

Confusion washed through Drago. Where had that come from? He thought she was upset because he had not provided her with a good meal. Instead, she was upset because she thought he didn't like cute and cuddly.

His gaze moved over her round face. Tiny brown dots feathered across her nose. Her cheeks were flushed the color of a soft red rose and he swore her skin would feel as silky as its petals. Her lips, especially her bottom one, begged to be teased and stroked. The tunic she wore hugged her figure. The neckline opened just enough to tease him with a glimpse of her ample breasts. He swore they would not only fill his palms, but overflow his hands. His mouth watered with the thought of wrapping his lips around each bud.

Carly's low hiss told him that he was gripping her hand tightly in his. If his eyes were not blazing with the fire of his dragon, they should be. He was more than ready to claim her as his. If not for his concern for her safety when he had felt the slight vibration against the wards he had placed around the island, he would have joined her in the shower this morning.

"I very much appreciate cute and cuddly," he replied, shifting uncomfortably in his seat when he felt the extent of his appreciation begging to be released. "Why would you think I do not?"

"You are plump like my mother," she mimicked, pulling her hand free.

Drago gazed at her with a frown before it cleared, and he grinned. "She is… was the envy of all the females in the kingdom. My father told of how he had been captivated by the curve of my mother's hips and her ample…," his voice faded and he held his hands out, cupped, as if holding a pair of large melons – or breasts. "The females on the Isle of the Dragon tend to be long and lean, but every once in a while there is one of such beauty, with curves that capture a male's imagination and make his mouth water to taste…," Drago's voice faded when he saw Carly looking at him with a wary expression. He dropped his hands back to the table and stared moodily at the food. "You need to eat."

Carly slowly reached for the plate of fresh fruit. Her gaze kept flickering to him as if she was trying to see if he had been telling her the truth. Drago wanted to groan out loud. He had to stop talking because the images that had formed when he was explaining had made his cock hard as stone.

"So… you like plump women?" Carly stated more than asked in a nonchalant tone.

Drago reached for the plate of fruit she was holding out. His fingers curled around the edges. What he really wanted to do was toss the plate aside, pick Carly up, and carry her back to his bed.

"No, I like cute and cuddly women, Carly, and they don't get any more cute and cuddly than you, my little thief," he replied.

Pleasure and excitement lit up Carly's eyes. Drago's gaze followed the movement of her lips. He bit back the curse that threatened to escape him. She was not making his resolve to find out more about her easy.

"After we break our fast, I must check the Isle," he said.

"Is something wrong?" she asked, glancing out over the wall.

Drago shook his head. "I am sure it is nothing to be concerned about. Most likely, another pirate ship wrecked amongst the rocks," he replied.

"Oh, just a pirate ship," she murmured, picking up her fork and taking a bite. "Thank you again for breakfast and the clothes."

"There is no need for thanks," Drago said.

"So, tell me about the Isle of the Dragon. What was it like, well… before?" she asked.

Drago's fork paused in midair. He glanced at Carly's face. She was leaning forward in her chair, gazing at him. He slowly lowered his fork to his plate and thought about her question. For the first time, he realized he had always taken for granted the beauty of his kingdom and its people.

"It was a wondrous kingdom filled with wealth and prosperity. During the day, the sounds of laughter and the daily lives of my people would drift through the air. I can remember the scent from the Baker's cottage. If the wind came in from the Southwest, you could smell the freshness of his baked bread. My mouth waters at the thought of it," Drago shared in a quiet, reflective voice.

"Mine, too. I love fresh baked bread with lots of real butter on it," Carly admitted.

Drago turned to look at her and smiled. "I would bring you a fresh loaf to break your fast each morning," he responded before turning to look out over the wall. "Dragons come in many different shapes and sizes. Some are more powerful than others, but they all have one thing in common."

He pushed his chair back and rose. Stepping closer to the railing, he gripped it and looked down on the deserted streets far below. A choking pang of regret swept through him.

"What do they all have in common?" Carly asked, setting her fork down and rising out of her seat so she could stand beside him.

"Family… A dragon's family is the most important thing to a dragon. We can feel each other. We are all connected in our dragon form so we are never alone. When…. I heard their cries of terror – each and every one of them, down to the smallest dragon – I could feel their fear as if it were my own. By the time I returned, they were all gone. The silence was deafening. I never realized that silence could be so loud," he explained, clenching the stone railing and leaning forward as if in pain.

"Oh, Drago. I'm so sorry," Carly whispered.

The muscles along his back tightened when he felt her hand slide across his shirt. Years – more than he wanted to remember – had passed since he had felt the touch of another and heard the sweet music of a voice. A shudder ran through his body and he closed his eyes.

"There was always music in the air," he continued in a thick voice. "The children would dance in the streets, their parents occasionally scolding them if they became too boisterous or got in the way of the vendors. The cove would be filled with ships from all the other Isles. Merchants would shout out orders while sailors would flirt in the hope of capturing some of the dragon's gold from an unsuspecting resident. It was all a game. Anyone who knows about dragons knows we would never let anyone steal our gold. It can only be given freely."

"It sounds like it was a wonderful place to live," Carly said, dropping her hand to the balcony and gazing down as if she could see what he was telling her.

Drago opened his eyes and straightened. "I would train with my guards each morning down in the courtyard. Afterward, we would break. Sometimes we would fly out to sea or to another Isle. Other times, I would go to a quiet place on the island to be alone. I never truly appreciated what it meant to be a part of a family until it was taken from me. I thought losing my parents was devastating, but it was nothing compared to losing everyone. My father… My parents used to warn me that one day I would understand. With their deaths, I gained the power to hear each and every voice inside me. It was no longer muted, but loud and pulsing. I resented the responsibility, thinking it a burden instead of the gift it was. I did what was expected of me because I had to, not because I wanted to," he stated in a rough voice.

"I can't imagine what it must be like to be responsible for a whole kingdom. I mean, I've read about kingdoms and stuff during history class, but to actually be a king or queen…. I'd be scared," Carly said, glancing at him.

"I am not scared, Carly, I am filled with rage. Now that I have awakened, I will try once again to find the Sea Witch and when I do, I will kill her – slowly, drawing out her last breath until she begs me to end her life," Drago stated.

"I… don't think that would be a good idea, Drago. Revenge usually doesn't end well for either party," Carly started to say.

Drago turned to look down at her, his expression hard. "I have to go. I will return later. Do not leave the safety of the palace," he ordered a moment before his body shimmered and he shifted.

Once again, the feeling of uneasiness hit him, as if something was pushing against the boundaries he had set. He moved back several meters to avoid crashing into Carly and the table. Stretching out his wings, he pushed upward in strong, powerful strokes. From high above, he glanced down at where she stood gazing up at him. In this form, he could see the delicate red threads of magic between them.

A snarl of rage was ripped from him when he felt another tug against his magic. He turned his head and focused on the intrusion. Sweeping his wings in strong, powerful strokes, he sped off to the north.

CHAPTER 10

Carly sighed as her gaze remained glued to Drago's fading figure. She would never get tired of watching him shift into a dragon. She lifted her hand to push her hair out of her eyes when a gentle breeze caught it. Lowering her hand, she couldn't resist pinching herself to see if all of this was real.

"Ouch! Yep, it's real," she said with a disbelieving shake of her head.

So much had happened in just twenty-four hours that her head was swirling. She froze as she turned when a horrible thought popped into her head. Her gaze swept over the walls of the palace to the ocean.

What if time moved faster here than it did back in Yachats?

"Jenny could be a little old lady! I have to find a way back. I have to at least let Jenny know I'm okay," she said, glancing back at the table where the barely touched breakfast was before looking in the direction Drago had disappeared.

With a determined nod, Carly turned back to the table and gathered the dishes. She would take the fruit and nuts with her. There was no telling how long Drago would be gone or how long she would be for that matter.

Carly thought about what she would do and Drago's warning for her to stay in the palace. Since where she was going was still technically a part of the building, she wasn't disobeying him. She was smart enough to know that if a dragon said to stay put, that meant there might be bigger and meaner things out there than he was. She might be clumsy, but she wasn't too stupid to live – well, most of the time. Exercising didn't count.

First, she would find a way down to the lower levels. From what she could see, there were a lot of levels in the palace. Then, she would find a way beneath it until she found the cavern with all the gold and jewels. Once she found that, it wouldn't take long to find the passage, hike the rest of the trail, hope she hadn't gotten a parking ticket – or worse, her car had been towed – then drive home, call Jenny, tell her that everything would be fine, quit her job, gather all her personal belongings, drive back, hike up, squeeze through, and be back.

"All of that should only take me about a week," Carly sighed, walking down the hallway to get her backpack. "I'll have to leave Drago a note. Argh! What if he can't read it? What if our written language is different and the only reason we can talk to each other is because of the magic here? There is no guarantee that it will work for writing."

She groaned in frustration. Opening her backpack, she placed it on the bed and rummaged through it, searching for the small notepad at the bottom. She grunted in triumph when her fingers closed over the paper and pen. Pulling them out, she sat on the edge of the bed and thought about what she could write to convey what she was doing.

She decided that stick figures worked. She carefully drew out a picture of herself with her backpack going down the stairs to the cavern below. Next, she drew a figure of herself going through the passageway to her world. Drawing out the mountain and a line for the trail down to her car, she added a series of stick figures.

Turning the page, she continued drawing pictures of herself in her car going to her house. There, she added her backpack bulging along with a suitcase. By the time she was done and coming back to the palace, she had used up ten of the small square pages of the notepad she'd gotten from the bank. Numbering the corner of each page, she placed them in sequence on the bed.

"That should work," she said, gazing down at the drawings and following them to make sure they made sense.

Carly thought the added touch of her hugging Drago in his dragon form should be enough to reassure him that she was coming back. Satisfied that she had done everything she could to communicate clearly with him, she picked up her backpack and crossed the bedroom to the door. She turned and glanced at the bed, remembering waking up in Drago's arms just a few hours ago.

"I'll be back. I promise," she swore before turning and hurrying down the hallway and out of the doors.

∼

The warmth of the sun caressed his scales and heated his body as much as the anger coursing through him. Drago soared through the air with a deadly purpose. His piercing gaze swept over the land below him, searching for the cause of the unease building inside him.

His lips tightened when he caught sight of the ship offshore. He swerved over the tall trees and down along the treacherous cliffs. Weaving in and out of the towering rocks rising from the sea, he flew closer to the ship. Reaching out, he slowed enough to grasp onto one of the large, black rock towers. He gripped the uneven rock face, clinging to it with his claws, and worked his way to the side until he could see the ship.

Monster! he thought with distaste.

His lip curled as the large ship touched down on the water. Each of the four winged creatures which were carrying it landed on a long perch – two in the front and two in the back. The four beasts were sleek, covered in blue-green feathers, and had long, wispy tails that snapped in the wind. Small bolts of lightning interconnected them, effectively warning any to keep their distance. Each beast had four translucent wings that folded back against their bodies. Drago could see the lines of electricity running through the veins in their wings. Their heads were long and narrow and their beaks filled with razor sharp teeth.

Drago watched as a slender, dark skinned woman climbed up the steps to the bow of the ship. He would have recognized that confident stride and jerk of her head anywhere – Nali. The Empress of the Isle of the Monsters was as beautiful as she was deadly. She was also smart enough and powerful enough to feel the wards he had spun around the Isle and made sure that she kept her ship just far enough out to sea to let him know it was there without becoming entangled in the spell.

He pushed back against the rock. His wings opened and he twisted. Using the wind to give him the lift he needed to rise above the pillars, he soared upward.

Drago kept a healthy distance from the thunderbirds perched on each corner of the ship. High above the vessel, he locked gazes with Nali. She returned his heated gaze with a steady one of her own. The thunderbirds snapped their beaks at him as shafts of white hot energy danced along the veins of their translucent wings. Nali's chin lifted and her hands shot out in warning to the creatures protecting her.

"Drago! It is true. You have awakened," Nali called out when she saw him.

"What do you want Empress?" Drago demanded.

"I need your help," she admitted.

Drago's eyes narrowed. Unease washed through him at her admission. His first thought was to deny her, but something held him back. How had she known he had awakened?

"Calm your beasts, Empress," Drago ordered.

"*Yetiz!*" Nali ordered with a wave of her hands.

The thunderbirds immediately calmed. Drago's gaze moved to the crew warily watching him. Nali sensed his hesitation. A reluctant smile curved her lips. She raised her right arm and snapped her fingers. Within seconds, the men and women aboard disappeared below deck.

Drago circled the ship once before coming in for a landing. His wings folded and he shifted less than a meter from the ship, landing on the upper deck near the helm. He ignored Nali's raised eyebrow at this maneuver which placed him above her.

"How did you know I slept?" Drago demanded, folding his arms across his chest and watching Nali walk toward him.

"No dragons have been seen for years – since the Great Battle ended. It was known those who came to trade with the Isle of the

Dragon either returned empty handed, unable to find entrance through the mists, or did not return at all," Nali stated.

"That does not explain how you knew I slept and that I had awakened," Drago retorted.

Nali's expression softened. "Your dragons were not the only ones affected by the Sea Witch's magic. When one of my cyclops' ships did not return, I sent another and then another. One by one, each ship failed to return. Finally, two of my crew members were rescued. They explained what they had seen to me. I came to see for myself and felt the wards you had spun. I could see beyond the veil and saw the tainted remains of the Sea Witch's evil. I knew from the spells cast that you lived, but all the Goddess' Mirror revealed was your slumbering form," she admitted with a rueful smile.

"You would use the Goddess' magic to spy on me?" Drago demanded, dropping his arms to his sides and stepping toward Nali.

Nali warily moved from one foot to the other on the bottom step. Drago paused at the top and placed his hands on each side of the railing. His fingers dug into the wood at the violation to the sacred magical agreement between Kingdoms not to use the Goddess' gift against another kingdom.

"I was desperate, Drago. The Sea Witch's darkness is threatening my kingdom also. I fought it as long as I could, but even we are not infallible. My powers are weakening, dark threads are creeping up out of the ocean and slowly killing my kingdom. My people are in danger," Nali fervently explained.

"The Goddess' Mirror was given to you to protect your people, not to spy on me, Nali. It is against the Laws of the Seven Kingdoms to use a gift from the Goddess on another Kingdom," Drago argued.

"I did use it in order to protect my people! It does not show me everything, but I saw the strange woman who awakened you, and I am certain she is the key to saving us all. The Goddess gave you the Dragon's Heart to protect your people, Drago, do not tell me that you would not have used it to save them if you could have," Nali retorted, suddenly angry. She waved her hands toward his kingdom. "What do you want me to do – let my subjects perish like yours have done?"

Drago paused to contain his fury, then spoke in a measured voice.

"You have brought the Goddess' Mirror out into the open – into the *ocean*, and it did not occur to you that doing so tempts the Sea Witch to take it from you?" he challenged.

"If she did obtain it, she would see nothing," Nali insisted in a quiet voice.

Drago shook his head. "You do not know that," he said.

Nali lifted her chin in defiance. "The mirror is a reflection of the Goddess' soul, Drago. It reflects the hope inside her and cannot be used for evil – despite what the Sea Witch wishes. The Goddess' Mirror was only banned because you and the other rulers do not understand it. As an extra precaution, I also ensured that neither she nor anyone else can see what the mirror holds," she informed him.

Drago's gaze narrowed on Nali's face. For a brief second, sorrow glittered in her eyes before it was replaced with a confident mask once again. His gut – and his dragon – told him that he *would* have done anything to save his people, even if it meant violating their most sacred treaty. These were truly desperate times. He also knew without a doubt that she had told him far more than she wished to about the mirror, and he would learn nothing more about it. Releasing a tense sigh, he shook his head.

"There is nothing I can do to help you, Nali. My people are gone. My only desire now is to find and kill the Sea Witch," he stated, looking over the bow to his kingdom.

"I know what happened to your people. Many sea monkeys saw your people beneath the waves near the cliffs, their bodies turned to stone," Nali said, climbing the steps until she stood in front of him. "There may be a way to save them, but not if you kill the Sea Witch. I saw it in the mirror. Something otherworldly controls her. If you and Orion can capture her, you can kill it. Once free, the Sea Witch could reverse her spells."

Drago looked down at Nali with a hard expression. "Nothing controls the Sea Witch but her own greed for power. I will capture her, but only to end her life. Leave the waters around my kingdom, Empress, there is nothing left here for you or anyone else," he ordered.

"You are wrong, Drago. If you kill the Sea Witch without killing the creature that has taken over her body, you will condemn all of us," Nali warned.

Drago shook his head. "There is no creature, Nali. I saw her. I saw what she did. Return to your kingdom. I hope you are more successful at protecting your people than I was at protecting mine."

"Drago… You obstinate dragon! The creature is not from…," Nali began to insist before she threw up her hands in exasperation. "Fine! If you will not listen to me, then I will seek Orion's support to stop you!" she threatened.

Drago heard Nali's reply, but didn't respond. Stepping back, he shifted into his dragon and swept upward. The thunderbirds, sensing his turbulent emotions, glowed with the electricity inside them. Turning back toward the land, Drago soared upward and landed on one of the tall spires of rock that rose from the ocean floor.

Nali stared at him for several long minutes before he saw her turn and snap out a command. Her crew appeared from the companionway and lower hatches, pouring onto the deck. The thunderbirds' wings spread wide, electricity crackling in the air. The crew harnessed the energy using long, iron rods that channeled the energy to the engines. The beasts rose into the air, lifting the ship by the harnesses attached to them.

Drago watched from his perch as Nali cast him one last, frustrated look before motioning for the ship's helmsman to turn the craft around. It wasn't until the ship was a distant smudge on the horizon that Drago turned his attention away. He twisted on the rock and pushed off. He would fly around the isle to ensure he had no more visitors, then he would return to Carly.

CHAPTER 11

"I'm not lost. I'm not lost. Oh, man, I am so totally lost," Carly said in exasperation, turning in a tight circle on the dark landing. She glanced up at the narrow stairway leading upward before turning to look over the edge at the never-ending steps leading down. A loud groan escaped her, echoing in the underground cavern and mocking her attempts to find a way back to where she had entered yesterday. "How many frigging levels does this place have? Whoever heard of a building needing this many rooms and doors? I don't even think Buckingham Palace has this many!"

Okay, well, it might. It wasn't like Carly had ever been to Buckingham Palace. Heck, she had never been out of the country before! One thing was for sure, finding her way back home was a lot harder than she had thought it was going to be.

Releasing another loud, echoing sigh, Carly adjusted the backpack on her shoulders. She had already been heading down for a long time, there was absolutely no way she was going back up. Her thighs and calves were already killing her.

"Stairmaster, I'll just think of this as the ultimate, gym training session– one of those iron man super courses that the gym downtown offered last spring," Carly huffed as she held onto the wall so she wouldn't get dizzy looking down the long, long drop on the other side. "Handrails... I'm going to recommend handrails and more lighting. Maybe I can convince Drago to install an elevator or escalator, too. Mm, not an escalator, that would be the world's longest one and I'm not sure they can build one that big. I wonder if they have magical elevators. Now, that would be cool – step in and pop out on the other end."

Carly decided that focusing on how to get to the top without having to climb all the stairs would be better than thinking about what she was going to do if she got to the bottom only to find out she was in the wrong place and had to crawl out. She had no doubt that crawling was going to be her only recourse if she planned on ever getting out of this miserable labyrinth of stairs.

She began to shiver even more the lower she descended. Soon, she was shivering uncontrollably and her teeth were chattering. She paused and pulled out her jacket and gloves before pulling her backpack back over her left shoulder. The extra clothing wasn't helping. It felt like she was freezing from the inside out.

"I su... sur... sure... don... don't... remem... remember... it... being... this... col... col... freezing!" Carly groaned.

She stumbled on the next step, unable to see in the dim light and around the edge of her jacket. She reached out to grip the wall, but it was slick and her hand slipped against the polished stone. A horrified gasp escaped her when she began to fall forward. She stumbled, her hand slipped again, and she fell onto the landing. Her backpack slid off her shoulder. Before she could grab it, the backpack skidded across the smooth stone and over the edge. She found herself frozen to the landing, staring into the bottomless chasm where her bag had disappeared.

Shaken, Carly pushed back from the edge and rolled over until she could sit with her back against the wall. The cold had soaked into her bones until she felt like she would never get warm again. Tears of frustration and defeat glittered in her eyes, but she blinked them away. Crying wouldn't get her out of this mess.

A sudden wave of exhaustion washed over her. Her eyes felt heavy and she swore the fog was moving into her brain the way it did over the shoreline in Yachats – thick and seemingly impenetrable. Shaking her head to clear her mind, Carly felt herself slipping again, this time to the side. She protected her head with her arm, folding it up under her head to keep her face away from the icy stone step that she was now using as a pillow.

"I'll… just… close my eyes… for a… minute," she murmured, her voice fading as her eyelashes fluttered closed, weighted by a sudden, overwhelming fatigue. "Drago…."

Carly's softly spoken call echoed upward through the maze of stairs, carried by the magic that had been cast to confuse and trap those unlucky enough to get caught in the endless maze that led nowhere. The magic captured the single name in a bubble that floated and bounced as it rose higher and higher.

Carly was completely unaware of the deadly magic that had closed around her. Tired from her journey and frozen from the plummeting temperature, she fell into a slumber that pulled her deeper and deeper into its greedy clutches until her heart barely beat.

∼

Drago carried the limp body of a fish in one clawed hand and several large pieces of ripe fruit in the other. He had picked the fruit at the last minute from a large bush full of ripe red treedrops. The fish he had caught from a nearby freshwater lake.

Swooping down, he landed on the railing, balancing for a moment before he hopped down. He placed both the fish and the fruit on the balcony before he shifted and looked around. The table was cleared of the morning breakfast several hours before.

Glancing toward the French doors, he saw they were closed as well. Bending, he picked up the fish and the fruit. He would clean the fish after he let Carly know he had returned.

Gingerly opening the door with a wave of his hand, he stepped inside. He caught the door with his foot, preventing it from slamming closed behind him when a gust of wind blew in off the ocean. This was probably why Carly had the doors closed.

Drago frowned at the silence. The room was immaculate. Walking through the living area to the kitchen, he noticed the dishes from earlier were washed and left to dry next to the sink. He walked over and placed the fish in the sink before releasing the two melons. His nose wrinkled when he noticed the smell on his hands and he quickly washed and dried them.

"Carly?" Drago called out before frowning again.

Perhaps she is taking a rest, he thought.

It wouldn't surprise him if she had returned to bed. She had traveled a fair distance yesterday, and besides the fact that she had to be exhausted from her trip, she had cleaned his living quarters as well. That was a task which normally was a day's work for three or more of his staff to do in previous years.

Walking down the hallway, the twist in his gut grew, warning him that something was wrong. He picked up his pace, entering the room at almost a run. His gaze swept over the empty bed. He crossed the bedroom, already knowing the answer to his question – the open door and empty bathing chamber confirmed his suspicion – Carly wasn't in his living quarters.

Drago turned on his heel to retrace his steps. He glanced at the bed once more and paused when he noticed something spread out on top. Shifting his direction, he walked over to the bed. A frown creased his brow when he saw the long row of papers spread across the dark blue bedspread.

He bent and picked up the first paper, staring down at the illustration. A confused expression, part exasperation and part intrigue, crossed his face as he 'read' Carly's message. It took a few tries to finally get her meaning. When he finally understood that she was trying to return to her world, fury poured through him.

"Never!" he snarled, crushing the paper in his fist.

He paused, then lifted the paper to his nose and breathed in a deep breath. The fragrance of Carly, mixed with the soap from the kitchen, teased his nostrils. Turning, he followed the faint trail she had left behind. He snorted in displeasure when he realized that she had left his living quarters before he grimaced at his unreasonable irritation. He had just cautioned her to stay in the palace, not his rooms.

He continued down the corridor to the far set of steps. Once again, a sense of urgency gripped him. Pausing on the lower level, he released his grip on the white sheet with the drawings on it.

"Take me to her," he ordered, casting a Finding spell over the foreign material.

The crumpled ball of paper unfolded and reformed into a small bird that turned to look at him with a somewhat confused expression. A wry smile curved Drago's lips. Finding spells took on a part of the essence of the person who had left the item. The bird had emulated Carly's personality perfectly – especially when it wobbled and almost fell to the ground when it turned.

Drago quickly scooped the paper bird into his palm and waited for it to refold one wing. Tiny wisps of dust brushed across his palm when the bird sneezed. He raised an eyebrow at the magical paper creature and impatiently waited while it smoothed out its tail feathers.

"Are you finished yet?" he demanded.

The tiny creature wiggled its tail at him and opened its beak. It must have thought better than to push its luck any further when Drago flexed his fingers in warning. Drago watched the creature turn on his palm and wiggle one more time before fluttering up into the air.

"Find her," he ordered again.

The paper bird nodded and turned. With much more speed than Drago had anticipated, it took off down the stairwell. Drago darted after it, taking several steps at a time to keep up with the creature ahead of him. It wasn't until they reached the main floor of the palace and the bird turned to the corridors leading to the lower levels that Drago realized exactly where Carly had gone and the danger she was in.

Drago rushed down the corridor. His hands opened wide and the door at the end opened. The bird disappeared through the opening and down the long spiral staircase. Drago followed as quickly as his human form would allow.

On the lower level, the bird fluttered impatiently at the door at the end. It disappeared through the narrow iron bars across the rectangular opening. With another muttered spell, the door opened for Drago.

He had descended almost a dozen flights of stairs before he saw the shimmer of a colorful light rising from the dark labyrinth toward him. His steps slowed as the bubble drifted closer to him. The paper bird fluttered around it, curious.

"Come to me," Drago ordered the bubble, holding out his hand to the floating apparition.

The bubble twirled as a current of warm air brushed against it, gently pushing it closer. Drago's fingers itched to grasp it, but he dared not. If the bubble broke before he could touch it, the message held inside would be lost. The staircases below the palace were a never ending maze, constructed and spelled to confuse any who tried to enter the treasure cavern far below. For those seeking it, only one staircase, taken in the correct sequence would lead them to the Dragon's Treasure. All the other staircases would take the intruders on an unending search where they would be lost forever unless rescued by the King of the Dragons.

Drago reached out both hands and cupped the bubble when it floated close enough. He opened his hands and stared down at the image locked inside. Carly was lying on one of the landings with her head resting on her arm. Ice crystals clung to her eyelashes and her lips held a tinge of blue. Fear gripped him. She could be anywhere in the maze.

The paper bird must have felt the pull of Carly. It landed on his hand, hopped along his finger and peered at her slumbering form. Drago was about to issue a command when the bird pecked at the bubble. The translucent shape burst in a kaleidoscope of colorful sparkles.

"Drago...." Carly's faint voice, captured inside the sphere, called to him.

"Where...?" Drago choked out.

The paper bird, decorated by the remains of the magic from the bubble, shook and chirped before launching off of Drago's finger. Time was of the essence. Shifting into his dragon, he plummeted off the edge of the steps after the tiny, now colorful bird.

CHAPTER 12

*D*rago weaved in and out between the maze of steps, cutting through tall, narrow doorways, following the paper bird as it sped through the deep cavern. Sweeping over a large boulder, Drago tucked his wings and rolled as they passed through another doorway. His stomach rubbed against the stone pillar, but he refused to let it deflect him from his mission.

Nearly twenty minutes later, the bird passed through a large opening. Against the far wall, Drago could see the glowing light lying near Carly. Spinning upward, Drago swept past the bird that headed for Carly. He shifted, landing on the platform above her.

He took the steps down two at a time. The paper bird chirped at him as it hopped onto Carly's shoulder. Drago knelt next to Carly. He picked up her hand. Her slender fingers were almost blue. Leaning forward, he tenderly rolled her enough so that he could slide his arm under her and lift her up.

Her head rolled and her cold nose touched his neck under his chin. He couldn't feel her breathing. The tightness in his stomach grew along with the unfamiliar sensation of panic. He lifted her frozen fingers to his mouth and blew on them.

"Drago…," Carly moaned in a barely audible voice.

"Ah, my little thief, what did you think you were doing?" Drago gently chided.

"I left you a note," she said in a voice that slurred. "You… need… an…."

"What do I need, little thief?" Drago asked, holding her closer to his warm body.

His breath caught when she didn't answer. The paper bird landed on Carly's knee and chirped at him. He drew in a deep breath and nodded.

"Yes, I need to get her warm," Drago agreed.

His body shimmered. One second Drago was holding Carly; the next, a dragon was. They were one and the same, both determined to protect the fragile creature who was quickly capturing their hearts with her fierce personality.

Drago grunted to the paper bird. It took off first, its tiny, delicate wings fluttering madly to lead the way back to the upper levels. Unwilling to chance dropping or harming Carly, Drago murmured the spell, causing the ground to open up as he flew upward until Carly, the paper bird and he burst through to the courtyard and out into the fading sunlight.

He rose even higher until he reached the balcony of his living quarters. Shifting even as he landed, he tightly cradled Carly's unconscious form against his body. He decided the best way to warm her was in the large bathing pool in the bathing chamber. The doors opened at his command and he walked through to the bedroom.

Gently laying Carly down, he methodically removed her boots before removing her jacket and the tunic he had given her this morning. His fingers paused for a moment on the waist of her pants before he muttered a curse under his breath and removed those, along with her pink panties. Once she was undressed, Drago removed his own clothing. Worried that her breathing was too shallow, he shot a glance at the fireplace. His fist clenched for a moment before opening. With a flick of his wrist, he tossed the fireball in his hand at the fireplace. Flames flared in a brilliant display of colors, igniting the enchanted wood.

The room would quickly warm with the fire. Returning his attention to Carly, he gently picked her up and cradled her in his arms once again. Her body was icy and her skin a pale, unnatural shade of blue.

"I will not lose you, Carly," Drago said in a quiet voice. "I cannot lose you."

Drago crossed the room and into the bathing chamber. He stepped over the side of the deep bath and down the steps. The sensors imbedded in the pool flashed and jets of warm water began to fill the large tub. Drago used the controls on the side to adjust the water until he was satisfied with the heat level.

He sank down onto one of the built in seats and held Carly close to his body. A soft whimper escaped her when the water swirled around her feet and moved up her legs. Drago held her when she jerked and tried to escape the warm water. Her fingers moved against his skin, as if she were trying to clutch at him but couldn't quite get her fingers to work properly. It wasn't until the water swirled around their waists that she melted back against him and quit trying to fight him. A low groan escaped both of them, the sounds of their voices blending in harmony with the intense feelings coursing through them. For Carly, it was her body beginning to defrost. For Drago, it was the feel of Carly's body pressed against his own.

"What am I going to do with you, my little thief?" Drago asked in a quiet, remorseful tone. "I have been alone for far too long, Carly. The thought of losing you is more than I wish to bear." Drago relaxed against the seat. "I will tell you a story, one that you will not remember and one that I have never shared with anyone else. Perhaps, this is the best time to tell you since I am not sure I would share it otherwise," he reflected with a wry smile, rubbing his thumb along her arm. "It is the story of my people… and myself."

CHAPTER 13

Pain radiated throughout every nerve ending in Carly's body. She swore even the ends of her hair hurt, which was ridiculous since hair had no pain receptors. She couldn't remember ever being so cold in her life.

When Drago's warm hand touched her, all Carly wanted to do was snuggle against him. The sound of his voice had washed through her numb body, slowly penetrating the fog that had wrapped around her mind. She had been unable to silence the moan of pain that escaped her. The heat from his body felt like it was searing her. At the same time, she was reluctant to move for fear she was just imagining that he had found her.

Her memories of him picking her up, talking to someone, chiding her, and their journey back to his living quarters were interspersed with periods of darkness. She liked the darkness because then she couldn't feel the agonizing fire licking at her skin. Carly was vaguely aware when he laid her down on the bed. She had wanted to turn over and curl up, but Drago had started tugging at her clothing. Her lips parted to protest – she would surely freeze more quickly without them – but it had been too much of an effort and she had allowed the darkness to swallow her once again.

That darkness had begun to fade the moment she felt the warm water strike her like the sparks from a welder's torch. She had immediately noticed two things: she was alive; and Drago felt utterly wonderful with his warm, strong, and naked body against hers. There was no way she was going to burst this bubble in case she was still unconscious. She much preferred this fantasy to the reality of the endless staircase.

Carly relaxed against Drago when the pain began to fade. The warm water bubbled around them, melting the ice that had sunk deep into her bones. She relished the feel of Drago's thumb brushing against her skin.

Remaining still, she listened to his heartbeat under her ear. Above the sound of the water, his deep voice rang clear in the large bathroom. Carly listened when he began talking.

"The dragons are among the oldest peoples of the Seven Kingdoms – only those of the elements are older. Next came the people of the sea, followed by magic, then the monsters and giants… and then there are the pirates – the outcasts of the Seven Kingdoms. They, especially their king Ashure Waves, are a pain in everyone's backside but brilliant opponents when it comes to bartering – and stealing. The old archives say that our world formed after a fight between the Goddess and her mate. In her rage, she split the world in half, leaving her mate to rule one world while the Goddess ruled over this one," he explained, stroking his hand over her bare arm.

Unable to pretend she was still unconscious, Carly tilted her head back and gazed up at Drago. She could visualize so clearly his description of this world's riveting beginnings. He turned his head to look down at her. His hand rose and he drew a damp finger along her still pale cheek.

"Why did you leave me?" Drago demanded in a voice thick with an emotion Carly wasn't sure she understood.

Carly frowned and shook her head. "I was planning on coming back. I needed to let Jenny know what happened to me. We're like sisters. If she were to disappear, I'd never stop looking for her," she said, running her hand up his chest and laying it over his heart. "I promise… I was coming back. I couldn't leave you alone again."

Drago reached over, gripped her hand, and pulled it to his lips. Carly watched him press a kiss to the back of her fingers. A swell of emotions rushed through her – compassion, warmth, hope, determination, and something else – the beginning of love. Her eyes widened at the thought that this was a man she could fall in love with. For a brief second, she swore she saw tiny glittering red threads weaving around their entwined hands.

"Drago…." Carly blinked and shook her head. "Tell me more about your world," she requested, laying her head back against his chest.

Drago regained her hand and began speaking again. "First came the elements: earth, wind, fire, water, and sky. The Goddess created elementals to control them and created the Isle of Elements for them. Next, the Goddess created dragons. We were born from the fire that burned in her heart for the creatures she loved so much. She created the Dragon's Heart, a powerful red diamond that contains a part of her. The Dragon's Heart captures the very essence of who we are and gifts us the ability to change forms," he said, rubbing her hand against his heart.

"What happens if you lose it?" Carly asked, tilting her head back to look up at him.

Drago paused, deep in thought before he continued. "The Seven Kingdoms will cease to exist," he replied with a shake of his head. "Each ruler was given a gift from the Goddess. Ours was a piece of her heart. It is the responsibility of each kingdom to protect the gift they were given – at all costs. The dragons received the Dragon's Heart, the elementals were given the Gem of Power, the sea people the Eyes of the Serpent, and so forth. Each contains a part of the Goddess," he explained.

"So, what happens if one person has all the pieces?" Carly asked with a frown.

Carly knew from the sudden stillness in Drago's body that it wouldn't be a good thing. His expression hardened with anger and his lips tightened. A shiver shook her frame, drawing him back from whatever dark thoughts he was having.

"Whoever controls all the pieces, controls the Goddess and the fate of the Seven Kingdoms. If one piece is destroyed, it would be a mortal wound to the Goddess – and the death of our world," he finally said.

"What exactly happened to your people, Drago?" Carly asked, sitting up to gaze back at him.

"If you are feeling well enough, I will show you," he replied in a quiet voice.

Carly nodded, then bit back a groan when she felt him move under her. She felt like an idiot for forgetting that they were both naked… in a bathtub together… and she was sitting on his lap.

Only I could blow such a perfect opportunity, she silently berated herself. "That's it, I've pissed off someone in a past life and I'm destined to end up having to live on erotic dreams and my battery operated boyfriend for the rest of eternity."

"I will make sure that your erotic dreams are fulfilled and when you come, it will be by my hand – and more. Though I do find the idea of watching you reach orgasm by your own hand very pleasing," Drago replied, turning to gaze down at her with an expression of amusement in his eyes.

"I said that last part out loud, didn't I?" she groaned, her face flaming with embarrassment and her body suddenly overheated.

"Yes," Drago chuckled.

Carly looked at him in resignation when he held out his hand to her. She couldn't hide under the bubbling water forever. Self-conscious about her weight, she reluctantly slipped her hand into his and stood up. She started to run her hand down over her stomach, but the heat shimmering in his gaze stopped her.

"You make my blood boil with desire, Carly. I want you, little thief," he informed her in a tone touched with awe.

"I…." Carly paused and licked her lips. "I'm not a thief," she whispered.

Drago bent down and brushed a kiss across her lips. Carly leaned up to meet him halfway. Her body exploded with desire and the hand that had moved down to her stomach reached out instead, wrapping around his pulsing cock.

Drago pulled back with a hissing breath. The flames that had been dancing in his eyes now turned into a raging inferno. Carly swallowed. Her eyes widened even as her hand tightened around him.

"Yes, you are. You have…," his voice faded and he looked down.

Carly followed his gaze. He was looking down at where she was holding him. Instead of being embarrassed or shy at her current faux pas, she felt empowered by his reaction to her. Stepping closer to him, she raised his hand to her breast.

"I want you, Drago," she said, refusing to look away.

"What I claim, I do not give away nor let go, Carly," Drago reminded her.

Carly felt Drago's hand splay over her breast. The water churned around her thighs, stroking her sensitive flesh. Her hand moved along his swollen shaft to the head. She might technically still be a virgin, but that didn't mean she hadn't read her share of erotica romances, watched a few late night videos, or had her own personal battery operated boyfriend. Even she realized when she was being offered a chance of a lifetime. She might be clumsy, she might occasionally behave like an idiot, but she wasn't going to look a gift-dragon in the face and turn him away.

"I claimed you, remember?" she replied in a slightly broken voice.

Drago's eyes widened in surprise before his lips curved into a smile. Carly felt his left hand sliding down her arm and around her back even as his right hand kneaded her breast. She took another step closer when he wrapped his arm around her and drew her closer to him.

"Yes, I remember," he said before he bent and captured her lips in a deep kiss that made her forget about everything else.

Carly released him, and her hand slid up his arm until she could wrap it around his neck. She rose up when his left hand dropped to her buttock and he firmly massaged it. Deciding two could play the teasing game, she slid her right hand down and caressed his ass while rubbing against him. A startled gasp escaped her when he pulled away and lifted her up in his arms.

"Drago, put me down! You'll…," Carly started to protest when he stepped out of the water.

"If you want to dry off, you'd better grab a towel as we walk by; otherwise, expect to get the sheets very wet," he interrupted.

Carly giggled and reached for the towels on the shelf when he swept by it. She pulled the towel over his shoulder and against her chest. A moment later, she was standing next to the bed and the towel was now in his hands and he was….

"Oh yes!" Carly breathed, her eyes lighting up when he caressed her aching breasts with the towel, then bent to suck on her nipples. "You are making me wet again."

"It will give me a reason to dry you off," Drago teased, sinking down to one knee. "…here."

Carly's hands shot out and she gripped Drago's broad shoulders. Her breath hiccupped and her eyes glazed with pleasure when he leaned forward and she felt his warm breath against her. For a moment, she wished that she shaved between her legs, but that thought faded into a haze of pleasure when Drago tugged on her soft brown curls. Her legs immediately parted in anticipation.

"Drago," Carly begged.

"I've decided I like you wet," he replied in a rough voice.

Carly melted when he suddenly stood and gently guided her back to the bed. She sat down, scooted up a little, and sank back. Her gaze never moved from his. When his hand slid up the inside of her right leg, she opened for him again.

"A dragon is a very tactile creature," he informed her in a silky tone.

Carly tilted her head back and released a blissful smile. "I knew there was a reason I loved dragons," she retorted before she closed her eyes and moaned softly.

CHAPTER 14

Fire licked through Drago as he parted Carly's legs, opening her to his touch. Her responsiveness to him solidified his certainty that she was his mate, the one destined to stand by his side as his partner. The red threads of their connection danced along his fingertips and across the inside of her thighs.

Drago's breath made the threads swirl in delicate circles. The heat from his breath drew a moan from Carly and she shifted impatiently under his hands, her hips slightly rising off the bed. Following the line of red threads, Drago slid his fingers through the soft, tight, brown curls covering the triangle of her mound. He was rewarded when her legs opened wider. Sliding his other hand up under her, he pressed a hot, open mouth kiss to her left thigh before he nipped it.

"Oh, for goodness sake, will you quit tormenting me!" Carly growled, lifting her legs and placing them over his shoulders. "I am so thinking of revenge if you continue to tease me for too long."

Drago couldn't contain the chuckle that escaped him at her impatient threat. His body was feeling the throb of impatience. It would appear his little thief was going to be a demanding lover – something he would not complain about.

"Did I mention dragons are very tactile creatures?" he teased.

"Did I mention that I am too?" Carly retorted on a loud moan.

"Goddess!"

The word slipped out of Drago before he could contain it. The thought of Carly's hands running all over his body created a visual image that challenged his promise to himself to give her pleasure first before seeking his own.

Carly pressed her heels into his shoulders, pulling him forward. Drago did not need a second invitation. His fingers slid through the tight curls and down along the slick folds. She opened for him like the petals of a flower and he bent forward to savor her like a bird sipping the nectar from the rich fruits that grew from the vines.

Drago ran his tongue over the taut nub that swelled under his teasing. He was rewarded by Carly's strangled cry and trembling body. His fingers slid between her moistening folds.

Drago kept his attention focused on every response, pausing when she stiffened, continuing when she moaned and relaxed. He slowly worked one, then another finger into her, stretching her so that when he entered her, she would feel pleasure and not pain. He didn't stop his tender caresses until her body stiffened and her wild cries grew louder and she came around his fingers.

He continued stroking and sucking on her, drawing her orgasm out until she frantically reached for him. Releasing her, he gently slid her legs off of his shoulders and moved up her body. He pressed hot kisses against her stomach as he slowly worked his way up her writhing form. When he reached her taut nipples, he couldn't resist capturing each one in his mouth.

Carly raised her hands, burying them in his hair and pulling him down to her even as she rose to meet him. He sucked on each rosy peak until they were the size of small pebbles. His own breath caught when Carly wrapped her legs around his waist and aligned her desire swollen entrance with his cock. The heat and slickness from her orgasm brushed against his swollen, over-sensitized head and he groaned loudly from the pulsing need to thrust his hips forward.

He released her right nipple and gazed down between their bodies where he was connected with her before he shifted his gaze to hers. Her eyes were clear, brilliant, melted pools of liquid mahogany. In their dark depths, he could see his reflection. His face was taut and his eyes flaming with need and desire.

"I want you, Drago," Carly said in a gentle voice, sliding one hand down to caress his face.

Drago's arms trembled for a moment. "Then you shall have me, little thief," he replied.

He kept his gaze on her face as he slowly pushed forward. Her orgasm coated his cock. He could feel the muscle in his jaw twitching when her body wrapped around his, pulling him in and fitting like a glove, fisting him. Every inch was sweet torture and pure bliss. Lowering his body down so that he could slide his arms under her and hold her closer, he buried himself deep inside her.

"Sweet goddess, but you have stolen my heart," Drago murmured in a strained voice as he pressed his face against her left cheek.

Carly's arms wrapped around his head and she began moving her hips. The friction of her movements along his cock sent bursts of overwhelming pleasure through him. His body ignited with the fire of his dragon and the desire to claim Carly as his.

Wrapping his arms more firmly around her, his hips took over the rhythm of their primitive dance. He moved faster and faster, the heat between their connection and the slickness of their desire making his thrusts easier even as his cock thickened even more. Pain and pleasure exploded through him when Carly turned her face into his shoulder and bit him. The feel of her teeth was enough to snap his control.

"I want more, Carly," Drago groaned.

"Me… too," Carly breathed out.

Drago wanted to bring Carly to another orgasm. The need to have her completely melted with pleasure under his touch was more instinctive than his need to fulfill his own desires. His mate would always come first. Her desires, her needs, her wants would always be his primary concern.

Rolling, he pulled Carly with him so that she was lying on top of him. Her gasp and the way her eyes widened told him that she had not been expecting his quick move or that such a position would cause his cock to sink deep into the very depths of her womb. The position gave her power, but also allowed him to gaze up at her beauty and freed his hands to explore her swaying breasts.

"You were made for me, Carly," Drago swore, reaching out to cup both of her breasts.

Carly nodded in agreement. Her eyes were half closed with pleasure and she was leaning forward with her hands kneading his chest as she rode him. Drago rose up, pressing her breasts together, and captured both of her nipples. He sucked deeply and was rewarded by her thighs clamping down on his and her heated feminine core pulsing around him. His hips began a strong, rhythmic thrusting.

Drago felt the pressure building in Carly again. This time, he waited until she had peaked before he released the nearly nonexistent control he had on his body. His seed pulsed deep into her, compelled by the spasms of her orgasm. Locked together, they clung to each other before he melted back against the pillows, pulling her with him.

"Wow!" Carly shakily whispered against his neck.

"Wait until the next time," Drago chuckled.

He was rewarded with another nip, this time to his neck. His cock pulsed, reminding him that he had a lot of time to make up for. Rolling again, he captured each of Carly's wrists in his grasp and gazed down at her with a wicked smile.

"What…?" Carly asked, startled.

"Now, I take my time with you," he stated.

"Oh, boy! I really have fallen into a fantasy," Carly breathed with a happy grin.

CHAPTER 15

*L*ater that afternoon, Carly was watching Drago fasten his shirt and wondering if there was something wrong with her. All she could think about was how she wanted to rip Drago's shirt off again and just make him walk around without it – or without anything else on for that matter. It was probably a good thing she had already finished dressing first, otherwise she seriously doubted they would have left the bedroom. Her lips curved in a rueful smile when Drago turned to look at her when he heard her soft sigh. Her smile faltered when he raised an eyebrow in inquiry.

"Earlier… before…."

A blush stained Carly's cheeks and she glanced down at the tiny paper bird that was sitting in the palm of her hand. She had been surprised when she woke a short while ago to find it pecking at a strand of her hair. It had taken several long seconds to realize that it was made of paper. The magical creature had quickly captured her heart with its amusing behavior and curiosity. Drago explained that he had cast a Finding spell in order to locate her and this was what the spell created.

Carly gently stroked the paper feathers while trying to search for what she wanted to say without it sounding dorky. She felt the warmth of Drago's hand before he touched her chin. Lifting her head, she gazed up at him. A shy smile curved her lips when she saw the slight redness on his neck where she had bitten him.

"I left teeth marks on you," she continued in a distracted voice.

"I know, I felt them," Drago teased before his expression became questioning. "You were saying… Earlier…?"

Carly blinked, already feeling the need to be wrapped in his strong arms again. What had transpired between them earlier had deeply affected her. Their lovemaking was more than just physical to her. There was an emotional level to it that shook her, leaving her confused and wary of what she was opening herself up to – real heartache.

Granted, Carly knew she had a big heart and was an emotional person, but she'd always believed that the love she read about in books was make believe. Heck, even her parents hadn't loved each other. The moment she had graduated from high school, they divorced and went their separate ways. Her dad remarried and had a couple of kids and her mom had taken a teaching job overseas and had a new girlfriend. Carly hadn't seen either of them since she and Jenny had moved in together and they only called each other on their birthdays – though, even that wasn't consistent now with her mom in another country and as her dad had said – 'I'm too busy to remember birthdays anymore'.

"I just wanted you to know that I thought what happened was special," she said in an awkward voice.

"I agree," Drago replied, brushing a kiss across her swollen lips. "I wish to show you something."

Carly drew in a deep breath and nodded. The little bird flew up onto her shoulder when she slid her hand into his. She swallowed again when Drago stepped back and gently squeezed her hand. Together, they stepped out of his living quarters and into the outer corridor.

They walked together down the long hallway to the staircase she had walked down early this morning. It took several minutes to remember that he had been going to show her something before they were distracted. Darkness had fallen and now the magical torches ignited along the passageway, illuminating the beautiful tapestries and paintings along the walls. Once again, Carly was reminded that she had fallen into a world unlike anything she could ever have imagined.

"Where are we going?" she asked.

"Earlier you asked what happened to my people. I wish to show you," he replied.

Carly followed Drago as he guided her down the long staircase. At the bottom, they crossed a large open foyer that Carly recognized from her earlier adventures. Her gaze went to the door that led down into the labyrinth below and a shiver ran through her body. Instinctively, she moved closer to Drago. A smile curved her lips when the tiny paper bird on her shoulder hopped closer and tried to hide in her hair.

She lifted a finger to stroke it. Drago released her hand and paused in front of a set of massive doors. They had been locked when Carly had tried the doors earlier. Drago reached forward and gripped the handles, pushing the doors open.

"How...? Oh yeah, no doors remain locked against you," Carly said with a shake of her head.

Drago stood in the doorway looking into the interior. His face was a frozen mask. Carly, unsure of what to do next, peered into the darkness. One by one, the torches flared to life. Her throat tightened when she caught her first glimpse of what the room contained. Stepping past Drago, she entered the room.

"What is this?" she asked in a quiet voice.

"This is just a small gathering of my people," Drago replied, his voice echoing through the room filled with hundreds of statues.

Carly paused by the frozen figure of a dragon trying to protect a small boy. The boy was turned toward the dragon trying to protect him, his small hands desperately reaching around the large creature. The boy's head was tilted back, his mouth open, and Carly could see the traces of tears on his cheeks. The dragon, Carly suspected it was the boy's mother from the delicate features and the way she protectively encircled the boy with her body, was staring off into the distance with a look of fear and horror. Carly raised her hand and trailed her fingers along the little boy's face, wishing she could dry his tears.

"Her name is Morgan. The boy is her son, Arid. His father is – was – one of the gatekeepers," Drago said.

Carly moved among the statues. Each figure was frozen in a different position. Some statues were in their person form while others in their dragon. She gently traced over them with her fingers as she moved throughout the room, her heart nearly bursting with grief. On all of their faces was the identical look of horror and fear.

"Where are the others?" Carly asked, turning to look back at Drago with tears shimmering in her eyes. "You said… you said this is just a small gathering. Where are the others?"

Carly saw Drago's throat move up and down before he reached out and ran his hand down the long scorch mark on the dragon nearest him. She saw his hand pause over the mark before he continued down to the dragon's shoulder and rested his hand there. His gaze moved around the room before settling back on her.

"Many are still in their homes, others – others were lost to the sea," he said, turning away from her.

Carly could hear the grief in Drago's voice. Her gaze swept over the room filled with statues….

No, not statues, Drago's people, she thought, pausing on the figure of a large dragon shielding a woman and two small children.

The tears that Carly fought so hard to hold back spilled over and silently slid down her face. She threaded her way back to Drago. He must have sensed her approach because he turned toward her and opened his arms. Carly practically fell into them, choking sobs shaking her body as she cried for all the people who couldn't.

Drago held her tightly against his body. She could feel his cheek on her head. He held her to him with one hand and caressed her hair with the other. Carly felt the shudder that ran through his body.

"Come with me, I wish to show you my kingdom," Drago finally said, releasing her.

Carly nodded and wiped her hands across her damp cheeks. She released a watery laugh when the little paper bird tried to help her. It chirped when one of its wings stuck against her damp skin. Carly carefully pulled it free and shook her head.

"You need to be more careful, Little Knight," she gently admonished.

"Little Knight? It is just paper," Drago commented, glancing at the bird.

Carly shook her head and ran her finger over the bird's tiny head. "No, he's not. Little Knight saved my life, like a knight in shining armor," she said, turning to look up at Drago with a tender smile. "He showed you where I was. He's… magic."

"If you like the creature so much, I will make you a flock of paper birds," Drago stated, reaching for her hand.

Carly followed Drago out of the Great Room. Her resolve to stay with Drago strengthened when he shut and locked the doors. She never wanted him to be alone again. No one should have to live through what he had witnessed and remain alone.

His tender vow to create a flock of paper birds melted her heart. Deep down, Carly knew she was no longer falling in love, she was already completely in love. How an emotion so strong could happen so quickly, she didn't know.

She remembered the saying 'love at first sight' and had read about it in books, but she always believed it was a fairy tale made up to make little girls believe. Oh, she had seen couples in love. There were several older couples who were inseparable back home, but she'd figured it was more of a deeper friendship than actual love. She definitely knew that infatuation and lust were real, she saw that all the time and had felt it a few times herself. This emotion was different. She felt – whole, as if a piece of the puzzle that had been missing was suddenly found. There was a powerful physical attraction as well as a chemical reaction to him, yet she couldn't put her finger on why it was there – it just was.

Carly watched the massive front doors open when Drago waved his hand. The paper bird chirped and lifted off her shoulder. Little Knight turned in the opening and chirped again, as if telling her to come on!

"My, but you are an impatient little thing!" she giggled.

She followed Drago down the front steps to the courtyard. The last light of the day began to fade and the stars were coming out. Carly swore it looked like they were so close that she could reach out her hand and touch them.

"The kingdom is magnificent during the day, but absolutely magical at night," Drago said, pausing to look up at the night sky.

"It's magical to me all the time," Carly replied in a quiet voice.

Drago turned to look at her. Carly stepped closer to him when he reached out towards her. She tilted her head and pressed her face into his hand when he ran his fingers down along her cheek.

"You have stolen the heart of this dragon, little thief. That is something I never thought possible," Drago said in a soft, tender voice.

The corner of Carly's mouth lifted in a teasing smile when she realized why he called her little thief. She had finally come to accept his nickname for her as the sweetest, most special endearment she had ever heard. His softly spoken words just sealed the last of her doubts. She had fallen in love with the most magnificent man in this entire, fantastical world.

"I think I love you, Drago," Carly admitted with a wavering smile of uncertainty.

"Good," Drago replied, stepping back. "Now, you will fall in love with our kingdom."

An exasperated frown flickered across Carly's face. She declares her love for him and he responds with a 'good'. What the heck was that supposed to mean? She was about to point that out when his body shimmered and he transformed into his dragon form.

Carly watched in confusion when Drago knelt down. The little bird excitedly chirped near his shoulder, fluttering from Drago to her and back again. Drago turned his head and looked at her, raising his eyebrow when she remained rooted to the spot she was standing on.

"Well, do you wish to see your kingdom?" Drago asked in a slightly amused tone.

"My kingdom? How?" Carly asked.

"Climb onto my back," Drago instructed.

"Climb...? Okay, climb, like on a horse," Carly replied in a slightly uneasy voice. "Did I ever happen to mention that the only horse I have ever ridden was on a merry-go-round... and that I fell off of it?"

Drago's husky laughter filled the air. "I do not know what this merry-go-round horse was like, but I will not let you fall off," he promised.

"Yeah, well, those could be the last famous words I ever hear," Carly muttered under her breath.

She tentatively stepped closer to Drago's large body and looked up. His shoulders stood way over her head. There was no way she could climb up that far. Biting her lip, she started to shake her head. A startled squeak escaped her when she felt a strong scaled band wrap around her waist and she was suddenly lifted into the air.

"Drago!"

"I will not let you fall, Carly. Trust me," he said.

Carly's fingers curled against the scales of his tail. She muttered a soft curse when she looked down and realized she was several meters above the ground. She swallowed past the lump that formed in her throat and nodded when he gently lowered her to sit astride his shoulders and neck. Instinctively, her fingers clutched one of the large fin-shaped membranes that ran along the back of his head and down his neck. She tightened her thigh muscles and braced her heels against the front of his shoulders.

"I can already tell that this is a really, really bad idea, Drago. Don't you have a pair of binoculars or one of those machines you put a quarter in to look around? I mean... Eek!"

Carly's voice faded on a loud screech when Drago's muscles tightened under her and he pushed upward. Terrified, she leaned forward and wrapped her arms as far as she could around Drago's neck, buried her face against his smooth scales, and closed her eyes, all the while muttering dire threats and begging forgiveness for all her past sins.

"You will have to tell me about of some of these sins. Something tells me the list would not be very long, but it could be very entertaining," he chuckled.

"Oh, just shut up. I can't believe I am doing this," she sniffed against his neck.

"I swear I will not let you fall, Carly," he insisted.

She didn't respond. Her arms and legs trembled with the effort to hold onto him. Her stomach dropped when he started to fly in an upward direction. She was having trouble breathing. The fear and panic threatened to choke her. Black dots danced behind her closed eyelids. Her fear of passing out grew until she opened her mouth to cry out a warning to Drago. Her eyes snapped open at the same time.

The cry of terror she was about to release died on her lips. Her stunned gaze locked on the beauty of the stars and the faint wisps of clouds. On the horizon, the fading red, yellow, and orange glow of the setting sun was in stark contrast to the darkness of the night.

"The moons will rise shortly," Drago said.

"Oh, Drago, it is – breathtaking," Carly whispered, unsure that he could hear her, but needing to express the awe she was feeling anyway.

Breathtaking was an understatement. The view of his kingdom from above literally took her breath away. The setting sun illuminated the horizon like a blazing fire, igniting the ocean in an array of colors before it slowly dissolved and faded.

Carly turned her head to look along the coastline. She expected it to be too dark to see, but waves of brilliant green and blue bioluminescence lit up the water along the cliffs. A startled laugh escaped her when the little paper bird flew by them before turning back toward the palace after Drago snorted at it.

"Where is Little Knight going?" Carly asked in concern, trying to follow the bird's flight.

"I instructed him to stay close to the palace. Where we are going he might get damaged," Drago stated.

"Oh, good. Where are the lights coming from down in the forests?" Carly asked, leaning forward.

"Many of the plants and animals have a chemical that glows at night, much like those in the water. Hang on tightly," Drago replied.

Carly blinked when she realized that she was barely gripping the curved ridges along his neck. She tightened her hold on Drago just as he swooped downward. She gasped and then felt a sense of exhilaration sweep through her. She could feel the power in Drago's dragon body as he guided them down along the cliffs. His wings rose and fell in strong strokes before he caught a gust of wind and allowed it to lift them up again.

"This is just like being on a roller coaster," she laughed.

"What is a roller coaster?" Drago asked, turning his head to glance at her over his shoulder.

"It is a ride that goes up and down, in tight circles, and sometimes upside down really fast," she explained.

"You enjoy these roller coasters?" Drago asked.

"Yes. Not the real scary ones, but I do love the not-so-scary kind," she admitted.

"What do the scary ones do?" he curiously asked.

"If they have a really big drop or go upside down, I get sick to my stomach, but I love the ones that curve sideways," she said, staring down at the water below them.

"Then I will give you a not-so-scary ride," Drago replied with a firm nod of his head.

"Drago… Oh!"

A squeal of laughter escaped Carly when Drago swooped down again and began weaving in and out of the tall pillars that stood just off shore. She leaned forward, her hands firmly gripping him. The wind blew her hair back, and she could feel the fine mist rising from below as the waves crashed against the base of the pillars.

Together, they weaved in and out of the towers of rocks and up along the coast. Carly shouted for him to go faster. Their laughter combined when he soared up over the cliffs and turned inland. The first moon was coming up on the horizon, turning the glowing waves into a cache of multi-colored diamonds. If anyone had asked her at this moment if she had seen anything more beautiful in her life, she would have said one word – Drago.

"It's magical," she remarked in a quiet tone.

"Yes," Drago agreed.

Carly turned her head to focus on where they were going. Drago was flying high above the treetops. Bright colors flickered on and off like fireflies far below them. Drago continued his inland course for close to half an hour before he swept through a gap between two mountains and emerged in a long valley. She thought he would land in the meadow, but he didn't. Instead, he turned to the west.

She caught her breath again when he entered the thick forest. Her fear that he wouldn't be able to see soon died when he easily navigated through the forest. Massive trees that reminded Carly of the Redwoods near her home rose up to block the bright light from the rising moon. To the left, she saw the movements of a herd of animals. It was hard to tell exactly what they looked like in the darkness, but the shadows were enough to make her thankful that Drago was there.

"Where are we going?" she asked.

"To a special place that I used to go to before.... I wish to show you the old palace," he replied.

"Oh!" Carly hissed out when they broke through the darkness of the forest and into another clearing.

A lake at the base of the mountain stretched out in front of them. The second moon had begun to rise, illuminating the tranquil water. At the far end, carved into the mountain were the ruins of an ancient castle.

"The ruins of Arkla," Drago announced, skimming the water of the lake with his hind legs before soaring upward.

CHAPTER 16

Mists from the waterfall to the right of the ruins made the white stone glisten. This was the one place where Drago had found peace during the hectic days before the silence. He had also come here shortly after his confrontation with Nali.

His gaze swept over the ancient palace that had stood for almost a thousand years before his ancestors had built the new palace closer to the coast and near the cove. This was a sacred spot preserved as a reminder of their origins. Eleven of the fifteen tall, dragon-shaped pillars remained supporting the remnants of ornate arches. Parts of the other four pillars were submerged beneath a waterfall, while their other remains lay scattered near the palace's entrance. Pride filled him when Carly released a soft exclamation of pleasure. Turning, he flew down for a landing along the front steps.

"What was this place?" Carly asked, sitting up and gazing around.

"Arkla was the original stronghold of the dragons," Drago said.

He knelt down and stretched out his wing. Turning his head, he lifted his tail out to Carly. She gave him an uncertain smile before lifting her leg over his neck. She held onto his tail to steady herself before sliding down his wing to the ground. He transformed once she was standing on her own.

"Oh! I swear I could watch you do that all day long," she said before turning to walk over to the edge of the courtyard. "This is incredible."

Drago watched Carly run her hand over the smooth stone. He walked up behind her and wrapped his arm around her waist. They stood there, staring out over the vast lake. The first moon had risen high enough to cast its light across the water.

"As the population of my people and trade with the other kingdoms grew, it became necessary for our city to be near the coast. The final decision came after a fierce winter snowstorm covered the mountains with a record snow. The combination of the snow and an earthquake sealed the fate of this palace," Drago explained.

"It is amazing," Carly said, leaning her head back against him.

"I used to come here as a boy," he reflected.

Carly looked up at him in surprise. "I can imagine it was a lot of fun to explore," she said.

Drago chuckled. "It was forbidden. My parents warned me that the structure was unstable when I asked about it. My mother soon realized that the combination of danger and saying it was forbidden was like waving a bag of gold in front of me. She worked with the engineers to stabilize the structure to preserve it for future generations. At least that was the excuse she gave my father when he protested the gold she was exchanging for the work," he replied with a grin before it faded.

"You must miss them very much," Carly said, turning in his arms to gaze up at him.

Drago sighed when she wrapped her arms around him and laid her head against his chest. He ran his hands down her back to her hips and pulled her close. Closing his eyes, he allowed the peacefulness of the night and the warmth of Carly's presence to wrap around him.

"I do. I miss them and my people. I wish...." He paused and opened his eyes to gaze out over the moonlit water again.

"You wish...," she asked.

Drago swallowed. How did you tell someone that you wished you could have one more second with someone? He couldn't remember his last words to his parents before they had left. All he could remember was the sound of his father's heartbroken roar before it too became silent. That was the first time in his life that he had really felt the emptiness of losing someone close to him.

He shook his head. "It is nothing," he said, releasing her and stepping to the side to hold onto the stone railing.

"I had wishes," she said.

Drago's lips twitched and he turned his head to gaze at her. "More than one?" he asked with a raised eyebrow.

Carly waved her hand in the air. "Oh yeah, probably like a hundred or more, but not all at the same time. I finally decided if I ever met a real live genie that I needed to have my three wishes ready," she stated with a toss of her head.

"A genie... I do not believe I have ever met one of those," Drago replied with a thoughtful look.

Carly sighed and stepped closer to him. Drago decided he liked the way her hair shimmered in the moonlight. He could see strands of gold running through the dark brown tresses.

"Well, so much for being a magical land! No genies, what is the world coming to?" she grumbled.

"I did not say they did not exist, only that I had never met one. What is a genie and why would you wish to meet one?" he asked.

Carly leaned forward on the railing and released another loud sigh. Drago bit back the retort he was about to make when the movement gave him a full view of her breasts and the curve of her buttocks that made him want to slide up behind her and....

"You aren't listening, are you?" Carly asked with a knowing grin.

"What?"

Carly shook her head again and turned to gaze out over the lake. "I said a genie can grant you wishes, but you have to be very careful what you wish for. If you wish for the wrong thing, bad things can happen. Oh, and you only get three wishes. No wishing for more wishes," she firmly stated.

"That is not much fun," he retorted with a grin.

Carly laughed. "No, it isn't, but you can imagine the problems it could create for the genie," she replied.

"What would you wish for?" he asked.

Drago leaned closer when she didn't immediately answer. The light-hearted mood from a moment ago had changed to a quiet reflection. He raised his hand to brush her windblown hair back from her face.

She turned to look at him. In the moonlight, he could see the expression in her eyes. It was sad, more like resigned. A rueful smile curved her lips.

"When I was a kid, I wished for my parents to love each other, a dragon, and to free the genie because I couldn't imagine how hard it must be to never be free," she admitted.

"And now?" he asked.

Carly straightened and turned to him. "It hasn't changed much. My parents have found love with someone else. It turns out my dad was not the right person for my mom. She has a new girlfriend and is finally happy. My dad found a woman who loves to cook, doesn't nag him about watching football, and has three boys to take fishing and play sports without nearly killing anyone else on the field. As far as my dragon wish – well, I chose you. Since I never met my genie, I'll just have to hope he or she was set free. Overall, I can't complain…." Her voice died and her expression changed as she turned her head away from him.

Cupping her cheek, Drago gently turned her head so that she faced him again. "Except for?" he encouraged.

"Jenny – I miss Jenny and I can't help but worry about what she must be going through after my disappearance," Carly confessed with a strained smile.

Drago pulled his hand away and turned toward the ruins. He could feel a muscle in his jaw pulsing as he clamped it tight to prevent the harsh words from escaping. He knew the words were born of fear – his fear of losing Carly and being left alone once again.

Deep down, he understood her worry and regret. He had felt the same emotions when he had lost everyone. How could he justify allowing Carly to live with that feeling?

A strange burning in his eyes and a swift pain in his chest struck him. He raised his hand and rubbed the spot over his heart. His jaw tightened with resolve.

"We need to return to the palace," he said.

"What? Oh, okay," Carly replied with a slight frown.

Drago stepped away and shifted. He reached down and scooped Carly up in his claws. Holding her against his chest, he pushed off the ground. Carly sat in his palm, leaning against one clawed finger with her arms wrapped tightly around it. Neither one of them spoke during the return trip, both lost in their own thoughts. Drago wished he could read Carly's thoughts. His own thoughts were swirling with memories of their brief time together. He desperately wanted to remember each and every second of it. The knowledge that those fleeting moments might be the only things he would have of Carly pierced his heart with a sharper blade than that of any sword or arrow.

He glanced down when he felt Carly move. She was stretching out a hand to touch the cloud they were flying through. The simple, innocent move was like another knife through him. Her joy and awe was captured in his mind to join with the other precious memories. Facing forward, he released a low roar.

∼

"Where are we going?" Carly asked nearly an hour later.

"To the treasure room," he replied in a clipped tone.

Drago pulled her closer to his chest as he turned in a downward spiral and whispered the magical words that would split open the ground. His body twisted and turned through the jagged opening, the ground closing in behind them within seconds of his passing through the gaping hole formed in the compacted dirt, rock, and roots.

Within minutes, they burst through to his hoard of treasure far below. His wings opened and he glided over the rolling mountains of treasure. His back legs extended and he landed, sliding along the loose gold coins before coming to a stop near the archway where Carly had first appeared.

He reached out and gently set Carly on the steps before he shifted.

She turned toward him with a frown. Her face was tight and she had that look of defiance on her face.

"What is going on, Drago? Why are we here?" she asked.

Drago returned her steady gaze. He lifted his chin and unclenched his fists. He would not change his mind. As a leader, it was his responsibility to think of those under his protection first, even if that meant great heartache and loneliness for himself.

"I am setting you free – like your genie. You must return to your world and let Jenny know that you are safe," he stated in a low, fierce tone.

"You are… Drago…?" Carly's voice faded and her eyes filled with tears. She stepped toward him, her right hand raised in a silent plea. "What if I can't come back? What about you?"

Drago reached up, grabbed her hand, and placed it against his cheek. He closed his eyes for a moment when he felt her caress. His fingers tightened around her hand and he opened his eyes.

"Go while I can still give you this, Carly. Go!" Drago ordered in a harsh voice.

Carly looked at him and started to shake her head. He released her hand and took a step back. His throat tightened when he heard her choked sob and saw the tears dampening her cheeks.

"I will be here when – if – you return. I will never forget you, Carly Tate. You are my greatest treasure, little thief," he swore.

Drago continued backing away from her, knowing that if he didn't, he would never let her go. Carly wavered on the steps, looking at the arched doorway she'd first entered into his realm and then back at him. She started toward him, but Drago shook his head.

"I'm coming back, Drago. I promise," Carly choked out.

"I will be waiting," he vowed.

Carly turned and slowly climbed the remaining steps. She paused under the arch, her hand on one of the dragon pillars. She glanced over her shoulder at him and her lips parted as she drew in a shaking breath.

"I love you, Drago," she said before turning and disappearing into the corridor.

Drago stood frozen, gazing at the empty doorway. Pain radiated through him to the point that he almost sank to his knees. His fists clenched and the burning in his eyes increased until he had to blink in an effort to clear his vision.

"Come back to me, little thief. Please, if I could have only one wish from your genie, it would be to have you come back to me," he whispered.

CHAPTER 17

"You can do this, Carly. You just have to put one foot in front of the other."

Her loud sniff echoed in the narrow passageway. She wiped a hand across her face, but it didn't help. The tears kept flowing.

Carly sniffed again. How could he let her go? True, she wanted to let Jenny know she was okay, but how could Drago just let her go?

I will be waiting.

His words echoed through her mind. It was that statement that gave her hope that she would be able to return to this magical world. She stumbled at the thought of not being able to find her way back to him – or worse, that the crack between the two worlds had already closed before she could.

"Please, if it closes, let it be before I go through. I'm so sorry, Jenny, but I can't leave him. I can't," Carly said in a quiet voice.

Carly reluctantly turned the last corner that she remembered on her journey here. The rough stone opening to the cave should be at the end. From there, it would be a short walk across it to the narrow opening of the crack in the rock and then the trail.

Carly fumbled for her phone before she remembered that she had left it in Drago's bedroom on the nightstand. Wiping at her face one last time, she drew in a deep breath. It wasn't far to the opening, but it was still very dark. She stopped and reached up to pull one of the burning torches free. Holding it in front of her, she turned and continued down to the end of the passageway.

~

Drago paced back and forth on the platform. His body shimmered – changing from his two-legged form to his dragon and back again. The power of his connection to Carly and the thought of losing her were driving him mad. This wasn't the same as the silence of losing his people, this was the desolation of losing a part of his soul.

"Now I understand my father's cry," Drago said, running his hands through his hair. "I have to stop her. I can't let her go. No, I must think of her needs before my own. I must – but, I can't."

His gaze swept up to the arched doorway and he froze in mid-stride. Standing at the top was Carly. Her hands were tightly clasped in front of her and her eyes were wide. A trembling smile curved her lips.

Impatient to gather her in his arms to see if she was real, he shifted into his dragon and launched off the platform with a single, powerful burst of energy. He soared up the mountain of gold and jewels before landing in a spray of coins. His body slid to a stop at the bottom of the steps.

Drago lifted his head and shook it, sending pieces of treasure scattering in all directions. He followed Carly with his gaze as she walked down the steps. She paused on the step above him. Reaching out a hand, she caressed his left nostril.

"Can I keep you?" she asked in a soft voice.

"A dragon never gives up his treasure," Drago warned.

"But – I'm not a dragon. I'm just a girl who loves one very, very much," Carly vowed, gazing at him.

Drago shifted and reached for Carly's hand. Pulling her into his arms, he held her against his body and buried his face in her hair. It took several minutes before he felt in control enough to pull back and look down at her. A dark scowl creased his brow.

"You were supposed to go. I set you free once. I won't be able to do it again," he warned in a fierce tone.

"There is a saying where I come from," she said in a quiet voice. "If you love someone, set them free; if they come back, your love was meant to be."

"And you came back," he said, cupping her face.

Carly giggled. "I made a wish for the passage to be sealed so I couldn't go through it. I guess it worked," she admitted with a sheepish grin.

"I wished it as well," Drago confessed.

Bending, he pressed his lips to hers in a deep, passionate kiss. She eagerly responded, tightening her grip around his neck and stretching up on her toes to get as close as she could. Their tongues dueled while their hands roamed in a desperate attempt to make sure that they were both real and together.

Drago pulled away to sweep Carly in his arms. Turning on the steps, he shifted into his dragon form. He spread his wings and pushed off the stone step. Drago murmured the spell to open the ground and swept upward through the quickly widening gap.

Outside, the tiny paper bird flitted up to greet them as they emerged. Carly clung to Drago as he swept up the side of the tower to the balcony of his living quarters. High above, both moons shone against a canvas of black ink dotted with brilliant stars.

"I love it here," she said, resting her head against his chest.

"Good," Drago replied.

A smile curved his lips as he transformed back into his two-legged form – Carly still nestled in his arms. The paper bird darted around them. The doors opened to his living quarters and the three of them disappeared inside. Drago left the doors open to the gentle breeze and the sound of the waves crashing against the cliffs.

"I really need to talk to you about what you mean when you say 'good'," Carly complained with a teasing laugh.

"We can talk later," he stated, the flames in his eyes dancing with mischief.

"Oh… Good!" she breathed when he turned toward their bed.

The next several weeks passed in a blur for Carly. She went on the twice-daily flights he made around the isle. They often stopped and had a lunch of fish, fruit, and nuts that he caught and gathered for them. Each day he would show her a new region of the isle.

"Is there any way you can create a spell to protect the isle without anyone getting hurt?" she asked, leaning forward as they flew over the remains of a shipwreck.

"If they are not smart enough to stay out of the mist, then they deserve their fate," he retorted.

"But... What if they can't, through no fault of their own? I mean, accidents happen and they might not have meant to come through it," Carly argued.

"They should not have accidents near my wards, then," Drago replied.

"I just think it would be better to help people," she insisted.

"The last time I opened my isle up to help someone, she turned my people to stone," he replied in a somber tone. "Besides, it is only those that ignored the wards and insisted on landing that met with disaster – I'm sure a few escaped unharmed."

Remorse swept through Carly at his reminder of the dangers this world posed. Magic was as powerful as the weapons back in her world. Still, she felt a need to protect those who were unwittingly caught in the pull of Drago's spells.

"Not everyone is like the Sea Witch, Drago. You didn't harm the monster lady and I've heard you speak of this Orion guy with respect. Surely, that counts for something," she said.

"Why do you care so much about those who you know nothing about?" he asked.

"Every life matters. You know what it feels like to lose someone you care about; well, think of the poor families of those who died here. They have no idea what happened to them. They could be someone's father or brother or uncle or... partner," she explained in a softer tone.

Drago was silent for several long minutes before he released a loud sigh. Carly couldn't keep the grin from her lips when he muttered under his breath that things were much simpler when he was just sleeping. She ignored his grumbling. Over the last few weeks, she had noticed he might grumble and growl in response to some of their discussions, but he always listened and tried to see it from her point of view.

"I guess now that I am awake, it would not hurt to lift them," he finally conceded.

"I think that is a brilliant idea," she exclaimed, wrapping her arms around his neck and giving him a hug.

Drago chuckled, the huge body of his dragon vibrating with his amusement. Carly grinned and straightened. Lifting her arms up into the air, she laughed with delight at the freedom she felt whenever they soared over the forests and along the cliffs.

Closing her eyes, she imagined what it would feel like to be a dragon. She would fly beside Drago over the forests and along the cliffs. Maybe one day, they would think of having children.

There was so much hope for the future now, and Carly wanted to embrace it all. Drago had not mentioned finding and killing the Sea Witch since the day the Empress of the Monsters came to visit. Hopefully, he had given up on his need for revenge and could look to the future.

CHAPTER 18

"We need food," Drago stated several days later.

"You mean, we can't live on love?" Carly teased as she placed the last dish in the cabinet.

Looking over her shoulder, she gazed at him with twinkling eyes. Drago wiped his hands on the dishtowel he was using to dry the last of their morning dishes. He tossed the towel onto the counter beside the sink, wrapped his arm around her waist, and pulled her back against him.

A smile tugged at his lips when she giggled. Bending, he pressed a kiss to the mark he had left on her neck. He was amazed at how 'normal' their routine had become. If any of his guards had told him that he – Drago, King of the Dragons – would be doing such menial work and enjoying it, he would have laughed at them.

"Fruit and fish are not enough. I need energy to keep up with you, woman. You are insatiable," Drago groaned.

Carly laughed. "I know," she quipped, turning in his arms, sliding her hands up over his shoulders to play with his hair. "I'm glad I claimed you, Drago," she added in a more serious mood.

"I am, too, little thief. I regret that you could not assure your friend that you were safe, but I could not risk losing you," Drago admitted.

"I feel the same way. I'm hoping Jenny will know somehow that I am safe and happy. So, what are we going to do about food? I'm pretty sure you don't have a magical grocery store nearby. I have to agree that we need more variety. I like fish, but not for breakfast, lunch, and dinner. Right now, I'd give anything for a pizza," Carly replied with a sigh of longing.

Drago's expression softened. He wasn't kidding about needing food. Carly deserved more than fish, nuts, and fruit. They had been eating it for weeks and even he was growing tired of it. What concerned him the most, though, was that he could see that Carly was losing weight from their limited diet.

He lifted his hand and brushed her hair back from her face. "I do not know this grocery store, but I do know that we cannot live on fish, fruit, and nuts forever," he said.

"I will see if there is anything preserved in the village. If there is not, I will have to negotiate with some merchants from another isle. It could mean a trip to another kingdom," Drago said.

"Oh! I would love to see the village. These past couple of weeks has been wonderful, but I'd love to see more," she admitted.

"I have been negligent in my care of you," Drago stated, running his fingers down her cheek.

"Don't get me wrong, I'm not complaining. If you want to call making me feel like the most special person in the world neglect, sign me up for it any day!" Carly retorted with a grin.

Drago's body reacted to her teasing and he slid his hands down over Carly's hips to cup her buttocks. Oh, yes, he would sign her up if it meant what he thought it did. He gently kneaded her cheeks with his fingers, enjoying it when she tightened her muscles and pressed against him.

"I think it is time to neglect you some more," he stated, bending to capture her lips and pulling her up against him.

Carly was already working on the front of his shirt. His tongue danced along the inside of her mouth, caressing, teasing, and demanding her response. He shivered when he felt the cool air against his bare flesh and Carly's nails lightly scraping across his skin as she pushed his shirt off his shoulders.

He released her lips and straightened, allowing his shirt to fall to the floor. He thought he was the one seducing Carly, but he was quickly discovering it was the other way around. He tilted his head back when she pressed her hot lips to his distended nipples.

How could something so small be so sensitive? he wondered, tightening his hands on Carly's buttocks.

"Carly!" Drago hissed, staring down at her tangled brown hair and bent head.

"My turn… You promised…," she said in a muffled voice.

"When…? Goddess, woman, what are you doing to me?" Drago groaned when her hands moved down his chest to the front of his trousers.

"Undressing you, kissing you, depleting your energy," she replied, unsnapping his pants and sliding her hands inside.

"Please deplete me," he groaned, lifting his hands to bury them in her hair when she pushed his pants down and forced him to step out of them. She bundled the material together and knelt on it in front of him, her face level with his throbbing cock. "Goddess!"

Drago fought for control and willingly lost. The touch of Carly's lips around his cock was pure ecstasy. Her hot mouth against his sensitive flesh sent shivers through him. He watched her slowly swallow his length before pulling back and doing it again.

His breath caught when she raised her hands to cup his balls. She gently massaged them as she turned her head from side to side. The pressure of her movement caused a friction that heated his blood. She was in complete control of his body. While he wanted nothing more than to release his tight control into her mouth, he wanted her pleasure to come first.

"No, you can make me come afterwards," she protested when he tried to stop her. "Let me do this."

"Carly…. Goddess, woman! How can any man deny such a thing?" he hissed.

"You can't. This is my turn," she insisted.

Drago clamped his teeth together to keep a curse from escaping. He wouldn't last long at the rate she was going. He reached up and gripped the counter, spread his legs slightly, and leaned forward. The position gave Carly better access to him. She didn't waste any time. Her hands stroked his long length at the same time as her lips and tongue did.

He watched his cock slide in and out of her mouth. His hips rocked back and forth, picking up speed as his balls tightened to the point that he thought he would explode. The tingling along his spine increased to fever a pitch.

Drago could feel the pre-cum begin to seep from him. Carly took advantage of it to help make him even slicker. Her hand fisted him, sliding up and down. A moan escaped him when she ran her tongue up and over him before he felt the scrape of her teeth down along his cock. She did that three times before he lost control and his body jerked with his orgasm.

Shock and fascination gripped him when she swallowed, refusing to release him. His body felt like it was melting into a puddle of hot, molten lava. Her skill at bringing such pleasure had to be a gift from the Goddess. He had never experienced such an emotional connection in his life as he did when Carly and he made love.

"Now… Now, it is your turn," he said in a hoarse voice. "I will begin by laying you out on the table."

"Oh, boy!" Carly responded in a breathless voice. "Dinner will never be the same again."

"I will make sure of that!" Drago vowed.

∼

Later that morning, Carly hummed as she walked along the deserted street of the village. A smile curved her lips as she reached out to run her hand along the short wall of a fountain in the center of the street. Over the last week, she had explored more and more of the palace and grounds while Drago made sure that the wards that were protecting the isle were still in place. Her heart hurt for the residents who had once lived here.

The devastating helplessness of losing everyone you ever knew would have been more than Carly could have understood – if she hadn't experienced it herself. Fortunately for her, she wouldn't have to live through the suffocating loneliness that Drago must have felt – she had him.

This was the first chance that she'd had to explore the village portion of the kingdom. Drago explained that there were many small villages dotted around the isle, but Dragon's Keep was the largest.

"Did you find anything?" she asked when he emerged from one of the buildings to her left.

"Flour," he replied, holding up a large sack.

"Oh! I can make bread and biscuits – and pizza dough! We just need eggs, oil, spices – you have some, but I'd like to find some more...." Carly waved a finger while she was talking, her mind on all the ingredients she would need.

"I do not know where to find half of the items you are mentioning – except...," Drago's voice faded and he frowned.

"Except?" Carly asked.

"The Isle of the Pirates would have what you want. They have everything," he grudgingly admitted.

"Pirates? You mean like real-live-honest-to-goodness pirates?" she asked excitedly.

"Yes, and the worst one of the lot is the King of the Pirates, Ashure Waves," he said.

Carly laughed and danced up to him. Drago's lips curled upward at her excitement. He knew he had already lost any argument he might have made against visiting the pirate kingdom when she rose up on her toes to brush a kiss across his lips.

"When can we go?" she asked, biting her lip.

Drago shook his head and chuckled. "We might as well go now. It will take at least two days flight on a good wind to reach the kingdom," he stated.

"How will we bring everything home if you are flying?" she asked.

"Come and I will show you," he said.

Drago turned and placed the bag of flour inside the doorway of the building he had exited a few moments before. He shut the door, then held his hand out to her. A quick glance at her showed her excited expression. Her eyes gleamed with delight, she was biting at her bottom lip, and she had a tight hold on his hand.

"Will the isle be okay while we are gone?" she asked with a sudden frown.

"Yes," he answered.

"This is so exciting," she admitted.

"I hope you think so after we arrive. Stay close to me and whatever you do – don't trust a pirate!" he cautioned.

"Got it – stay close, don't trust a pirate – but can I do some of the shopping? Will there be stores? I've never been to a pirate grocery store before," she said, twisting to walk backwards so she could look up at him.

Drago released an amused chuckle and steadied her when she almost fell. He stopped and gazed down at her. For the first time, he realized that Carly might enjoy interaction with someone other than himself and the flock of magical paper birds he had given her.

"I will take you to the market. It is famous throughout all the kingdoms for its choice of merchandise. They are said to have the finest fabrics and spices in all the lands. Of course, the pirates tend to be a boastful bunch of thieves, so I do not give much credence to what they say," he dryly remarked.

"Well, I'm a thief, too, don't forget! Can one of those pesky pirates claim to have captured the heart of the dragon king?" Carly demanded with a teasing smile.

Drago tilted his head back and laughed. Carly telling that to Ashure was something he would love to see. The Pirate King would believe Carly had stolen the Dragon's Heart. He would be trying to pick Carly's pockets to see where she had it hidden away. The thought of Ashure touching Carly quickly sobered him. That conniving pirate was known for his love of flirting. If he so much as looked at Carly wrong, Drago would burn the man to ash.

"I think you should keep that information to yourself, my little thief. The pirates might think you have the Dragon's Heart and they are not above using treacherous methods to get their hands on anything that is not safeguarded from their sticky fingers," he warned.

This time it was Carly's turn to laugh. She tilted her head and grinned up at him. Her eyes sparkled with delight.

"I'm a walking hazard, remember? I'll find a broom or a mop and then they'll be sorry," she promised.

Drago grimaced and his hand instinctively dropped to the front of his pants. A wry smile curved his lips and he nodded. That kind of pain was not something he would ever forget.

"I will make sure you have an arsenal of brooms at your disposal during our visit," he chuckled. "Now, if we are going to leave today, we need to pack."

"Yes!" Carly exclaimed with a fist pump.

Drago caught her around the waist when she swirled around and promptly lost her balance again on the uneven cobblestone road. Bending, he pressed a kiss to her neck before he steadied her. He put her back on her feet and recaptured her hand. He was soon caught up in her excitement and already planning the fastest route to the Isle of the Pirates.

CHAPTER 19

It was early afternoon by the time they left. Drago kept a wary eye on Carly, fearful that in her enthusiasm she would fall over the side of the great ship. She must have realized he was watching her because she suddenly turned and grinned up at him.

Drago couldn't keep the sigh of relief from escaping when he saw her step away from the side and gingerly navigate the deck of the airship to the steps leading up to the helm. The Dragonriders were much like the great ships that Nali used to travel. The difference was the Dragonriders used the dragon's fire to power the great engines instead of the electricity of the thunderbirds.

Powered by the engines, guided by the wind, and with two massive wings and a rudder, the ship soared out of the protected cave in the cliff and into the sky. Drago was proud of the Dragon's fleet of airships. Before the Great Battle, their fleet of ships had soared through the skies along with their dragon escorts. He turned the wheel and steered them to the southeast.

"This is unbelievable," Carly said, climbing the stairs to stand next to him.

"The ships allowed us to increase our trade with the other kingdoms," he explained.

"I don't understand physics or aeronautics, but I do know this isn't something my world has ever seen. Of course, they've never seen dragons, mermaids, or monsters, either," she laughed.

"You live in a very strange world," Drago replied with a shake of his head.

Carly's laughter wrapped around him. She stepped forward to grip the railing. The warm breeze blew her hair back and once again he was reminded of the glitter of gold as the sunlight caught the different colors in her hair.

She turned and grinned at him to show she had heard his comment and found it amusing. Drago glanced around the ship, trying to see it from her point of view. The things he took for granted, she found magical. He couldn't imagine not being able to shift into a dragon or live in the world he did without having the ability to use magic or fly through the air in the great ships. Life would be – difficult, at best.

He adjusted the sails with a slight twist of a knob and increased power to the engines. They had a good tailwind behind them and should make good time if it continued. They maintained a height of about three hundred meters above the ocean. He adjusted the wings to ensure a smooth flight. Locking the controls, he stepped around the helm and walked up behind Carly.

They stood in silence, gazing out over the vast ocean. Time seemed to stand still as they took in the beauty of the blue sky dotted with white clouds and the dark, sapphire blue waters below. The flock of paper birds darted about the ship, some landing on the ship's rigging while others hopped about the deck.

"You said it would take us two days to get to where we are going?" Carly asked, leaning back against him.

"Yes. Just remember what I told you," he cautioned.

Carly laughed. "I know. Stay with you and never trust a pirate. No worries, Captain. I'll have my trusty broom and Little Knight and my flock of paper birds for protection," she stated with a small salute.

"And me," he added.

"And you," she repeated with a giggle when he bent to press a kiss to her neck. "For always."

Two days later, Drago was already having doubts about his decision to travel to the Isle of the Pirates. He should have known his arrival would cause a stir. After all, it had been more than a decade since the last dragon had been seen.

Their entry to the Pirate's Cove was through the skull shaped rocks that were heavily guarded. This was the only entrance into and out of the isle's port – at least the only one known to outsiders. The port was surprisingly empty compared to what Drago remembered.

"Prepare to be boarded!" an old pirate yelled from the aft side of his ship.

"Board at your own risk, old man," Drago growled. "Carly, take the helm and slow the vessel."

"Uh, Drago, I don't think…," Carly started to say before her voice died.

Drago had shifted into his dragon form and was snapping at the cables the pirates had thrown to connect the Dragonrider and the pirates' ship. Several pirates preparing to swing onto the ship via long ropes scrambled back when Drago sent several bursts of blue flames in their direction.

Drago paced back and forth snarling and growling at the pirates who watched him with unease. No one would board his ship unless he gave permission. Those dirty bastards would steal the linen off the beds if given half a chance.

"Uh, Drago, I hate to tell you this, but I'm not very good at driving a boat, even a magical one," Carly called down from the wheel.

The paper birds all rose and flapped around in alarm, drawing Drago's attention to the fact that the dock was rapidly approaching. The pirates must have realized that a collision was imminent as well because they turned their ship to starboard. Drago's eyes widened and he turned. With a single leap, he cleared the quarter deck and shifted behind Carly and the helm. Reaching out, he pulled back on the throttle and turned the wheel to the left.

The force of the sudden reversal and the dip as the ship turned threw Carly off balance. Drago reached out and grabbed her around the waist before she fell. He pulled her close while keeping his other hand firmly on the wheel. The vessel shuddered before gently bumping into the floats attached to the dock.

Several dock hands immediately threw a series of ropes up to secure the ship to the dock. With a flick of his wrist, Drago lowered the anchor. Water splashed up onto the deck and the paper birds scurried to safety in the Crow's Nest.

"All secured, my lord," one of the dock hands yelled.

"Good job. Keep the coin and if my ship remains intact until my departure, there will be two more to go with it," Drago said, tossing a gold coin to the man.

"Aye, my lord. We'll make sure nothin' is taken," the dock hand stated with a toothy grin.

"He even talks like a pirate!" Carly whispered in awe, turning her gaze from the man to the town.

"Yes, it gets a bit irritating after a while," Drago said, shutting down the engines.

"Drago!" a thundering voice called out.

"Who is that?" Carly asked, staring at a well-dressed man walking down the dock toward them.

Drago's face twisted into an expression of reluctant resignation. His gaze followed Carly's, narrowing in on the man who had yelled his name. The huge grin and speculative expression in the man's eyes meant that this was not going to be a quick shopping excursion.

"That is Ashure Waves, King of the Pirates, and lord of this miserable lot of thieves," Drago responded under his breath. "Ashure," he greeted in a louder voice.

"Well, well, well, what wakes the dragon after so long? Or should I say who?" Ashure asked, staring at Carly.

*

Carly didn't know what to think of the tall, elegantly dressed man standing on the dock. A faint blush colored her cheeks when he turned his gaze on her and gave her one of those assessing looks. Lifting her chin, she resisted sticking her tongue out and crossing her eyes –

barely. Her second response wasn't much better. She really wanted to tell him to take a picture, that it would last longer, but she bit her tongue. From the way Drago stiffened and the dark expression on his face, the pirate would be lucky if he didn't get a few of the feathers sticking out of his hat singed.

"I would be careful if I were you, Ashure," Drago growled when the man didn't look away from her.

"As surly as always, even after a decade of rest, I see. You know I lost a lot of men over the years waiting for you to wake up again," Ashure stated.

"That sounds like a personal problem to me," Drago blithely retorted, holding Ashure's gaze in silent challenge before he smiled and shrugged.

"Yes, I guess it is." Ashure replied, returning Drago's gaze. His steely expression quickly changed to a genial look and he grinned, replacing his unease with a slightly mocking expression. "Still, I would be remiss if I did not welcome you to my humble kingdom," Ashure stated with a bow. "Welcome, mighty – and may I add extremely wealthy – king of the dragons, to the Isle of the Pirates."

Carly bit her lip to keep from laughing. The long feather in the man's hat actually touched the dock. The man straightened and looked at Drago with an avaricious grin. Carly wasn't sure if the guy was just plain stupid or had a death wish. Who in their right mind would challenge a dragon?

She was just about to suggest that maybe they should leave when Drago threw his head back and laughed. Carly started in surprise and cast a puzzled glance back and forth between Drago and Ashure. The pirate was grinning as well.

"You haven't changed a bit," Drago said.

"Nay, not enough to boast about," he said genially. He continued in a suddenly serious tone. "I am glad you are here, Drago. Nali told me you had awakened. There is a matter I wish to talk to you about."

Drago's expression turned somber and he nodded. Carly felt his arm slide around her waist and she stepped forward when the dock hands secured the gangplank for them to descend. She breathed a sigh of relief when she saw that it had rope handrails that she hadn't noticed when the men were pushing the ramp closer. There was no way she would have trusted herself to make it down a narrow plank without falling off.

Once on the dock, she was startled again when Ashure stepped forward and grabbed her hand. He ignored Drago's muttered curse and raise her hand to his lips. Carly tugged on her hand in an effort to pull free after he finished.

"You have found a woman with fire in her blood, Drago. She has the heart of a dragon," Ashure said in a deceptively soft and playful tone.

"Be careful, Ashure. My temper is still as fierce as it has always been. Carly is not for you to toy with or to use your gifts on," Drago warned.

Ashure's lips twisted into a sardonic smile. "What you call a gift, others would call a curse," he said. "No threat intended, Dragon King."

Carly watched the pirate turn on his heel and snap out an order to one of the men waiting patiently behind him. Within seconds, a carriage drawn by two magnificent black horses appeared. Drago held her back for a brief second.

"Whatever you do, stay close to me," Drago warned.

"I will," Carly promised, a shiver running through her. "What's wrong?"

"I do not know, but I plan to find out," Drago said before straightening when Ashure turned back to them.

"Your harbor looks bare. I seem to remember more merchants," Drago said as he helped Carly up into the carriage.

"There is much we need to discuss, my friend, but not here. First, let me offer you a comfortable room and a good meal. Then, we will talk," Ashure said.

Carly didn't miss the look of warning in Ashure's eyes or the way he glanced around at the men and women milling around the docks. She frowned and followed his gaze. Everything looked okay, but looking and feeling were two entirely different things.

While everything appeared normal, Carly could feel there was a tension in the air, and it seemed to center around her, if the stares directed her way were anything to judge by. Carly sank down onto the padded leather seat and ran her hands down the soft fabric of her brown pants. Drago sat down beside her and slipped his hand into hers while Ashure sat across from them. Ashure waved his hand and the coachman slapped the reins. Carly gripped Drago's hand and held the side of the carriage as it began to move up the slope and through the town.

"Ouch! What was that for?" Drago asked, rubbing his arm where Carly had pinched him.

Carly looked up at him and grinned. "I just wanted to make sure that I wasn't dead or dreaming. I've already pinched myself. I figured I'd try pinching you this time to make sure," she teased.

Drago recaptured her hand and held onto it. "I can assure you that you are neither dead nor dreaming in a less painful way, little thief," he assured her with a chuckle.

Ashure laughed quietly. "As I said before, Drago, you have found a woman with fire. I love that she also has a delightful sense of humor," he stated.

"Just remember she belongs to me, Ashure," Drago said.

"I have enough worries without the addition of an offended dragon on the list," Ashure assured him.

Carly glanced again at the pirate king, but he was now smiling and waving to a group of women standing outside a tavern. Carly couldn't help but stare at the women. They looked like they could take on the Giant from Jack in the Beanstalk and defeat him with one hand. She had only seen muscles like that in the magazines at the gym.

She turned to look at Drago when he raised her hand to his lips. A rueful smile curved her lips and she rolled her eyes. His soft chuckle told her that he understood her silent message.

"I prefer cute and cuddly," he murmured.

Carly could feel the warmth of his words sweep through her and couldn't contain the brilliant smile that curved her lips. She settled back and enjoyed the ride. There were so many different shops that she couldn't decide which one she wanted to explore first.

"So, my friend, tell me the reason for your visit," Ashure prompted.

CHAPTER 20

Drago stepped back into the rooms that Carly and he had been given. Their quarters consisted of three rooms. They were as large as his living room back home. The sitting room was elegantly furnished with several large chairs, an oversized couch, a massive fireplace, and rich tapestries depicting different events throughout the pirates' history. Two sets of double doors led out onto a curved, covered balcony that overlooked the town and harbor.

The other two rooms were decorated with the same lavish touch. The finest silk sheets, soft down bedspread, and thick curtains around the massive four-poster bed caused Carly to swear she was the princess in a fairy tale.

"Nay, a queen, at least, my lady," Ashure had exclaimed.

The pirate king had quickly excused himself after Drago growled out yet another warning when he tried to kiss Carly's hand again. The devil would push Drago to a sparring match before their trip was over. Drago adjusted the sleeve of his shirt under his long coat. They were to join Ashure for dinner in a few minutes.

"This guy has way too much money," Carly stated, stepping out of the bedroom.

Drago looked up and started to make a sarcastic retort in agreement, but the words froze on his lips. His body was suddenly humming, and the last thing on his mind was dinner – with Ashure. He would much rather have dinner with Carly; or rather, have Carly for dinner.

"Do I look stupid?" she asked with a raised eyebrow.

Drago's gaze ran from her braided hair over her flushed cheeks and down to the tops of her creamy breasts peeking out of the bodice of a gown that hugged her full figure to perfection. The rich, dark red gown made the golden highlights in her hair glow like the fire in the Dragon's Heart. His first and only thought was how much he was going to enjoy taking it off of her.

"I do not remember my mother ever wearing that dress," Drago choked out.

Carly laughed. "Ashure had it delivered while you were talking to the guard earlier," she said, spreading the long skirt to show the pair of leggings through the front slit. "I feel like I'm ready to either go to a ball or, at the very least, the company Halloween party."

A scowl creased Drago's brow at the mention of Ashure sending the dress. He should have been the one to give her the gown, not that scurvy pirate. His expression changed to remorse when her smile died and Carly's expression turned to embarrassment.

"I guess I should go change into my jeans and T-shirt," she said.

Drago quickly crossed the room and reached for her arm when she turned away. Sliding his left hand around her waist, he reached up and cupped her face. He brushed a kiss across her lips before giving her a rueful smile.

"You look stunning. I am jealous that Ashure would think to give you something so fine while I have given you nothing but hand-me-downs from my mother," he admitted.

"Oh, well, I've loved everything you've given me. It is more comfortable than wearing something with enough material to make a bedspread," she responded.

"I will take you shopping for clothing tomorrow. There are many fine seamstresses here," he promised.

Carly shook her head. "If I can't pay for it, I'd rather not get it. I wouldn't mind looking, but the last thing I want is to feel like I am some damsel in distress needing to be clothed. I mean, borrowing clothes is bad enough, but at least I can give those back. Buying them is another thing. At least with something like food, I can contribute by cooking," she insisted with a stubborn thrust to her jaw.

"You would allow Ashure to clothe you, but not me?" Drago demanded.

"Of course not! We bartered. I gave him a finger spinner and he gave me the dress," she said.

"A finger spinner?" Drago asked, puzzled.

"It's a toy that lights up when you spin it," she laughed. "I paid less than ten bucks for it. He liked it and insisted it was a fair trade. Who am I to argue with a pirate?"

"You traded a toy for this?" Drago chuckled, standing back to look down at the gown.

"It lights up and spins," Carly stated with a grin.

Still laughing, he pulled her back into his arms. His little thief was a brilliant negotiator. It would appear he had a few things to learn from her.

"You are an amazing woman, Carly Tate," he said, sliding the back of his hand down her cheek.

"I'm just cute and cuddly," she replied, reaching up to slide her arms around his neck.

Drago groaned softly when he felt her fingers playing with the ribbon holding his hair back. He bent his head to meet her halfway when she rose up to kiss him. Their lips were a breath away from each other when a knock sounded at the door.

"Dinner," she whispered, gazing up at him.

"Dinner," he grudgingly repeated.

Drago reluctantly released Carly, but not before she brushed a quick kiss across his lips. He started to reach for her again when the knock resonated through the room, this time louder than the first one. Irritation flashed through Drago. It would be just like Ashure to give Carly a dress that he knew Drago couldn't resist peeling off her only to interrupt him.

"We are coming," Drago snapped out in a loud voice.

He strode across the room and opened the door. The scowl on his face darkened when he saw Ashure's amused face gazing back at him. He curled his fingers into tight fists when he noticed Ashure's appreciative expression when Carly stepped up behind him.

"A barter well worth the price, my lady. May I say you are more beautiful than any who have graced the doors of my palace. If you ever tire of this fire-breathing lump of dragon meat, you have only to cast your gaze in my direction and I will forever be your willing servant," Ashure stated with an elaborate bow.

"I swear if you kiss her hand one more time, I'll bite off your arm," Drago threatened.

Ashure straightened with a laugh. "I detest blood, especially my own. Come, dinner will be ready shortly and the others await," he said, stepping to the side.

"Others?" Drago asked with a wary glare.

"Nali, Koorgan, Gem, and Isha have come to meet," Ashure said in a more serious tone.

Drago's gaze narrowed on the calm mask that Ashure wore. Rulers or representatives from most of the kingdoms were here. Drago's stomach tightened at the meaning – the Sea Witch was up to something.

"Where is Orion?" Drago asked.

Ashure cast him a quick, sad glance. "He is unable to attend. He lost his mate, Shamill, during childbirth and has remained under the sea since, to care for his sons. It is said he still searches for Magna, as well," he explained.

"Isn't Magna the Sea Witch?" Carly asked.

"Yes," Ashure said.

Drago wrapped his arm around Carly. He was shocked to learn of Shamill's death. This would be a devastating blow to Orion and to his kingdom.

"I did not know," Drago replied.

"It was a shock to all," Ashure agreed.

∽

Carly wasn't sure who Orion and Shamill were, but it was obvious the news of Shamill's death had shaken Drago. She quietly walked next to the men, listening to their exchange and appreciating the pirates' castle. Rich, dark, wooden beams in varying shades of color, including a red that matched her gown, held large chandeliers with flickering, white-blue flames. The doors were made from the same wood. Each door was intricately carved with a different scene and in the center was a cast metal door knocker. Some were in the shape of fish while others were in the shape of animals.

The walls were covered with bright tapestries that hung from the ceiling to the floor. Instead of knights in armor standing in the hallway, there were statues carved out of marble – only these statues moved and followed their progress. Carly scooted closer to Drago when one of the statues winked at her.

"How do they do that?" she asked.

Ashure grinned. "A gift from the king and queen of the Isle of Magic. I saved their dog once," he said with a sheepish grin.

"You stole their dog and returned it, more than likely," Drago dryly retorted.

"I will never admit to such a devious action," Ashure stated.

Carly giggled at the snappy banter between the two men. Despite the things Drago said, it was obvious that he admired the Pirate King. She couldn't help but wave at another statue that bowed to her.

She wound her arm around Drago's when he held it out and they descended the staircase behind Ashure. At the bottom, several men and women stood quietly talking. Each of them stopped and turned to stare at them as they descended the stairs. Carly blushed when all eyes turned to assess her.

"Drago," a huge man greeted with a bow of his head.

"Koorgan," Drago replied.

"Lord Drago, on behalf of the royal family of the Isle of Magic, I wish to convey my heartfelt sorrow at the devastation to your people. The Queen also asked that I tell you she is searching all of the spell books known to our people for a way to reverse the spell," the young man stated with a stiff bow.

"The way to break the spell is to kill the Sea Witch, Isha," Drago answered in a hard tone.

"And I have told you that it would doom us all if you do that," a dark-skinned woman argued, stepping forward.

"Nali," Drago greeted. "I did not see your ship in the harbor."

"I did not want to scare you away," she replied.

Drago's expression darkened. "You know my thoughts about using the mirror," he warned.

"Before we begin another war, let me introduce Drago's beautiful companion, Carly. Carly, may I introduce you to Koorgan, King of the Giants," Ashure said, stepping between Nali and Drago.

"Hello," Carly said.

"I am Gem from the Isle of Elements," a young woman announced with a stiff bow of her head.

Carly knew she was staring, but she couldn't help it. She glanced at the huge man who had first been introduced to her. Giant was an excellent word to describe him. The man was taller than all of them, including Drago. His features were hard and he looked like he would rather be anywhere else but there. The young ethereal woman who called herself Gem was a stark contrast to this man. Gem's long, brown hair was floating around her and there was a slight glow around her body. Carly swore she could almost see through the woman at times.

"I am Isha, Captain of the Guard to the King and Queen of the Isle of Magic. The king has been… unwell and the queen asked that I come in their stead," Isha greeted.

"Hi Isha," Carly said, trying not to feel overwhelmed.

"And last, but never least, is the lovely – and very dangerous – Nali, Empress of the Monsters," Ashure said with a grimace when Nali shot him a heated glance.

"Trying to charm me won't work, Ashure," Nali stated. "Welcome, Carly. I am honored to meet you."

"Thank you, Nali," Carly responded.

Carly was surprised when Nali stepped forward and gave her a hug. The warmth and sincerity in the woman's eyes and posture told Carly that Nali meant what she said. Carly gazed at the other woman for several long seconds. In that short space of time, Carly felt as if she had met a true friend – something that she had never felt since meeting Jenny.

"What is going on?" Carly asked in a quiet voice when the others started to move toward the dining room.

Nali slipped her arm through Carly's, ignoring Drago's disapproving glare. Carly fought back a giggle when Drago mouthed a curse. He was distracted by Koorgan who slapped him roughly on the shoulder.

"You are the hope our world needs to conquer the darkness sweeping through it," Nali replied.

"Me! I'm just – I'm just a bank teller from Yachats, Oregon. How am I supposed to fight anything?" Carly asked in an incredulous tone.

"Your presence has started a chain of events that will change our world, as long as…."

Nali's voice faded and Carly looked at her, waiting for her to continue. A frown creased Nali's brow and she appeared uncertain for a moment. In frustration, Carly stopped and placed her hand on Nali's arm.

"As long as what?" she demanded.

Nali glanced toward Drago and shrugged. "As long as Drago does not kill the Sea Witch," she said before pulling away. "I would be pleased if you would tell me about your world."

CHAPTER 21

"No! I will not agree to this!" Drago declared, slamming his fist on the polished wooden table.

"The taint of the Sea Witch has already been felt on the Isle of Magic. Her darkness is spreading. It is imperative that the Sea Witch be found and stopped," Isha stated.

"My father and mother are doing what they can to stop the Sea Witch, but even with their extreme measures, they fear it will not be enough. The darkness in her is unlike anything we have ever seen before. I agree with Drago. The Sea Witch must be stopped once and for all," Gem argued.

"I will search her out and kill her," Drago vowed.

"You can't. You will doom us all if you do," Nali snapped in aggravation.

"Drago, be reasonable. At least listen to what Nali has to say," Ashure said, raising his hand in a gesture to calm Drago's anger.

Drago stood up and glared at the group sitting around the table. His gaze flashed to Carly's pale face, and he slowly sank back down into his seat. He clenched his fists to contain his anger and directed his displeasure to the root of it – Nali.

"You are wrong, Empress. The death of the Sea Witch is the only way to save our kingdoms," he growled.

"No, I am not. The mirror showed me a vision. The Goddess is never wrong," Nali argued.

"You see what you wish to see," Drago retorted. "Where was your vision when the Sea Witch turned my people to stone? Where was the Goddess for that matter?!"

"The Goddess is not wrong, Drago! The mirror showed me the creature inside her. It will not stop with her death. It will only move to another and another until there is no one left to stop it. Somehow, someway, the Sea Witch is preventing that from happening. I don't know how or why, but she is!" she snapped. "Do not stand in my way, Drago. My kingdom is in danger and I will do anything to protect my people."

"Do you think I would have done any less for my people, Nali? They were gone before I could reach them. Their cries of horror still echo through my soul! The sounds of mothers and fathers begging the Sea Witch to spare their children only to have them turned to stone in their arms. You speak of an alien creature, but I never saw any such thing! Magna's insane cackle plays over and over in my dreams and you want me to ignore her? To let her go?" Drago choked out over his rage.

"No, I ask that you listen to me, Drago. That you all listen to me," Nali pleaded. "The darkness in her is from beyond our world. Only someone from another world can defeat it."

"There is no one from another world, Nali," Drago said, running his hands through his hair.

"That's not true," Carly said, breaking her silence.

Each person around the table turned to look at her as if they had forgotten her presence. Drago turned to her and reached for her hand. He did not want Carly involved in this. She was all that he had left.

"Carly," Drago began.

He stopped when she raised her hand and laid her fingers against his lips. Drago shook his head when he saw the determined expression that came into her eyes. His little thief was about to stand her ground.

"I am not from your world. I don't know what is going on. Where I come from we don't have magic, Sea Witches, and alien creatures or whatever is doing this, but what if Nali is right? What if you kill her and it is something else that is doing this? Can you blame this Magna when it might be beyond her control? I'm not saying what she did was right. I'm just saying that killing someone is wrong and… and doing it out of revenge never works out well for anyone," Carly explained in a quiet voice.

The muscle in Drago's jaw throbbed. He could see the worry and sadness in her gaze. He lifted her hand to his lips and pressed a kiss to her fingers, his grip hard. He turned to look at Nali.

"Tell us what you saw," he ordered in a gruff tone.

Nali relaxed in her seat and nodded. "I saw mostly fragments, things that are not completely clear. A black shadow moving over the Sea Witch and her fighting with it. I saw her fear – but, also her determination," she said.

"That does not tell us how to stop her, Nali," Gem stated in frustration. "What is this black shadow? Where did it come from?"

Nali shook her head. "I don't know. I saw a flash as something fell from the sky," she said.

"How can she be stopped?" Koorgan demanded.

"I saw Orion, Drago, and two others – a man not from our world and a woman. They will fight a great battle and the creature will be killed," Nali admitted.

"Then I *will* kill the Sea Witch," Drago stated.

"Yes – no – I don't know. All the mirror shows me is the same thing over and over," Nali admitted.

"None of this matters if the Sea Witch cannot be found," Isha reminded everyone in a quiet voice.

"What do you propose, Nali?" Ashure wearily asked.

"That we allow fate to play out. When I saw Carly's appearance, I knew that it would set in motion the events that would save our world," Nali said.

Drago's eyes narrowed on Nali's face when she turned it at the last moment. There was something else Nali wasn't telling them. Perhaps that feeling was what made accepting what she was saying all the more difficult.

"I vote that once the Sea Witch is located, she be detained and a gathering called in order to determine what should be done next," Ashure said. "We will see if the visions from the Goddess' Mirror come true. I hope for all our sakes that they do, Nali. All in agreement say aye."

"Aye," Isha said with reluctance.

"Aye," Nali agreed.

"Nay," Gem stated, rising from her seat with a scowl and folding her arms in defiance.

"Aye," Koorgan said.

"I'll agree – unless I see her again. Then I make no promises," Drago stated.

"Aye. Gem, inform the king and queen that we will do all that we can to find and contain the Sea Witch," Ashure instructed.

"I will kill her myself if she attacks my people," Gem retorted before pushing away from the table, fading, and then disappearing through the ceiling.

"What?! Where did she go?" Carly asked in shock.

"Gem is an elemental. She can become any element, including air," Drago explained.

"Wow! That is... really cool," Carly whispered.

～

The sun shone through the windows early the next morning, waking Carly from a sound sleep. She lay on her side and stared out the windows at the first rays of light. A smile tugged at her lips when she saw the flock of paper birds stretch their wings and wiggle their tails. They had made a point of nesting on the balcony outside of the bedroom.

She lifted her hand to run it down Drago's arm. The coarse hair on his arms felt good against her palm. She laid her hand over the one he had wrapped around her waist.

A shiver ran through her when she felt his hot lips against her bare shoulder. She had given up trying to wear any clothes to bed. He always took them off of her – or she did – before their heads hit the pillows. From being a girl who was a little self-conscious about her body, she had become a lot more comfortable with it.

"It is still early," Drago complained.

Carly giggled when he slipped his arm under the covers. She grabbed his hand and pulled it up to cup her left breast. She moaned softly when he pressed his aroused length against her.

"I thought you said it was too early," she teased.

"I said it was still early. That gives us time to enjoy the morning," he countered, pressing another kiss to her shoulder.

"That… sounds good… to me," she moaned.

She didn't protest when Drago reached down between them and began to arouse her. The feel of his fingers teasing her clit soon had her ready for more. She leaned up when he slid his other arm under her so he could play with her nipples.

"This position is much safer," he teased.

"Oh, shut up. I didn't mean to knee you," she groaned, rocking her hips back and forth.

"This is still much safer," he replied.

Carly scooted back, arching her back so that he could align his cock with her wet entrance. She was ready for him. The feel of him, pressing into her, stretching her, sent a powerful wave of pleasure and desire through her. How this happened every time they came together amazed her.

"Drago," she moaned.

He raised his hand and gripped one of hers, pulling it down to continue rubbing her clit while he tightened his hold on her hip and began pinching her nipples until they swelled. His lips continued to tease her neck and shoulder. The sound of his aroused breathing echoed in her ear in tempo with the movement of his hips.

She gasped loudly when he rolled both of them over so that he was draped over her back. He used one hand to pull her hips up in the air while he braced his other one near her side.

"Come for me, Carly," Drago hissed.

Carly felt the powerful thrusts increase. She could no longer tease her clit. The feel of his thick cock, moving back and forth was all the stimulation she needed now. Her nipples, already swollen and tender from the night before and the teasing from this morning, were extra sensitive to the friction caused by the bed covers as he thrust into her.

Carly's hands curled into the fabric and she buried her face in the pillow to smother her loud cry when she came. Drago wasn't as quiet. He arched his back to press deeper into her when he came, his voice loud enough to startle the paper birds which fluttered outside the open doors. Carly turned her head and moaned.

Drago groaned and bent back over her. His arm wrapped around her waist and he collapsed to his side still holding her. Carly groped for the covers, but gave up when Drago laid his leg over her.

"I swear the town knows what we were doing," she informed him with a sigh.

Drago's chuckle made her giggle. "They will all be jealous of me," he boasted.

"Men!" she teased.

"All the men will be jealous of me, Carly. I have captured a treasure of true beauty," he swore.

Carly relaxed against him. She raised his hand to her lips and pressed a kiss against it. Pulling back, she frowned when she saw the tiny silver threads shimmer before disappearing. She blinked, wondering if it was a figment of her imagination. She had seen it several times now. She was about to ask Drago about it when her flock of magical birds decided to join them.

"We're being attacked," she gasped in a fit of laughter.

"Ungrateful creatures! I should have burned them instead of giving them life," Drago growled in amusement when several tried to burrow into his hair. "Be off with you, creatures."

"Be careful! You might hurt them," Carly said, grabbing his hand and pulling it back against her. "Drago...."

"Yes, little thief," Drago replied.

"I love you," she whispered, reaching out to touch one of the birds with a gentle finger.

Drago leaned up and pressed a kiss near her ear. "I love you as well, Carly."

CHAPTER 22

"I hear you had a good night and a good morning," Ashure said with a knowing grin.

"Keep your voice down, Ashure. Carly is not like the women here. She is shy," Drago warned.

"Shy? Fascinating," Ashure replied under his breath.

Drago saw the inquisitive expression on Ashure's face and knew the pirate wanted to ask him more questions. Drago did not want to answer them. Deciding to remove Carly, along with himself, from the other man's presence was the best way to avoid upsetting her, Drago turned and walked over to where she was talking with Nali.

"Nali, I promised Carly I would take her shopping today. There are many supplies that we need before we return to my kingdom," Drago stated in a quiet voice.

"We could establish trade again if you lifted the spells that protect your kingdom," Nali suggested.

Drago shook his head. "The only thing I have to trade is gold. With my people gone, there is not much else," he replied.

"I understand. Dragon's gold is not a bad trade if you should decide you wish to barter. My cyclops would appreciate the added revenue," Nali laughed.

"You never told me what is happening on the Isle of Monsters. Is there anything I can do to help?" Drago politely asked.

This time it was Nali's turn to shake her head. She glanced over at Ashure. Koorgan and Isha had already departed before daybreak – each of them feeling the weight of their responsibilities.

"Nay, I have no proof that the Sea Witch has touched my kingdom," she admitted.

"Yet…," Drago pressed.

Nali released a dry laugh and lifted her chin. "I will let you know, dragon, if I need your help," she said.

Drago studied the other woman's face for a moment before he nodded and turned his attention to Carly. She silently studied the two of them. He knew from the expression in her eyes that she had not missed Nali's brief hesitation or Nali's evasive response.

"Thank you, Nali. I hope you have a safe trip home and that I get to see you again soon," Carly said, reaching out to hug the other woman.

"I hope one day you will see your friend, Jenny, again. I would be honored to meet her. She sounds like a wonderful person," Nali stated.

Carly wiped the corner of her eye. "She is, and I'm sure she'd love to meet you, too," she said.

"Safe journey, Carly. Until we meet again, dragon," Nali said with a bow of her head before she stepped back, turned, and walked out the door.

"Don't forget to take those eels with you! They are terrorizing my herd of sea dragons," Ashure called out.

"Orion will have something to say about that, Ashure!" Nali retorted with a wave of her hand.

"Eels?" Drago asked, turning to look at Ashure.

"I made the mistake of suggesting a race between her eels and my new herd of racing sea dragons. I forgot the creatures were over thirty meters long and electric. Two of my fastest sea dragons bolted when she brought the eels in," Ashure explained.

"When are you going to learn not to antagonize the other kingdoms?" Drago asked.

"Where is the fun in that?" Ashure demanded with a confused expression.

Drago shook his head and looked at Carly who was trying to smother her laughter. He rolled his eyes, something he couldn't remember ever doing before. The laughter he was trying to hold back escaped and together they enjoyed Ashure's exasperated confusion.

"You have become a very strange dragon," Ashure complained. "Go spend your gold, Drago. I have more important things to do while you shop."

∽

"I believe that is the last of the items we need," Drago said.

Carly nodded and surveyed the items as they were being loaded onto the wagons. After this, there would be four full wagons of supplies ready to be transported to the Dragonrider and stored below deck. Carly didn't know what they would do when they got back home. It would take a week to unload everything with just the two of them.

"I'm starving! Do you think we can get something to eat?" Carly asked.

"Of course. I could use something to eat as well. Are you sure you do not mind that we are leaving this afternoon to return home?" Drago asked.

Carly shook her head. "Not at all. I thought it would be nice to see other people, but I honestly miss having you to myself," she admitted with a sigh. "I think the birds would like to return home as well."

"I noticed they did not stay long," Drago observed.

The only bird to remain behind was the first one Drago had made. This little one had become her protector. It sat nestled in the loop of the red scarf she wore around her neck.

"I will order some food for us at the tavern. There are some tables protected from the wind on the side of the tavern. Would you prefer to eat inside or out?" Drago asked.

"Outside! I love to people-watch, even if I am looking forward to returning home," Carly laughed.

"I will reserve the table," Drago stated.

Carly nodded. They cut across the busy street and stepped under the covered entrance to the tavern. A tall woman with flowing black hair stepped out of the entrance and greeted them.

"Two for the table in the corner," Drago stated.

"This way," the woman said.

Carly noticed the woman's respectful expression when she looked at Drago, but she regarded Carly with curiosity. She should be used to it. It seemed as if everyone knew who Drago was, but all of them had gazed at Carly like they had never seen a regular human before.

"Drago!"

Both of them turned when they heard a voice call out behind them. Carly stifled her giggle when Drago muttered a curse under his breath. Ashure was weaving his way along the walkway toward them.

"I thought we had lost him," Drago said under his breath.

"King Ashure, welcome," the woman said in a warm tone.

"Are you dining here?" Ashure asked.

"Yes, and you are not...," Drago started to say before his voice faded when Carly elbowed him in the ribs.

"Hi Ashure. I thought you were busy," Carly said.

Ashure waved his hand. "A simple beheading, a few tortures, nothing that takes a full day and it leaves me famished," he replied.

"Really?" Carly asked, aghast at the thought of anyone being beheaded or tortured.

"Ashure," Drago growled.

Ashure shook his head and chuckled. "No, not really. Beheading and torture are too bloody and tend to displease the fairest citizens of the kingdom. I spent the day in boring meetings trying to decide who to pillage and loot next." He paused, looked around, and leaned forward and told them in a hushed voice, "Now that Drago has awakened, my captains believe it is time to visit the Isle of the Dragon again. I hear there is an impressive blood red diamond and a room full of treasure to be found," he teased.

"More like a huge cavern... not that I've ever seen any of the gold and jewels in it," Carly hastily corrected.

"A cavern! Please do share the details of this amazing cache you have never seen," Ashure begged, reaching for her hand.

Carly giggled when Ashure ended up with Drago's hand instead.

The pirate king quickly released Drago and wiped his hand across his shirt. Carly shook her head and turned to follow their hostess to the table.

"We hoped we wouldn't see you again," Drago said.

Carly murmured her thanks when Drago held out a chair for her before he and Ashure took the seats on each side of her. A waitress appeared with three menus. She placed them in front of each person before standing back a short distance to wait for their orders.

"Three ales, please," Ashure asked, ignoring Drago's rudeness. Once the waitress disappeared, he returned his attention to Drago. "I wanted to discuss a matter with you in private before you left."

Carly didn't miss the side glance Ashure gave her. She quickly scanned the menu and made a choice before placing it next to Drago. She needed to visit the ladies room and this would give the two men time to discuss whatever they needed to without worrying about her.

"I'll take the grilled bird with the fresh vegetables and soup. I need to visit the ladies room," she said, rising to her feet.

Both men rose as well. Drago had a slight scowl on his face that cleared when she rested her hand on his arm. She leaned forward and brushed a kiss across his lips.

"I'll be right back," she promised.

"Do not leave me alone with him too long. I cannot promise I won't kill him," Drago said.

"I heard that," Ashure dryly replied.

Carly laughed. "You'll both be fine. Nature calls," she said with a grimace.

"It was definitely calling last night and this morning," Ashure chuckled.

Carly's face flamed and she shot Ashure a stern glare before she turned to brush another kiss across Drago's lips. Drago may have some competition when it came to killing the Pirate King if he wasn't careful. She shook her head and stepped away from the table. She really felt sorry for any woman who tangled with Ashure. They were going to need a huge sense of humor, a long leash, and a whip or two to keep him in line.

"More like a Taser and a choke collar," Carly muttered to herself.

Carly stepped into the tavern and politely asked where the ladies room was located. After several attempts, she finally found it down a long, narrow corridor. She quickly used the facilities and refreshed herself before weaving her way back through the growing crowd.

She stepped outside the front entrance again and drew in a breath of relief. She was about to turn to the left and return to the table when a small table set up to the right caught her attention. The scarves hanging from the merchant's cart were beautiful.

Biting her lip, Carly decided a few extra moments wouldn't hurt. Drago had given her a few coins to buy anything she wanted, but Carly had been reluctant to spend any of it. For one, she didn't know the monetary system here. She could give the wrong coin and never know that she had given someone way too much or too little.

Walking over to the cart, she fingered several of the scarves. On the table was a wide variety of brooches to hold them in place. One of the brooches caught and held Carly's attention. It was of a small dragon. What made it unique were the tiny white birds that flew beside it. It reminded her of Drago and the paper birds.

"That is one of my most unusual pieces," the woman said, emerging from the shadows behind the cart.

Carly jumped in surprise. She hadn't seen anyone there. She blinked and pulled her hand back from the delicate piece.

"Oh, I didn't see you," Carly said, smiling at the pale young woman standing across from her.

"The piece would look lovely against your red scarf," the woman said, tilting her head to the side and staring at Carly with vivid green eyes.

"I... yes, it would. I.... How much is it?" Carly asked.

"A small silver coin – or your magical paper bird, if you wish to barter," the woman replied.

Carly instinctively reached for Little Knight. The tiny bird chirped and tried to burrow deeper into her scarf. Carly noticed that the other woman looked as if she were ill. Her eyes had dark circles under them and she appeared shrunken. The woman wore a long, black cape with the hood up to protect her from the chill of the breeze coming in off the harbor. Her black hair hung limply over her right shoulder.

"I'll pay the coin; the bird is not for sale," Carly said, reaching into the front pocket of her trousers for the small bag of coins Drago had given her. "You said a small one?"

"Yes," the woman replied, picking up the brooch. "I will wrap this for you unless you wish to wear it now."

"No, no, you can wrap it up. I'll take it with me," Carly replied, holding out the coin to the woman.

Their fingers touched for a brief second in the exchange. Carly's gaze jumped to the woman's face and she froze. The woman's fingers were like ice. Deep within the green eyes, Carly thought she saw a swirl of black, but the woman blinked and the vision vanished.

"The Dragon's Heart," the woman whispered.

"I beg your pardon?" Carly replied with a frown.

"You have captured the Dragon's Heart. You have started a chain that cannot be broken," the woman continued in a barely audible voice.

"How did you…? Who are you?" Carly asked.

The woman smiled. Carly could see the warmth and joy in the movement, as if the woman was unused to feeling either. The woman shook her head and pulled the hood closer around her head when a stiff breeze swirled around them.

"I hope you enjoy your gift, my lady," the woman said.

"Yes… Thank… Thank you," Carly responded, tucking the small bag with the brooch in it into her pocket. "Have a nice day."

"I will, my lady," the woman replied.

Carly turned when, out of the corner of her eye, she saw the waitress walking toward the table with a tray full of food. She hurried back to the table. Murmuring her apologies when both men stood, she sat down and the waitress began serving them.

"I was afraid you lost your way," Drago teased, leaning closer to her.

"I was just freshening up a bit," Carly replied.

"Carly, can you please tell me more of this wondrous cavern that you did not see?" Ashure asked as they began to eat.

CHAPTER 23

Early waved to Ashure and the dock hands one last time. She smiled broadly when Little Knight and the small flock of paper birds swept by the group and made their way to the top of the mast. Drago called out an order to release the lines and she watched as the great Dragonrider slipped from the dock and out into the protected harbor.

Before long, they were sailing through the narrow opening beneath the oddly shaped rock that was the entrance to Pirate's Cove and the Isle of the Pirates. The sun was low on the horizon, but the sky was clear. As soon as they were clear of the towering rocks, Drago unfurled the massive wings and sails, and the ship began to rise above the waves.

Carly leaned forward to watch as the great ship left the water and slowly gained altitude. A sense of peace settled over her, and she watched the pirate kingdom slowly fade into the distance. Reaching up, she tucked her hair behind her ears and turned to climb up to the bow.

Her mind played through all the different things that had happened since she had left for her hike. The days had blurred to weeks and in all honesty, she couldn't remember exactly how long she had been here – just that it felt natural.

"What has you so deep in thought?" Drago asked, coming to sit beside her.

Carly turned and smiled at him. She reached up and pulled her hair back again, tucking it once more behind her ear then turned to face the wind. A smile of appreciation curved her lips when Drago scooted closer to her and wrapped his arm around her waist.

"Nothing really, just a lot of different thoughts. It seems like another lifetime ago that I was just Carly Tate from Yachats, Oregon, going for a hike to try to lose some weight and get fit. All of this...." Her hands rose and she waved at the flying ship. "All of this seems so normal now and that other life – well, it feels more like a dream," she tried to explain.

"Do you miss your life there?" Drago asked.

Carly immediately shook her head. "No. Well, except for Jenny," she quietly amended.

She looked down at her hands where they lay on her lap. By now, Jenny would know that something had happened to her. She couldn't help but think that Jenny must feel the same way she did. As each day went by and the knowledge that Carly wasn't coming back became more of a reality, Jenny would only have her memories to comfort her.

"If I could bring your friend here, I would," Drago replied.

Carly heard Drago's heavy sigh and a sense of remorse swept through her. She felt too good to let regret rule her life. She had learned a lot about that when she was growing up; so had Jenny.

"I know you would. I didn't mean to make you feel guilty. Jenny will always have a special place in my heart. Still, I wouldn't change anything else about what has happened. I belong here – with you, Drago. I'll never regret that. I hope one day that she knows I'm safe and happy. Who knows, maybe whatever magic brought me here will send her a message. Either way, life is too short to have regrets about things you can't change," Carly said.

They sat in silence, each lost in their own thoughts and watched the sun set. There would be no moons until late tonight. They were both waning and wouldn't come up until after midnight. Twilight soon turned to darkness and the stars shone like brilliant diamonds in the sky. Below them, bioluminescent organisms illuminated the water as sea creatures small and large followed the ocean currents in search of food and migration.

The paper birds retreated through the open doorway to the Captain's cabin below deck. Drago rose to check their course and Carly prepared a light meal for them, which they ate above deck. After several hours, lack of sleep and exhaustion from their long day caught up with her and she couldn't keep her eyes open any longer.

"Go down to our cabin, Carly. You are exhausted," Drago ordered in a tender voice.

"What about you?" she asked.

Carly grimaced when she ended her question with a wide yawn. That wasn't a very sympathetic gesture. She blinked, but even raising her eyelids felt like a major chore. With a sigh of resignation, she reluctantly nodded.

"I can go weeks without sleep," Drago chuckled. "Make sure Little Knight and your flock are safe. I feel a storm gathering."

The thought of a storm perked Carly up for a brief moment. She glanced around with a frown. Sure enough, in the distance, she could see flashes of lightning and the sky was so dark that all the stars had disappeared.

"Will everything be okay?" she asked with a worried frown.

Drago brushed a reassuring kiss across her lips and nudged her to go below deck. Carly wanted to protest, but she felt like the wilted stem of a flower. She could barely stand up.

"The Dragonriders can handle the weather. Go curl up in bed. I will come later once we have passed through it," he promised.

"Okay," Carly replied. With a shiver, she glanced once more at the dark sky in front of them. "What about you? Will you get wet?"

"Only when I am thinking of you," he chuckled. "There is a control center below deck. Once you are safely tucked in our cabin, I will secure the ship and move down to the bridge there. I will not be able to leave as long as the weather is foul. It is best if you stay in our cabin as it may get rough. This way I know you will be safe and comfortable. I will come find you as soon as we are through the storm."

"Oh, good," she said, remembering briefly seeing a room in the very front of the ship. "Okay, if you are sure. I'll see you after the storm."

"I'm sure. Good night, little thief," Drago replied.

"Good night, Drago," Carly murmured.

"Carly," Drago called when she started down.

She glanced back over her shoulder at him. "Yes."

"I love you," he said.

"I love you, too, Drago," she responded with a tired but happy smile.

She turned back and slowly walked down the stairs to the lower decks. Passing through the door, she descended the next short set of steps and made her way to the end of the corridor. A soft, sympathetic smile curved her lips when she heard the frightened chirps of the paper birds.

"Come on. You can sleep with me," Carly instructed as she walked through the door and closed it behind her. "It is getting cold and going to be very wet out there. You need to stay inside where it is dry and hopefully warmer."

Walking over to the built-in vanity, she pulled open the drawer and picked up the brush. She pulled off her red scarf and brushed her hair out before rising to wash her face and brush her teeth in the small adjoining bathroom. Returning to the bedroom, she sat down and removed her boots and socks. She placed them next to the chair that was in the corner near the vanity table before rising to remove her trousers.

The soft sound of something hitting the wooden floor drew her attention. A dark blue velvet bag lay on the floor. Carly bent to pick up her trousers and the bag. She tossed the trousers over the back of a nearby chair before turning the bag over in her hand.

A shiver escaped her when the chill from the dropping air pressure swirled around her bare legs. Walking over to the bed, Carly pulled the covers back and slid under them before pulling them firmly around her and laying back. She fingered the bag, remembering the beauty of the delicate brooch inside.

Opening the bag, she pulled the wrapped brooch out. She carefully unfolded the cloth covering the brooch and touched the midnight black gems, tiny white shell birds, and the etched gold surrounding the design. What caught her attention was the tiny red jewel where the dragon's heart should be.

Carly's fingers brushed over the red gem before she turned it over. A slight cry escaped her when the sharp pin on the back pricked her finger. She raised her finger to her lips to stop the blood. Her hand trembled and she tried to shake away the sudden dizziness.

"I... I must be... more tired... than I realized," she whispered in a slurred voice.

Carly was unaware that her hand had fallen to the side and the brooch slipped between the folds of the covers. Her wounded finger slipped from her lips and fell to the side as well. Carly's eyelashes fluttered for a moment before settling like twin crescents against her pale skin.

Little Knight sensed the unnatural magic and frantically tried to wake Carly. When the paper bird was unable to wake her, he flew to the door. The other birds, realizing what was happening, joined Little Knight. They flung themselves against the door in a frantic attempt to get to Drago. Unable to open the door, Little Knight landed on the floor. With a shake, the paper bird unfolded itself and slipped under the door. One by one, the flock followed, driven by the urgent need to get help for Carly.

Little Knight quickly refolded his small body and lifted off the floor. The tiny paper bird soared down the passage, once again unfolding, slipping under the doorway at the end, and refolding his body with the flock following closely behind. The fierce wind tossed the birds around, scattering them. No matter how hard or fast they tried to fly, they were no match for the swirling storm. One by one, they were swept over the side, caught in a turbulent force beyond their power until only Little Knight remained – and then, the sky opened up and the rain began to fall.

The sound of the thunder drowned out the desperate, pitiful chirps of the paper bird. Large raindrops began to soak the paper it was made from, dissolving the pictures Carly had drawn and weighing it down. Little Knight fought against the elements, focused only on reaching

Drago. The Dragon King did not see the tiny speck of white against the flash of the lightning nor hear its cries over the rolling of the thunder. He was busy securing the sails.

Little Knight bowed his head, pushing at his heavy wings to continue the fight, but a gust of wind swept him over the side. Unable to use his wings, he spiraled downward into the raging ocean, his desperate chirps swept away on the winds. The last of his magic melted away with the rain until he became lost in the dark, angry ocean that had claimed the rest of the flock – and so many of Drago's people.

∽

The storm swirled around them for almost a day and a half. Unable to leave the bridge, Drago was surprised when he realized how much time had passed. It wasn't until the Dragonrider emerged on the other side of the sprawling cyclone that he relaxed his grip on the controls.

He rolled his shoulders to relieve the stiffness and rubbed his neck. Normally, there would have been a full crew on duty to handle the needs of the ship through such a storm. He hoped that Carly had been able to get some rest. There were a few times when the trip had been a little rough.

Engaging the auto-navigation, he turned and strode toward the door. His first thought was to check on Carly, then he would assess if there was any damage to the ship. He should probably reverse that, but he needed to make sure she wasn't too shaken by the storm.

Striding down the passage, he pushed open the door leading to the deck. Brilliant sunshine and crisp, clear skies greeted him. It was so bright that he had to blink several times to adjust his vision. He walked across the deck, noting any obvious problems. One of the sails looked as if it was ripped and several of the coils of rope now lay twisted like a confused snake across the deck, but otherwise it looked to be minor damage.

He was almost halfway across the deck when he glanced down as he stepped over a bundle of rope. A speck of white was caught underneath. Drago bent to retrieve it as a nagging feeling began to build. He lifted the rope and gently peeled the torn, white clump away from the coarse fibers of the rope.

Gently prying it free, he straightened and turned the fibrous mass in his hand. His fingers trembled ever so slightly when he saw the faint smear of black. The trace of his magic was still barely visible.

"Carly!" he hissed, his gaze shooting to the closed door leading down to their cabin. "Carly!"

Drago urgently called out her name a second time. His fist closed around the wet paper. Striding across to the door, he flung it open and took the stairs two at a time. He was running by the time he reached the bottom step – his long strides eating up the passage to the door of the Captain's cabin.

"Carly!" Drago called again, even as his hand turned the door knob and he pushed the door open.

His gaze flew around the room. He noted her boots and pants next to the chair and the red scarf that she had worn laying on the floor next to the vanity table. His gaze moved to the bed. She lay against the dark silk sheets. Her pale face relaxed in a peaceful slumber. There was a stillness to her features that seemed unnatural.

"Carly.... Little thief...," Drago softly called, unwilling to alarm her with his fear.

The sense that something was dreadfully wrong grew the closer he got to the bed. He sank down on the edge and raised a trembling hand to run his fingers down her cheek. He raised his other hand and realized he was still holding the remains of one of her birds. He dropped it on the bedspread.

"Carly, little thief, sweetheart, wake up," Drago pleaded in a quiet, tender voice. "Please, wake up."

He cupped her outstretched hand with a trembling one of his own. He lifted her icy fingers to his lips and gently blew on them before pressing a kiss to the tips. His throat tightened as he tried to speak.

"Carly, I need you to wake up. Please, my love, I need you... I...." His throat thickened to the point he couldn't continue. Closing his eyes, he drew in a deep breath and tried again. Opening his eyes, he gazed down at Carly's unresponsive face. "I love you, Carly Tate."

She still did not respond. Leaning down, Drago pressed a kiss to her lips and knew then that she wouldn't wake up. He could taste the faint, tainted magic on her lips – magic that he had smelled once before. The denial and rage that slammed into him was quickly overwhelmed by pure grief. This was a different type of pain. This was a mortal wound. He could feel his heart stutter, as if it was slowly breaking.

His head bowed at the pain and his hand fell to the covers beside her. He felt something hard under his palm. Curling his fingers around the object, he picked it up and turned his hand over. In the center of his palm lay a delicate brooch in the shape of a dragon that glittered in the light shining through the windows.

Tears blinded him. Ashure had warned him. The Pirate King said he had felt the taint of the Sea Witch's magic pass through the entrance. He told Drago that he had members of his elite forces searching every building, every rock and crevice, for Magna.

Drago could have sworn that Carly had never been out of his sight the entire time – and she hadn't been except for the few minutes when she had excused herself to freshen up.

Turning the brooch over, he rapidly blinked his eyes to clear them. A trace of blood coated the tip of the pin. Magna had managed to accomplish what she had set out to do – she had struck at the Dragon's Heart – his heart. She had not silenced his connection with Carly as she had done with the others. Instead, she had snared Carly in an immortal sleep – one where Carly was trapped between life and death. He could not leave Carly's side for fear that she would cross over.

Another shaft of grief struck him with such a blow that he rose up off the bed with a loud howl. Turning, he threw the brooch at the window. The brooch spun through the air, striking the glass and shattering it before disappearing.

The shards of glass that rained down felt like they were slicing through the remainder of his control. Sinking down next to the bed, Drago blindly groped for Carly's hand. Wrapping both of his hands around her cold fingers, large tears slid hopelessly down his cheeks and he realized something in that instant – that losing Carly had done something he didn't think was possible... he learned that grown dragons could cry.

CHAPTER 24

More than a day later, Drago docked the Dragonrider in the cave. He methodically went through the movements of pulling the wings in to store them against the ship, lowering the useable sails, and securing the vessel. He closed the doors to the entrance and locked it. He ignored the supplies. Where Carly and he were going, they would not be needed.

Once everything was done, he returned to their cabin. He tenderly ran his hand along her cheek. His eyes burned, but he ignored it.

Drago pulled the bedspread and sheet free from the bed and carefully wrapped Carly in them. Picking her up in his arms, he cradled her against his body. Unable to resist, he rubbed his cheek against her silky hair.

"I will never leave you, Carly. As long as your heart beats, so will mine. When you draw your last breath, I will give you mine so that we may always be together," Drago murmured.

He turned without another word and left the cabin. His footsteps were silent as he walked down the long passage and made his way up to the deck. Once there, his body shimmered and he transformed into his dragon with Carly still tenderly held against his body.

The magic in his words opened the ground. He knew this would be for the last time. There would be no need for him to ever return. The time of the dragons had ended. With his death, it would be the beginning of the end for the Seven Kingdoms.

Drago swept down, spiraling in a free fall. He barely opened his wings in time to keep from crashing into the mountains of jewels. Even so, he was going too fast to land safely and was forced to turn his body to shield Carly when he hit a huge pile.

He slid down the pile, throwing coins, jewels, and other treasures far and wide. He curled around Carly, tightly wrapping his wings around her and rolled before coming to a stop when he hit the platform at the bottom. He lay on his side, his head against the platform and his wings still cradling Carly against his chest.

Drago's eyes burned again when he realized where he had landed. In his mind's eye, he could still see that first day when Carly had come into his life. Her wide, expressive eyes had been staring at him with awe and excitement and her softly spoken words *'Can I keep you?'* whispered in his mind.

"Always," he whispered back. "You can keep me forever, little thief."

Opening his wings, he shifted back into his two-legged form. He would make her a bed, then he would shift into his dragon and he would watch over her. He gently laid her on the platform and set to work.

Drago found a gold and jeweled lounge with the finest royal red velvet cover and a silk pillow for her head. He cleared the platform of all treasure except the bed and Carly. Picking her up, he tenderly laid her on the lounge and made sure that she was covered. Once he felt she would be comfortable, he turned his gaze about the treasure room. He would give all of it away if it would bring Carly back to him.

His gaze moved to the floating red diamond of the Dragon's Heart. Bitter rage filled him. This was the gift of the Goddess and all it had brought him was sorrow. Lifting his arm, he opened his left hand.

"Come to me," he ordered in a cold, hard voice.

He would crush the diamond. With its destruction, the Sea Witch could never gain the power held within. There was nothing left for it to protect. He was the last of the dragons and his life was soon to be over.

"Come to me!" he growled, pulling on the power inside him.

The diamond began to spin as it rose higher. As if gripped by an invisible hand, the gem floated toward him. Drago's gaze burned with the fire of his dragon – of his people. He reached up to wrap his fingers around the diamond only to see his fingers passing through it. Stunned, he turned when it floated past him and on toward Carly.

He started to take a step forward to grab it again when it danced away from him. His fury changed to confusion and doubt. The diamond began to glow with a brilliance that blinded him. Raising his arm, he shielded his eyes. A hoarse cry of protest escaped him when he saw a shaft of red pierce Carly's chest.

Dropping his arm, he rushed forward only to be struck by a powerful blow which lifted him off his feet and threw him backwards off the platform. He landed several meters away. Stunned, he watched in disbelief as Carly's body rose off the lounge. The covers he'd wrapped around her opened and fell away, leaving her in the long tunic.

"No, please! No...," Drago pleaded, raising his hand in protest. "Do not take her from me."

The glowing magic from the Dragon's Heart surrounded Carly. Soon, she was wrapped in the brilliant red energy. Tears streamed down his face and he fought the paralyzing force of the spell keeping him from her.

A brilliant flash suddenly exploded from the Dragon's Heart, blinding him. Drago covered his eyes with his arm. His heart felt like it was being ripped out of his chest. The pain was so great that he threw his head back and roared in agony. He had known their time was limited, but he'd wanted every precious second he could have with her. Now, even that was gone – all gone.

Choking on his grief, he turned and buried his face against his arm. His body turned from the devastating brightness. Soft moans of pain escaped him in gasping breaths.

"My little thief.... My heart...," he repeated over and over in an uneven voice.

Darkness spread around him as the light began to fade. Drago heard the sound of Carly's body being lowered back to the lounge.

Drawing in shuddering breaths, he slowly pushed himself back up. The red diamond that was the Dragon's Heart silently floated over his head and back to the large statue of his father.

A slight noise behind him caught his attention. He froze, afraid to turn around. The sound came again, a slight scraping against the stone of the platform. Sitting up, Drago slowly turned.

"Carly…," he said in a barely audible whisper.

∼

All that Carly could remember was a sudden warmth and the continued increase in body temperature until she felt like someone had dropped her into a hot tub and forgot to tell her that they were going to be boiling frogs in it that afternoon.

That, and the glowing red light that seemed determined to blind me, she thought in confusion, trying to figure out where in the heck she was.

Carly glanced around, surprised that she could see so clearly in the dim light. It didn't take her long to realize that she had somehow ended up back in the treasure room under the palace. A frown creased her brow and she tried to remember their return trip to the Isle of the Dragon. For the life of her all she could remember was picking up the brooch she had purchased and falling asleep. Lifting a claw to push back her hair, her arm froze in midair.

Claw…. I have a claw…. I have a claw, she repeated in her mind again, staring at the slender ivory claws surrounded by taupe and ivory scales.

She glanced down at her body. Her gaze continued down, running over her chest and over her shoulder. She stepped sideways and her tail caught on an ornate lounge. She winced at the unusually loud sound when the legs slid across the stone. It sounded like fingernails on a chalkboard to her.

Carly shook her head in disbelief. She raised her tail and flicked it back and forth. Yes, it was hers – or, at least it moved when she thought about it. She heard a hoarse voice call out her name.

Turning back around, joy washed through her when she saw Drago staring up at her. There was an expression of shock on his face, as if he couldn't quite believe what he was seeing. A grin, or at least she hoped it was a grin, curved her lips.

"I'm a dragon! Either that or I'm dreaming I'm a dragon. I haven't figured out which one it is yet," Carly giggled. "I have wings – and a tail!"

Carly expanded her wings and curled her tail around her. She couldn't help but admire how beautiful they were. If this was a dream, she hoped she never woke up. Carly couldn't help but think if she was a dragon, she could be with Drago in the truest sense of a mate.

"You are... beautiful, Carly," Drago said, rising from where he was sprawled.

Carly tilted her head and watched him slowly climb the steps of the platform until he was standing in front of her. She lowered her head and pressed her nose against his hand. He tenderly stroked her jaw.

"What happened to me?" she asked in confusion. "How did I become a dragon?"

"You have captured the Dragon's Heart. It now lives inside you," Drago said, stroking her neck. "It is the only way for this to have happened. The Dragon's Heart contains the soul of who we are as people and as dragons. You have the essence of us within you, just as you have my heart, Carly. You are a gift I can never thank the Goddess enough for returning to me."

"I'm not sure I understand, but I'm not going to complain. Wait a minute! Does this mean I can learn to fly with you?" Carly asked in excitement before it died. "What if I can't change like you can?" she asked in horror.

"Try," Drago said, still caressing her.

"But... how?" she asked.

"Think of yourself as Carly. Put what you look like in your human form into your mind," he instructed.

Carly nodded and closed her eyes. She focused on what she looked like in the mirror. A tingling sensation washed through her. Startled, she opened her eyes to see a mist of red shimmering around her. When she blinked again, she was standing in front of Drago – only this time she had to look up at him.

Raising a trembling hand, she laughed when she saw her five

fingers reaching up to stroke Drago's cheek. Turning it over, she studied her hand before glancing down at her body. She was standing on two legs. Carly raised her head and smiled. The smile faded when she saw the lines around Drago's eyes and mouth and the clear exhaustion in his eyes.

"What happened?" she demanded.

Drago cupped her cheeks with trembling hands. His eyes searched her face, as if he were trying to memorize her features and see if she was real or not. This was different from the other times. This time there was a hint of fear in them that changed to relief.

"I thought I had lost you. The brooch you touched was cursed with a sleeping spell," Drago choked out, tenderly brushing her hair back from her face.

"The brooch…. You mean the one I bought from the woman outside the restaurant. She looked sick, but she was really sweet," Carly said with a frown.

Drago shook his head. "She was not sweet, Carly. That was the Sea Witch. Ashure warned me that he sensed her enter the Isle of the Pirates," he explained.

"Oh, Drago. The brooch reminded me of you and Little Knight and the flock and it had a red stone like the Dragon's Heart…." She paused and looked around before glancing up at the ceiling. "Are Little Knight and the flock waiting for us? How long have we been here? They are probably going crazy."

Drago shook his head in regret. "They are gone. I found the remains of one of them. I suspect they sensed the dark magic and tried to warn me, but they were no match for the storm."

Tears filled Carly's eyes and she began to cry. "Oh no. Poor Little Knight. He and the others were so brave," she sniffed.

Drago pulled her into his arms and held her tight. Carly could feel the heavy beat of his heart and feel the tremors that rocked his powerful frame. It took a moment to realize that Drago, the mighty King of the Dragons, was struggling to control his emotions.

Her arms wrapped around him and she held him as if she would never let him go. They stood together for several long minutes before he released a long breath. Stepping back, he glanced down at her and smiled.

"I will make you another flock of birds, this time bigger and fiercer, so they can help me protect you better. Come, let us return to the palace above," he said.

"Can I fly?" Carly asked excitedly.

Drago laughed and shook his head. "Perhaps it would be best to wait until you have more room," he suggested.

Carly's expression fell, but she couldn't keep the amusement from shining through. She nodded and stepped back. Within seconds, she was once again wrapped in Drago's embrace. This time, she would be awake and eager to see just what she could do in her dragon form – once she had more room.

"Does this mean we get to make love as dragons?" she suddenly asked as he began to lift off.

A low groan escaped Drago. "You ask me this now?" he growled.

The island birds, nesting along the walls of the palace, flew off startled when the ground of the courtyard opened up, and the sound of feminine laughter rose through the opening followed by the low growl of a male dragon. True to his word, Drago swept out over the forest. He turned, already knowing where he wanted to take Carly. He soared through the air, his instincts guiding him back to Arkla, the magical, ancient palace where the dragons were said first to have appeared.

A wave of warmth filled Carly. She loved this man-dragon more than life itself. A contented smile curved her lips when he reached out to run his back claws along the smooth surface of the pristine lake. Her gaze was captured by the beauty of their reflections caught in the mirrored surface.

Several minutes later, Drago swept up over the majestic white stones of the palace. With the flow of the waterfalls as their curtain, Drago tenderly guided her on how to shift into her dragon again. She twirled in an arc, her wings opened and her tail raised in an instinctive mating dance. Her breath caught when Drago rose up, his larger body caging her beneath him, and his wings framing her smaller form. Their tails tangled and they came together in the ancient way of the dragon, connecting the last threads of their bond.

EPILOGUE

Two wo years later:

Carly stood on the edge of the cliff and stared out over the sapphire waves. Riding the currents of air were a brilliant flock of large white paper birds. Carly laughed when they swooped down and turned in a wide circle. They wanted to play.

Big Knight, the name she'd given to the largest of the birds and the leader of the flock, wasn't going to be happy with her. He had become just as protective of her as Little Knight had been. He hated when he was told to return to the castle without her.

There were thick clouds building in the east. A storm was coming. While Carly loved storms, paper and rain did not mix well together, even with the powerful spell Drago had cast, and there was no way she was going to risk losing her paper friends.

The wind blew her hair in front of her eyes, obscuring her vision of the flock and the departing visitors for a moment. With an impatient hand, she brushed the strands away. She would give the flock a few more minutes before she chased them back into the palace. Her gaze moved to the faint outline of several ships on the horizon. She could still see the flashes of lightning from the thunderbirds powering the cyclops' ships. She hoped they would be able to avoid the worst part of the storm.

Carly couldn't help but reflect on how much her life had changed. Two years ago, she would never have imagined that going for a walk and encountering a storm would lead her to such a magical world. A reluctant smile tugged at her lips as she remembered the reason behind her unbelievable journey. She would never again complain about exercising, after all, it had led her to this incredible place.

Carly turned when she heard the sound of footsteps approaching down the path. A smile curved her lips at the sight of the man walking down the steep path. Dark sapphire and gold eyes held hers for several long seconds. She shivered at the promise in them. It never ceased to amaze her that Drago could light her blood on fire with just a look.

"A storm comes," he chided her in a soft voice.

"I know. I'm watching it. The flock isn't going to be happy. They are having fun. I can't blame them," Carly replied, turning to look back out at the white capped waves.

She sighed when Drago wrapped his arms around her and pulled her closer. She tilted her head, exposing her neck to him. A low rumble escaped her when he pressed a hot kiss to her sensitive skin.

"One more time before we return to the palace," Drago chuckled. "I love you, Carly. Fly with me."

Carly's delighted laughter filled the air when he released her and stepped back to change. The brilliant light of sapphire and gold shimmered in the air before it was replaced with a fierce male dragon. Turning, Carly focused as she raised her hands to the sky. A ruby red glow surrounded her, encasing her in its magic as her body shifted. Sweeping her dainty wings back and forth, she rose up off the cliff and soared down over the churning waters far below.

Ever since the day the Dragon's Heart had transformed her, Carly had been filled with even more excitement and wonder. The power of being a dragon was unlike anything she had ever experienced before. Sure, she was a bit clumsy. Yes, she had accidently swept her tail in the wrong direction a time or two and poor Drago had learned the hard way that a dragon's balls were as sensitive as a man's – but he had quickly learned to give her a little more room when she was shifting.

She circled the area leading into the harbor. Her gaze scanned the area to make sure everything was safe. No one had seen or heard of the Sea Witch since Carly's encounter with her. Turning her head, she released a rumbled warning to the flock of white birds that came up to fly beside her. Big Knight chirped, and quickly turned back toward the palace with the rest of the flock trailing behind him. Following them back up to the cliff, Carly swept past Drago.

"I love this, Drago!" Carly laughed, turning back out toward the cliffs again when she heard Drago spread his wings and snap his tail.

∼

Drago stood for a moment, watching as his beautiful, strange little thief soared out over the waters that surrounded their home. Spreading his wings, he took off after her, the glimmer of a smile on his lips. He had plans for tonight.

The last two years with Carly had chased the years of loneliness away. She had ignited the fire inside him and given him a reason to live again. Tonight, he would spread that fire inside her and they would fill their home with children.

They had been talking about it for the last few months. He had been reluctant, fearful of something happening to her, but he knew she was right – they could not live in fear for the rest of their lives. He would protect her and his children from the Sea Witch and any other threat that might come their way.

Soaring down beside her, he carefully guarded her while she flew. There were others out there who would still challenge him for his treasure. Drago thought it was more to bedevil him than to antagonize him. He almost always ended up bartering for goods like he had with the cyclops who had recently sailed into port.

For him, it was not the gold that warmed his heart any longer, but the female at his side. Reaching over, he nipped at her neck to let her know that it was time to return to the safety of their home. He could feel the static of electricity in the air. The storm tonight would be fierce.

"Come, Carly," he rumbled above the sound of the wind and waves. "The storm draws closer."

"I know," she whispered, raising her head to the light sprinkle of rain before turning her warm brown eyes toward him. "Let's go home."

Drago reached out with his tail and ran it along her sensitive belly. Carly immediately knew what her mate had in mind. Responding, she turned back toward the palace. Sweeping over the cliff and the high walls surrounding the entrance to their living quarters, she shifted as she stepped onto the long, wide balcony.

Drago swept Carly up into his arms the moment he shifted. A sense of peace settled over him when she wrapped her arms around his neck. He strode through the wide doors and into their bedroom. With a wave of his hand, the doors remained partially open. The covered portion of the balcony would protect them from the rain while the storm building inside the bedroom would rival the one outside. Bowing his head, he captured her lips as he lowered her down to the soft covers of their bed.

"I love you, Carly," Drago said, pressing his hot lips against the pounding pulse at her neck. "You have given me so much, I do not know if I can ever show you how much."

"As long as we are together forever, that is all that matters to me. I love you, Drago. I can't believe how lucky we are to have each other," she said.

A shudder raced through him when Carly slowly opened his shirt and pushed it off his shoulders. The feel of her hands awakened the fire inside him that was always burning for her. Shrugging his shirt off, he tossed it to the side. Pulling back just far enough, he stared down at where she lay against the black satin sheets.

His fingers carefully opened each button on her blouse, baring her breasts. Her soft, smooth skin felt like the finest silk. His fingers glided over her in reverence. His heart swelled with love and he knew that she was the best treasure any dragon could hope to find.

Carly tilted her head and gazed up at him. "What is it? You have that strange look in your eyes that you get when you are trying to hide something from me," she teased.

"I was thinking that you are right. I think it is time we started a family," he said, watching her eyes widen with happiness.

That night, neither Drago nor Carly paid much attention to the storm outside. They were more focused on the one they were creating inside. The curtains blew inward, showing the magnificent display of lightning, but inside the dragon's palace the two souls who came together were caught in a firestorm of their own making, one that would bind them together for eternity. For when a dragon finds her treasure, she never, ever lets it go.

Seven Kingdoms, eight incredible tales
The saga continues with The Sea King's Lady…

Clutching the material of the gown in her hands, she lifted it just far enough to make sure she didn't step on it before raising her chin and straightening her shoulders. She was going to do this.

"I've totally lost my mind," she said, staring at the door and willing her legs to work.

"Completely, so you have nothing to worry about," Kelia informed her.

Jenny can't bring herself to give up the search for Carly, even after all this time. Orion can't stop the Sea Witch from using his child to seal the fate of the merpeople. An unlikely alliance between Jenny and Orion could change everything, but what will it take survive the evil lurking in the depths of the ocean?

Read on for a sneak peak into the full book!

THE SEA KING'S LADY

Prologue

Five years earlier:

"Your Majesty," one of the guards urgently called to Orion.

Orion turned with a frown. He nodded at Kapian, his Captain of the Guard, to wait for him. They needed to review the damage caused by a minor earthquake that had struck three hours earlier, develop a plan of action to help those affected, and send support crews to begin repairs.

He and Kapian had just returned from a scouting mission offshore. The quake had rippled along the rocky floor of the ocean, opening a crevice that almost sucked them into it. They had hastily returned to the Isle of the Sea Serpent after they realized that the quake would probably impact the island as well.

There was no damage to the underwater city when they returned there, but he had received reports of some damage to the city above. Though the intensity of the earthquake had been relatively minor, he was concerned about the possibility of a Tsunami causing further damage to the upper kingdom. The new buildings were designed to withstand much stronger quakes, but there were also many older structures that would be vulnerable. His frown deepened when he realized who had called out to him. York was his wife's personal guard and was normally never far from her side.

"Is there a problem?" he demanded, noting the worried expression in York's eyes.

"It is the Queen, Your Majesty. She was hurt in the earthquake," York stated.

"Orion, do you want me to...," Kapian said, turning to gaze at Orion.

Orion shook his head at Kapian's sympathetic tone. "Find out if anyone else has been injured for me, Kapian, while I see to Shamill," Orion ordered before he turned to face York again. "Where is she?"

"In her chambers, Your Majesty," York replied.

Orion brushed past the guard and strode toward his wife's chambers. Palace guards straightened to attention as he passed, but he ignored them. His thoughts were on Shamill.

"Your Majesty," York called from behind him.

Orion impatiently turned to the guard, his hand on the door handle to Shamill's living quarters. He waited for York to catch up. His lips tightened when he saw an expression of grief in the man's eyes.

"What is it?" he demanded.

"I should warn you...," York said before his voice faded and he glanced at the door. "The Queen's injuries were most grievous. I should have protected her better. Please accept my deepest regrets, Your Majesty."

Orion didn't wait to hear York's next words. He didn't need to—the man's expression told him that Shamill's injuries must have been worse than he had first thought. Turning around, he pushed open the door. Three healers turned toward him when he entered the room and bowed in respect. They did not speak as he continued through the sitting room to Shamill's bedroom.

He paused for a brief second in the doorway. In addition to the healers conversing in the sitting room, there were three women in the room with his wife. The first was one of Shamill's Ladies-in-Waiting who was brushing a damp cloth across Shamill's pale forehead.

Shamill lay against the pristine white sheets, her skin almost the same color. He moved his gaze to the second woman who stood near the window. This woman held a small bundle in her arms and was swaying back and forth.

"Your Majesty," the third woman, Kelia, murmured with a respectful bow of her head.

Kelia had been his nursemaid when he was young and had been attending to Shamill during the later months of her pregnancy. His gaze moved over Kelia's lined face before shifting to Shamill's peaceful one. He hadn't missed the sorrow in the older woman's eyes.

"How is she?" he asked in a low voice.

"Not good, Your Majesty. Her highness was walking along the upper cliffs when the earthquake occurred. A portion of the retaining wall along one of the walking paths collapsed on top of her, trapping her," Kelia explained in a trembling voice. "Her guard found her and called for assistance."

"The babe...," Orion hesitantly asked.

"Your son survived, but keeping him alive until he could be born has cost the Queen her life," Kelia replied.

Orion walked over to the edge of the bed. Shamill's Lady-in-Waiting rose and silently walked over to the window. Orion sank down onto the bed next to his wife.

In the background, he heard Kelia murmur quietly to the young woman standing next to the window. The young woman holding his son handed the infant to Kelia before she and Shamill's Lady-in-Waiting quietly exited the room. Kelia walked over and held out the infant to him. Orion tenderly scooped the baby into his arms.

"I will be outside the door if you need my assistance," Kelia murmured.

Orion nodded and gazed down at the round, rosy cheeks of the sleeping infant. He lifted a finger and gently ran it down the baby's cheek. Almost immediately, the baby turned his head and opened his mouth.

"He... is... well?" Shamill asked in a voice that was barely audible.

Orion moved his gaze to Shamill. Her eyes were open, but he could see the shadows of death in them. Her gaze was no longer sharp and clear. The light that usually glimmered in her eyes was now barely visible.

"Yes, he is," Orion said, adjusting the baby in his arms so Shamill could see him.

A hint of a smile curved her lips before it faded. She winced and drew in a shaky breath. Her eyelids fluttered and closed for a moment before she forced them open again. Their gazes locked, and a sense of sorrow filled him. While he and Shamill had never been in love with each other, they were good friends. He respected her quiet grace and gentle soul.

"Dolph…," Shamill whispered.

"He is safe," Orion reassured her.

"Let me… just one… time… before…."

Orion gently laid the baby on Shamill's chest. He instinctively reached out to catch the tear that escaped from the corner of her eye. She moved her left hand, but she was too weak to lift it. Reaching down, he cupped it and placed her cold fingers against their son's warm cheek.

"What… name…?" she asked in a threadbare voice.

"Juno. His name is Juno, just like you insisted," Orion said with a small, sad smile.

"Juno…," Shamill whispered.

Orion grasped her hand when it started to slide. Drawing her cold fingers to his lips, he pressed a kiss to the tips. His gaze remained fixed on her face as the last of the light swirled and faded in her eyes. Juno's faint cry pierced him, it was as if the child could feel that his mother was gone.

"May your journey bring you happiness, Shamill. I will protect both of our sons and the kingdom," Orion said in a quiet voice.

He bent forward and pressed a kiss to her forehead before he gently scooped the fretting baby into his arms. Grief swept through him as he rose from the bed. Turning, he saw Kelia standing just outside the open doorway. She started forward with her arms out, but he shook his head.

"Where is Dolph?" he asked.

"The young lord is in the garden with his nursemaid," Kelia replied.

"I want you to find a nursemaid for Juno. Tell her to meet me in the garden in ten minutes," Orion ordered.

"Yes, Your Majesty," Kelia said with a bow of her head.

Orion walked through the sitting room and out through the balcony doors. Shamill had insisted on a first-floor apartment when they married as she feared heights and enjoyed being near the gardens. His own apartments were located in the West tower. He preferred to be able to look out over the ocean when he was on the isle.

Walking across the wide, covered balcony, Orion descended the steps and continued along the stone path. He instinctively shielded the baby in his arms as he walked through the garden. Even though the sun was low on the horizon, he knew the babe would be sensitive to light. He paused under a nearby tree and listened. He smiled when he heard the squeal of his eldest son's voice, followed by a splash.

"Master Dolph, you are not to get wet! Dinner will be soon," the nursemaid sharply scolded.

Orion walked down the path to a small stream that ran through the garden. Dolph sat in the middle of it, laughing and splashing. His eldest son was already a handful and, if the frustrated expression on the woman's face was anything to go by, it appeared he would be assigning a new nursemaid before long.

"I will see to him," Orion said in a dismissive tone.

The woman turned in surprise. Orion saw her gaze move to the baby in his arms before returning to his face. She looked shaken.

"Yes, Your Majesty. I... My heart goes with the Queen," she said, lightly touching her fingers to her chest near her heart.

"My gratitude for your sympathy," Orion replied before he focused his attention on his oldest son. "Dolph, come here."

"Father, I can make the water dance!" Dolph giggled, wiggling his fingers.

Orion watched as the water rose and swirled at his son's command. There was no denying that Dolph would be a very powerful ruler one day. He smiled at his eldest son's delight. Life continued.

"Very good, son. Come, meet your new brother," Orion said as he walked over to a stone bench under a tree and sat down.

"Can I teach him to make the water dance?" Dolph asked, climbing up the bank.

Orion chuckled. "When he is older," he promised.

Dolph hurried over to his father. He paused and gazed down at the small bundle in Orion's arms before looking up at his father with a frown. Another smile tugged at the corner of Orion's mouth at the perplexed expression on his son's face.

"He is small," Dolph said, gazing down at his brother again.

"So were you when you were his age," Orion gently explained.

"Can I touch him?" Dolph asked, looking up at his father.

"Yes, but be gentle," Orion replied, readjusting Juno so his elder brother could see him better.

"Mother went away. Didn't she want to be with us anymore?" Dolph asked, sliding his finger along Juno's cheek.

"Who told you about your mother?" Orion demanded, looking intently at his son.

Dolph giggled when Juno opened his mouth and tried to suck on his finger. Orion's mouth tightened in annoyance. It was his place to explain what had happened to Shamill. If the nursemaid had said anything….

"The water," Dolph replied. "Will he get teeth?"

"The water…?" Orion asked with a frown.

Dolph nodded and looked up at his father. "The water told me that Mother had returned to her. She said not to be sad because we would have a new mother one day who would love us just as much," he replied. "Can I go play in the water again?"

Orion nodded, stunned by his son's statement. The sound of approaching footsteps drew his attention. Kapian, Kelia, and a young girl paused briefly near the path leading to the stone bench where he sat.

Orion rose to his feet as they approached. Kelia reached out for Juno, who was beginning to fuss again. He handed the newborn to her.

"We will see to his care, Your Majesty," Kelia said. "This is my granddaughter, Karin."

"Thank you, Kelia," Orion absently replied.

The realization of what had happened began to sink in as he watched Karin cradle Juno in her arms before she and Kelia turned and walked away. Orion turned to watch Dolph play in the water. Even at the tender age of two and a half, his eldest was showing the power of his birthright as Prince of the Sea People. Dolph would need a firm hand to guide him.

Orion glanced at his friend, Kapian. "I want to know exactly what happened. Shamill was terrified of heights. She would never have traveled along the cliff path," he stated in a grim voice.

"I will have a full report for you as soon as possible. I've also ordered construction of temporary safety railings along the cliffs. It will take time to repair all of the damage, but we will do everything we can to ensure such a tragedy does not occur again," Kapian promised.

Orion nodded, lost in thought. There was too much to do at the moment to give in to the grief pressing on him. Shamill's death would not only leave a void in his life, but also in the kingdom.

Chapter 1

Present day—Yachats, Oregon:

Jenny Ackerly's heart was telling her that her best friend was not dead —even as her head argued the opposite. The long, winding road through the redwoods along the Oregon coast felt a lot like her life over the last two years since Carly's disappearance—a never-ending journey of twists and turns. She was ready for the road of life to straighten out a little so she could see where in the hell it was taking her.

"She isn't dead. I would know, damn it!" she cursed under her breath.

The burning in her eyes and the sudden need to sneeze warned Jenny that she was about to start crying. She always did when she got within five miles of Yachats State Park.

She kept her eyes on the road as she leaned over the passenger's seat, opened the glove box of her Subaru Outback, and pulled out a handful of napkins she had collected from various restaurants. She had already used up the last few tissues she had left from her trip here three months ago.

She wiped the escaping tears from her cheeks before loudly blowing her nose into the damp napkin. Reaching over, she stuffed the used napkin in the empty tissue box. Next, she twisted the knob on the radio and cranked up the volume. Another loud, shuddering curse escaped her when a new song started, and she recognized it as one of Carly's favorites. Of course, that really turned on the waterworks. Pressing the button, she turned off the radio.

Grabbing another napkin, she dabbed at the tears threatening to blind her. If she started crying too hard, she would have to pull over onto the shoulder of the road. It wouldn't be the first time she had been forced to park until she could compose herself. Unfortunately, the only thing crying did was make her face red and eat up precious time she could be using to find out what had happened to Carly. Blowing her nose once more, she angrily stuffed the used tissue into the rapidly filling box.

"I swear, when I find out who did this to you, Carly, I'm going to toast their ass. I'll rip them apart, put them back together, ask them how it feels, and do it all over again," Jenny vowed, gripping the steering wheel so tightly her knuckles were white. "If they made you su… suff… suffer at all, I'll bury them in a fire ant bed in the middle of the desert and watch the ants devour them while sipping on an icy lemonade."

Okay, she wouldn't really, but she could imagine it. Yes, she could be a bit bloodthirsty when it came to anyone who hurt her friends. Jenny decided it was just part of having red hair. She was known to have a nice, even temperament—until someone did something to piss her off. Then, the temper she inherited from her dad came through in all its blazing glory.

Jenny slowed and turned on her blinker when she saw the exit up ahead. She turned left into the entrance to Yachats State Park, and followed the road to the ranger's booth. A light drizzle had begun, but that wouldn't stop her from her mission. Rain or shine, cold or fog, she would follow the last trail that Carly took. She would search every tiny inch of it in the hopes that maybe the weather and time had exposed some clue that all the police and volunteers might have overlooked two years ago after she reported her friend missing.

"How many?" the ranger asked when she pulled up to the window.

"Just one," Jenny replied, handing him her annual pass.

The ranger studied it for a moment before looking at her. Jenny could feel his gaze move over her face. It didn't take long for recognition to hit.

"You're the girl who keeps searching for the one that went missing, aren't you?" the ranger asked, leaning on the window sill.

Jenny grimaced and nodded. "Her name is Carly Tate. Has anyone found anything?" she asked, holding her hand out for the pass.

"Nothing. There have been a few people who still come out on occasion to look, but it's been a while," the ranger replied with an inviting smile. "I'll be off at three if you'd like me to go with you."

Jenny pursed her lips together and shook her head. "That's okay. I don't have much time today," she lied.

The ranger's expression drooped and he shrugged. "Be careful. There has been some erosion along the trail leading down to the cove," he said, handing her the pass and a parking permit. "Keep an eye out for sudden weather changes. Fog and rain can move in quickly at this time of year, making visibility difficult."

"I will, thank you."

Jenny didn't wait for the rest of his memorized spiel. Having grown up in this area, she was aware of the sudden changes in weather and how to deal with them. Pulling up on the power button to close the window, she gave the car a little more gas than she meant to and felt the jar of the speed bump. With a grimace, she eased up on the pedal and slowly pulled away.

Once she was out of sight of the ranger station, she accelerated again. She followed the long, winding road and turned at the appropriate signs without having to read them. She knew where she was going. Pulling into the parking space, she noticed with satisfaction that there was only one other car in the parking lot, and it looked like the owners of it were leaving.

Jenny sat in her car and waited as the man and the woman argued over the map they were looking at. Tapping her fingers on the steering wheel, she impatiently resisted the urge to get out and ask the couple if they needed some help. Turning the engine off, she undid her seatbelt and turned to reach into the back seat for her jacket.

Straightening in her seat, she blinked back the tears that threatened again and released a deep, shuddering breath when the car next to her finally pulled away. Opening the door, she slid out, pulled on her jacket, and zipped it up before she closed the door. Out of habit, she gazed around her for a moment before she locked the door and pocketed her car keys.

Ever since Carly disappeared two years ago, Jenny hadn't felt safe. She had moved away from the small coastal community of Yachats, Oregon, over a year ago in an effort to get on with her life. So far, she had to admit she wasn't doing a very good job of it.

∼

Jenny slowly walked up the trail and paused at a fork. The path ahead of her did a loop through the forest and along the mountain. The one to the right lead down to the cove and beach area.

She quickly dismissed that area. Carly had left a map of the park in her car with the longest path highlighted in green and the words 'I can do this' written next to it. Jenny smiled when she remembered the added note 'ice cream' written and circled in black at the end of the trail.

Shoving her hands in her pockets, she continued past the sign pointing to the beach. She breathed in the rich smells of evergreens, moist soil, and frigid sea air as she walked. She scanned the path as her mind focused on what it would have been like for Carly.

"She would have been grumbling a lot," Jenny reflected out loud after a mile along the trail.

Pausing to look around, she sighed. Tall trees, thick ferns, and sloping ravines greeted her intense gaze. It was possible that Carly had stumbled, rolled down the side into the ferns, hit her head on a rock, and then was swallowed by the thick vegetation. *Carly was known for her clumsiness. It's possible that there was no foul play beyond bad luck,* Jenny silently admitted to herself.

"Surely someone would have found her if that had happened," Jenny murmured before continuing up the narrow track.

~

Twilight was beginning to settle by the time Jenny drove back into town. It turned out to be another fruitless one with no new leads. She had one more stop before she'd call it a day.

Slowing down as she entered town, she glanced around for a parking space. Now that summer was starting and people were taking off for their vacation, there were quite a few tourists in town. She breathed a sigh of relief when she saw two open parking spots in front of the local police station.

Turning on her blinker, she waited for several cars to pass before pulling into one of the empty spots. A quick glance at the clock told her it was later than she'd thought. She shifted the gearshift to park and turned off the engine. Staring straight ahead, she could see a woman behind the desk. It looked like she was getting ready to leave.

Jenny didn't waste any time undoing her seatbelt and pushing open the car door. She hoped that the new detective she had been talking to for the past couple of months was on duty. She didn't see him through the window, but there was a light shining from an office down the hall. Slamming the car door, she locked it, and strode across the sidewalk. She pushed open the door just as the woman behind the desk slid the strap of her purse onto her shoulder.

"Can I help you?" the woman asked, looking up at Jenny as she entered.

Jenny smiled, remembering the woman from the last time she was here. She hoped Patty would remember her as well. It took a moment before recognition hit. Patty threw a quick glance over her shoulder.

"Mike, the lady about the missing person is back," Patty called out, walking around the desk. "He'll be with you in a moment. He is on the phone."

"Thank you," Jenny said with an appreciative smile before she stepped to the side.

"No problem. I have to pick up my son. Have a good night," Patty said with an easy smile before pulling open the door and stepping outside.

Jenny could hear the sound of a man's voice speaking quietly in the background. She turned and walked over to stand near the front window and stare blindly out at the street. She didn't want to give the impression she was eavesdropping on his conversation. Lost in thought, she didn't realize he was finished until he spoke behind her.

"Good afternoon, Miss Ackerly," Mike Hallbrook's rich, smooth voice greeted.

Jenny turned to face the tall, handsome man who looked to be in his early thirties. Mike Hallbrook had one of those quiet, calm demeanors that drew you in and gave you a sense of security. The undeniable authority in his posture told her that while he may appear relaxed, he was always on alert.

She reached up to tuck a stray hair behind her ear and nibbled her lip in indecision. She felt slightly guilty for stopping by when it was so late. In a small town like Yachats, there wasn't a huge need to have someone with Mike's expertise on duty after hours unless there was a major crime. Still, she had to ask.

Jenny gave Mike a tired, apologetic smile. After ten hours of hiking and searching every nook and cranny along the trail, she was exhausted and disheveled. She was just thankful he didn't appear to care that she was here so late.

"Hello, Detective Hallbrook. Thank you for seeing me," she responded.

Mike Hallbrook nodded his head. "Anytime. What can I do for you?" he asked.

Jenny could feel his scrutiny. She could just imagine what he was seeing—damp and wrinkled clothing, dark circles under her eyes, windswept hair, and red cheeks. She looked like something that had washed up on the shore. With a weary smile, she drew in a tired breath before she released it.

"I was checking to see if there were any updates on Carly Tate's missing person's case," she said.

"Nothing since the last time you came in three months ago," Mike responded in a compassionate tone.

"Oh… The… The case hasn't been closed, has it?" she asked.

∼

Mike Hallbrook took in the tired, disheveled appearance of the woman standing across from him. A moment of regret flashed through him that he couldn't give her the answer to the question she had been asking for two years—what happened to her friend. The fate of Carly Tate was still unknown—a cold case for their small town.

When the Yachats Police Department receptionist, Patty, had called out, as she left for the night, that the girl who was looking for the missing woman was back, Mike didn't need the case number to know who Patty was talking about. There were not a lot of unsolved crimes in the area.

"No, the case won't be closed until we know what happened to your friend. Unfortunately, there isn't a lot to go on. I'm continuing to investigate leads. Do you have any new information?" he asked.

Jenny shook her head and wrapped her arms around her waist. "No. Did you ever get a chance to talk to Ross Galloway again? He was the last guy Carly dated. I've been meaning to ask but kept forgetting," she asked.

Mike nodded. "Yes. He has a solid alibi for the day Carly disappeared," he replied.

Mike took a step closer when tears welled up in Jenny's eyes. It was times like this that he hated being a cop. He watched as she bowed her head and pulled a tissue from her pocket. He heard her draw in a shuddering breath before she looked up at him. A faint smile curved his lips when he saw the determination in her expression.

"I left my phone number with your receptionist the last time I was here. Can you please call me if you find out anything?" she asked.

"I'll make sure it's the same number I have marked in the file. If we find anything, I'll be sure to contact you," he promised.

"Thank you," she said, turning toward the door.

"Any time. If you think of anything that might help locate your friend, please don't hesitate to call," Mike added.

"I won't. I plan to be here for the rest of the week. Thank you again for not giving up on Carly," Jenny said, glancing up at him when he reached around her to open the door.

"We'll bring her home," he responded in a quiet tone.

Jenny's eyes glistened with unshed tears. She nodded and stepped through the opened door. Mike watched her hurry across the sidewalk to a dark red Subaru parked out front. He stood in the doorway, lost in thought.

The case puzzled him. From the few conversations he'd had with Carly's parents, he'd gathered that they had already accepted that their daughter was dead and would probably never be found. The cold, disconnected resignation in their voices was completely opposite to Jenny Ackerly's grief. During his investigation he had learned that Carly had been a warm, cheerful young woman who got along with everyone. Hell, even Ross Galloway shook his head and said he couldn't see anyone harming Carly.

"She is dangerous enough to herself," Ross had said in exasperation.

When Mike had pressed Ross about what he meant, he discovered Carly was known as a lovable, but klutzy woman. Ross' description of her setting his boat on fire—a very minor fire, Ross had hastily clarified—helped Mike understand some of the other references made about Carly by other people.

"Knowing Carly, she probably got lost in the woods or fell off a cliff," Ross had said with a shrug. "It wouldn't be the first time."

It was a possibility, but something told Mike it was more than a simple act of getting lost. The numerous search teams would have found something. If Carly had fallen from the cliff, the tides would have washed her up on the shore because of the way the cove was shaped. He had already checked the area.

Mike blinked when a resident drove by and honked the horn in greeting. He automatically lifted his hand to wave and realized he was still standing in the open doorway of the small police station. Shaking his head in resignation, he stepped back, closed the door, and locked it.

He was supposed to be off now. Instead, he turned back toward his office. Maybe he'd take another look at the file and see if there was something he'd missed. After all, it wasn't like people just vanished off the face of the earth! There had to be a clue somewhere that would point him in the right direction of what had happened to Carly Tate.

Chapter 2

Jenny backed out of the parking space and turned south. She had only gone a block when her stomach rumbled. Grimacing at the reminder that she hadn't eaten all day, she considered her options: stop at the grocery store or stop at one of the restaurants.

She quickly decided that fighting the crowds at the grocery store and then having to prepare something to eat was more than she could handle at the moment. That decision made, she focused on where to stop. She really didn't feel like going alone to one of the nicer waterfront restaurants. What she really wanted was a nice cold beer and a platter of fish and chips.

Turning right at the stoplight, she headed for one of the pubs that was popular with the locals. Five minutes later, she was pulling into the parking lot of the Underground Pub. It didn't look like much on the outside, but it had great food, cold beer, live music, and a nice ambiance.

Grabbing her purse and jacket from the passenger seat, she opened the door and slid out. The smell of the ocean mixed with the fragrant aroma of food made her stomach growl again in anticipation.

Jenny shut and locked the car door. Seagulls squawked as they landed on the docks in the hope of finding a meal from the fishermen cleaning their daily catch or from a generous patron willing to share a leftover French fry or two. A brisk breeze swirled around her, and she quickly pulled her jacket on when it sent a chill through her. Shouldering her handbag, she crossed the uneven gravel of the parking lot to the entrance of the pub.

∾

Jenny pulled the door open and stepped into the dim interior. She paused as her eyes adjusted. Glancing around, she saw the band equipment set up along one wall. Wooden tables laden with condiments and scarred but sturdy chairs filled the interior to the point that Jenny was amazed the waitress could squeeze between them.

It was still early in the evening, and close to half of the tables were already filled with patrons. Jenny nodded to the waitress when she called out for her to sit wherever she wanted. Squeezing between two tables, Jenny made her way toward one in the back near the large set of double doors leading outside to the patio seating.

She slid into an empty seat with her back to the dark hallway leading to the bathrooms. From this vantage point, she could see the docks outside but was still far enough away from the band to keep from going deaf when they started playing. She glanced at her phone —almost eight o'clock. The band started at nine. If she were lucky, she would be out of here before then. Otherwise, her head would be hurting a lot more than it was at the moment.

"My name's Dorothy. What can I get you to drink, darling?" Dorothy asked with a friendly smile.

"Beer, whatever local beer you have on tap is fine. I don't need a menu. I'll take the fish basket with fries and coleslaw," Jenny said.

Dorothy tucked the menu she was about to hold out back under her arm and grinned. "The two piece or three piece, sugar?" Dorothy asked.

"Two is fine," Jenny replied.

"I'll bring you some chips and salsa," Dorothy replied with another smile.

"Thank you," Jenny responded.

She watched Dorothy take another drink order on her way back to the kitchen. Turning her head, Jenny stared out of the glass doors, lost in thought. She absently watched three older men as they stood around chatting. She smiled when she saw several pelicans and seagulls vying for a spot near the cleaning table.

"Here you go, sweetie," Dorothy said, placing the frosted glass of beer and the plate with the salsa and chips down in front of her.

"Thank you," Jenny replied with a grateful smile.

Dorothy stood and placed her hands on her hips. "Haven't I seen you here before?" she asked with a frown.

Jenny paused as she reached for the glass of beer. "Yes," she replied, not really wanting to talk.

Dorothy nodded and smiled. "I thought so. Your food will be right out. We have a great band tonight, so be sure to stick around," she said before moving to a new group of people who came in.

Sure enough, Dorothy stopped by a few minutes later with her fish platter. Jenny picked at the food, eating more because she knew she needed to than because she was hungry. After the first few bites, her stomach stopped rumbling, and she lost interest in the delicious meal.

A wave of weariness suddenly washed through her and she decided she'd done enough damage to the food in front of her. She was wiping her hands clean with a paper towel when the chair across the table from her was pulled out and a man wearing a dark brown leather jacket, white T-shirt, and faded jeans sat down. Jenny glanced up, the sharp retort on her lips faded when she recognized the grim-faced man. Straightening, she placed the paper towel down next to her plate and scowled at him.

"I didn't invite you to sit at my table," she said in a sharp tone.

Ross Galloway lifted the bottle of beer in his hand and took a long swig, not responding to her blunt statement. Jenny could feel her temper starting to rise. If Ross wasn't careful, he'd be wearing that bottle upside his head. Her eyes narrowed when he lowered his hand and put the bottle back on the table.

"I didn't have anything to do with Carly's disappearance," he said.

Jenny shrugged and sat back in her chair. "I heard you had an alibi," she replied.

"I liked her. She was a bit too dangerous to be around, but I liked her," Ross said, leaning forward and resting his arms on the table.

Jenny returned his steady gaze with one of her own. He didn't glance away, his expression compassionate and intense. Ross might be a jerk, but he'd never struck her as being dangerous.

"She could be hazardous at times," Jenny reluctantly agreed.

Ross nodded and relaxed, leaning back in his chair. "Have you heard if the authorities have found anything more?" he asked.

"No, they haven't," Jenny replied.

They both sat in silence for several minutes, each lost in their own thoughts. Jenny watched Ross. He absently played with his bottle of beer. A slight frown creased his brow, and he looked like he was trying to decide if he should say something else.

"Do you…."

"I guess…."

They both spoke at the same time. Ross released a long sigh and motioned for her to continue. Jenny twisted her lip in sardonic amusement.

"I was going to say, I guess I should be going. It's been a long day, and I'd like to do another search tomorrow," Jenny said.

"Yeah, well, I was going to ask if you wanted any help. I know that the cops have searched. It's been so long now, I doubt there is anything left out there. Carly's bones would either be scattered to hell and back or gone if she fell into the sea," Ross muttered.

"She's not dead," Jenny retorted as a flash of anger and grief rose inside her.

Pushing her chair back, she stood up. She pulled some money from her pocket and counted out enough for her bill. She placed it on the rectangular plastic tray that Dorothy left with her meal.

"Aw hell, Jenny. I didn't mean to upset you," Ross said, standing up.

"She's not dead. I would know," Jenny stubbornly insisted, lifting a hand to brush her hair back from her face.

"It's been a long time since she's been seen," Ross pointed out.

"I know, Ross," Jenny replied in a soft voice. "Thanks for your offer, but I'm good."

Jenny stepped around the table and started to pass by Ross. She paused when he reached out a hand and touched her arm. Looking up, she could see the flash of regret in his eyes.

"Be careful," he finally said.

"Always," Jenny replied, pulling away.

She could feel Ross' gaze on her as she mumbled a thank you to Dorothy before pushing open the door and stepping out of the bar. Drawing in a deep breath of the salty air, she shoved her hands into her pockets.

The docks were empty now. The last of the fishermen were either visiting the pub or home with their families. Jenny wasn't ready to go back to the house where she and Carly used to live. The original owner had sold the house shortly after she'd moved out. The small cottage-style home was now available as a vacation rental. Renting that particular house might be a little morbid, but the new owners had completely remodeled the interior and exterior, and it felt like just a house instead of the home that she and Carly had created together.

Walking along the dimly lit dock, Jenny listened to the fading cries of a seagull and the occasional splash of a fish. The soothing sound of the water lapping against the dock and boats and the chill of the breeze drew the tension from her body.

She walked to the end of the dock and stopped. Pulling her hands out of her pockets, she gripped the railing and stared out at the fading light. Restless energy and grief made her feel on edge and uneasy.

"I have to move on with my life, Carly. Staying in Oregon isn't helping me do that. I thought moving away would, but I still feel like something is missing," Jenny murmured to the wind. She brushed the hair from her cheek and tucked it behind her ear. "Do you remember when we said we would go on a great adventure? You'd search the castles of Europe for dragons while I sailed the seven seas before we'd meet up to share our stories with each other." Jenny stood silently staring out at the horizon, lost in her memories of their childhood hopes and dreams. "After this week, I think it is time I took off for a while—maybe find a position overseas or on a cruise ship. There isn't anything here for me anymore. I miss you. Wherever you are, I hope we get to meet again one day."

Tears burned Jenny's eyes, but she blinked them away. She'd shed enough tears. Now it was time to embrace her belief that somehow, someway, Carly was safe and happy.

Jenny stepped back and pushed her hands into the pockets of her jacket. Her fingers closed around a small shell she had picked up along the trail earlier in the day. She tossed it over the railing, turned, and walked away. As she walked down the dock toward her car, she couldn't help but think that Carly was like the shell she had just tossed back into the ocean—a small, fragile treasure lost in a huge abyss.

Chapter 3

Late the next afternoon, Jenny dejectedly walked down the trail back toward the parking lot. She reached the section where the path forked. The path ahead of her would lead her back to her car, the other went down to the beach.

Jenny bit her lip in indecision. She had always focused on the longest foot-trail. Carly had never been as enthusiastic about the water as Jenny had. Carly complained it was too cold, too rough, and contained things that liked to eat people. The memory of Carly's adamant refusal to go in the water during their high school years drew a soft chuckle from her.

Deciding the sound of the waves would help the depression she was feeling, she turned left and followed the uneven path through the thick woods and along the rocky cliff down to the beach. She paused near the edge of the rocks and looked out over the water. Once again, she'd discovered absolutely nothing on her trek today, but that wasn't a huge surprise. She would have been shocked if she had discovered something. Besides, she reasoned, not finding anything continued to give her hope that Carly was out there somewhere—alive and well.

Jenny thrust her hands into the back pockets of her jeans. Gazing out at the waves breaking against the rocky sand, she thought about her original plans to stay the entire week in Yachats. She'd planned to search for clues every day, but she was seriously considering calling it quits and driving back home later tonight.

After talking to Ross last night and her fruitless search today, she was thinking maybe it would be more productive to start researching her next move. If anything, the last two days had shown her that she was deluding herself into thinking she would find anything new. Ross was right; any evidence would have been destroyed over the past two years.

Jenny thought about her life. She didn't have anything to rush back to except an empty apartment. She was officially on summer break from the elementary school where she worked, and she had completed all the scheduled workshops. Now was the perfect time to start applying for positions elsewhere.

"It's hard to believe today marks exactly two years since you disappeared, Carly. I swear I don't know where time flies," Jenny said with a shake of her head.

She pulled her hands free from her pockets and reached up to unzip her jacket. She kicked at a few loose pebbles before stepping onto the loose sand. Walking toward the water, she breathed in the salty air.

The sound of the waves was already working its magic on her. She could feel the tension melting away. Her mind wandered as she glanced around. Instead of shelving the memories of Carly, she focused on the beautiful, cheerful girl who she had known since kindergarten. Flashes of their life together made her chuckle. Even though they weren't related by blood, they'd been as close as twins when it came to their silly pranks while growing up.

Jenny tucked her hands into her jacket pockets and scowled for a moment. If she ever found out who had hurt Carly, she would dice them into tiny cubes, pour soy sauce on the chopped up pieces, and stir fry their asses, then feed them to the fish. Yes, it sounded gross, but Jenny didn't care. Anyone who could hurt someone as awesome as Carly deserved that and more.

She drew in a deep breath and focused on the small outcropping of rocks that rose out of the Pacific Northwest's cold ocean waters. Even with the unexpected sun streaming down, the air still held a distinct chill to it. A sad and reluctant smile curved Jenny's lips.

"You would totally hate this, Carly. You'd be ready to pack it in and head back home, call for a pizza delivery, and debate whether you should watch Dragonheart for the millionth time. God, I miss you and the way we could laugh together," Jenny murmured, staring out at the rocks.

A sense of peace washed through Jenny. In her own way, she'd said goodbye last night, and it was just sinking in now. It might not be closure, but it was as close to it as she could get. Releasing a deep breath, she turned to the left and started walking again down the beach when a brilliant sparkle brought her attention to the water's edge. Bending, she picked up an unusual stone half buried in the sand and seaweed. She straightened and gazed down at the colorful swirls embedded in the surface. Jenny rolled the smooth, cold stone in her hand, studying the vibrant lines running through it. Her fingers slowly tightened around the sea-polished gem that looked more like a priceless jewel than an unusual shell or piece of colorful sea glass. She turned her gaze back out toward the ocean.

Jenny closed her eyes and muttered a silent wish as she listened to the sounds of the waves, the birds, and the wind. She really did love the ocean; it was the one thing she missed the most besides Carly since her move to the suburbs of Portland.

She had spent just about every weekend coming here to swim, surf, hunt for shells and sea glass, or just to enjoy the sounds. Carly had thought she was nuts and suggested they move to some place like Florida or Hawaii, where at least the water was warmer, but Jenny didn't mind the cold. A dry suit and vigorous exercise were enough to keep her warm, even on a chilly day like today.

Jenny drew in a deep breath, enjoying the smell of the moist, chilly air as it coursed down into her lungs. A frown furrowed her brow when a child's laugh rose above the natural cadence of the waves and drew her out of her reverie.

Opening her eyes, she turned in time to see a shirtless young boy, around seven or eight, running toward the water not more than a dozen feet from where she was standing. She frowned when he didn't stop at the edge of it, but plowed forward into the rolling waves, heedless of the cold. She started forward in concern, scanning the beach for his parents or another adult, but the area was empty.

"Hey! Stop!" Jenny yelled. She shoved the rock she'd found in her front pants pocket before she took a step forward and held her hand out in warning. "Hey, you! Boy! Kid! Stop!"

The boy paused and glanced at her with wide, mischievous eyes before he grinned and dove under the next wave. Her summers as a lifeguard kicked in, and she kept her eyes glued on the tousled, white-blond head as she shrugged out of her jacket.

She let it fall to the ground behind her as she started running. Her tennis shoes would be a problem. She could kick them off once she hit the water. A part of her was concerned that her shirt and jeans would hinder her, but she didn't have time to strip out of them. The boy wasn't staying in the shallows, he was swimming straight out towards the horizon.

Her adrenaline spiked as she hit the freezing water. At the same time as the water closed around her thighs, she saw a flash of bright hair further ahead. The boy turned to look at her, amusement and an intense emotion she couldn't quite get a read on shining from his eyes. He smiled at her one more time before he slipped beneath the surface.

Jenny dove beneath the wave as it rolled over her. Kicking out with powerful strokes, she swept her arms out and cupped her hands to propel herself forward. She caught a glimpse of green when the sun broke through a cloud to shine down on the water. The boy had been wearing green pants. Hope built inside her as she swam harder than she ever had before. She ignored the burning in her lungs as long as she could, afraid that if she surfaced for air she would lose sight of the boy.

Frustration rose in her when the boy remained just out of reach. Unable to continue, Jenny rose to the surface and drew in a deep breath, the chilly air stinging her wet face. Panic began to sweep through her when she realized that the boy had not come up for air. She dove down, and swam in the direction where she had last seen him.

The water was deeper here, and Jenny could already feel the cold threatening to pull her down into the inky darkness. If not for the adrenaline and fear for the boy, she would have given up and returned to shore. Ignoring the stiffness in her limbs, she propelled herself downward. Her burning eyes caught sight of the boy a short distance in front of her. A sense of renewed determination filled her. She would NOT let him drown!

Just a little more, Jenny whispered to herself as she frantically kicked her legs. *You can do it.*

Jenny reached out, trying to grab the boy's foot. She didn't know how the kid could hold his breath so long or swim so fast. Her fingers skimmed the tips of his toes, startling him. She jerked her hand back when he suddenly turned and looked at her. Blinking, she paused when he pointed at a dark recess in a rocky formation. Her gaze involuntarily followed his arm in the direction he was pointing before darting back to him. A small stream of bubbles escaped past her lips when he motioned for her to follow him.

Shaking her head, she started to reach for him when he twisted away. A low cry of dismay resonated through her when she saw him disappear into the gap in the rock. Surging forward, she frantically grabbed at his foot again, missing it by less than a finger's width. Jenny gripped the rough edge of the rock and pulled herself forward until her head was just inside the narrow opening.

Her eyes widened when she saw a colorful kaleidoscope of water swirling in front of her. She barely caught a glimpse of the boy as he passed through it and disappeared. Unsure of what was going on, she gripped the rocky entrance to the cave with one hand while she reached out with the other to touch the colorful anomaly. The moment her fingers skimmed across the surface, she felt her body being pulled forward. A silent scream echoed in her mind as she was sucked forward into the whirlpool of colors.

The Sea King's Lady

READ ON FOR MORE SAMPLES!

MAGIC, NEW WORLDS, AND EPIC LOVE IN
THE MANY SERIES OF S.E. SMITH…

ALEXANDRU'S KISS

Far from home...

Alexandru Carson has a major problem and it isn't with the woman who captured him - it is the fact that he can't remember anything but his name. He doesn't know where he is or how he ended up in the middle of a forest that feels completely alien. And he definitely doesn't know why it is so hard to keep his hands off the woman who claimed him as her prisoner.

Chapter 1

Alexandru Carson watched from the shadows of a Juniper tree as two men approached his parents' house. He had been waiting for one of the men – the tall man with the blond hair and an aristocratic air that clung to him. An aura of power and danger surrounded Simon Drayton. It spoke of someone who had lived for a very long time.

If Alexandru had his way, that life was about to come to a very painful end. A sardonic smile curved Alexandru's lips. Simon was so focused on his destination that the possibility of walking into a trap was the furthest thing from his mind.

His gaze moved over the dark-haired man walking beside Simon. Alexandru had spoken with Simon's personal bodyguard on many different occasions. Youssef Sharif was a quiet, dark-skinned man, and Simon respected the man's attention to detail. It was obvious that Youssef was aware of what Simon was, yet he remained loyal to the man. Alexandru hoped it would not be a loyalty that cost the younger man his life. Youssef Sharif was human and of little threat to immortals like Simon and him.

Alexandru's eyes narrowed when Simon stepped first onto the path near the front steps of the house. On silent feet, Alexandru surged forward. He struck Simon hard in the side, lifting him up into the air, before tossing him away from the steps. If Simon had been human, the blow to his side would have broken several ribs – but, Simon wasn't human. Even as he twisted in the air, Simon shifted, the beast inside him recognizing he was in danger.

Alexandru circled around the enraged werewolf. Hatred burned through him when he thought of what Simon had done to his little sister, Tory. The fire of his magic licked through his veins. It grew more intense when Simon sniffed the air, searching for Tory. Determined to pull Simon's attention away from his sister, Alexandru sent a powerful burst of electricity toward the werewolf. Simon jumped at the last second, barely avoiding the stunning electrical surge.

"I knew you would come," Alexandru snarled. "I hope Youssef told you that I plan to kill you. Youssef, I would stay out of this fight," Alexandru added when he saw Youssef start to take a step forward. "I have no desire to kill you."

His gaze flickered to the handgun in Youssef's hand. With a snap of his fingers, the gun disappeared. The clear threat drew a soft, menacing growl from Simon.

"She doesn't want to see you, Simon," Alexandru continued. "I'm just going to make sure she never has to worry about you coming near her – ever again."

In the split second before Simon charged, he saw the tension grow in the werewolf's body. Simon's back paws kicked up bits of dark, red clay, grass, and rocks, scattering them behind him. The nails of his front paws grew longer and cut deep grooves into the soil.

Alexandru braced himself. The second Simon lunged forward, Alexandru leaped to meet him half way. The two figures collided. Simon knocked Alexandru back several feet, but Alexandru was able to twist and wrap his hands around Simon's throat.

He jerked his head back when Simon snapped at him. The heated breath and snapping jaws was a powerful reminder that one bite could inflict serious or fatal damage. The force of Simon pushing his massive back legs against the ground had both men struggling for purchase where they grappled. Alexandru felt his grip loosening on the werewolf, and he twisted, extending his canines and slashing his fangs across Simon's left ear.

"You are dead, Simon. What you did to Tory.... The penalty is death," Alexandru snapped in fury, throwing Simon to the side.

"Mr. Carson," Youssef interjected from his position a safe distance from the fighting pair. "Your sister returns Simon's affections. She is his mate."

"She was an innocent," Alexandru retorted.

"She loves him," Youssef insisted.

Rage engulfed Alexandru and he attacked with deadly intent. He jumped at the last moment and vaulted over Simon's back. Reaching out, he wrapped his arms around the middle of the werewolf. Simon struggled to throw him off, but Alexandru locked his arms and began to squeeze. Simon fell backwards in an effort to dislodge Alexandru's grip, but Alexandru just applied more pressure.

Out of the corner of his eye, Alexandru saw Youssef rush forward to help Simon. Drawing a ball of energy in the palm of his hand, he gripped his left wrist with his right hand and twisted his left arm until he could release the ball of energy at the human. The powerful bolt struck Youssef on his left shoulder. The sound of bones breaking and Youssef's cry of pain mixed with another sound – Tory's cry of horror.

"Stop! Nonny! Help! Alexandru, Simon, stop!" Tory cried.

Hearing the voice of his sister sent a powerful surge of energy through Alexandru and he squeezed hard enough to feel Simon's rib crack under the pressure. Alexandru released the werewolf and rolled away while Simon writhed in pain. His gaze remained focused on the werewolf. In the background he heard his sister's panicked cry for help. Determined to finish the fight while he had the advantage, he started forward.

Alexandru's eyes widened when a dark hole suddenly appeared in front of him. The sound of Tory's voice rising as she intoned a spell that he'd heard before. The swirling colors of a magical portal and his forward momentum all added up to his having a very, very bad feeling of how this was going to end.

Unable to stop before he passed through the portal, Alexandru felt the magic surround him. Tory's magic was unpredictable when she knew what she was doing. It was chaotic when she did it without realizing what she was saying. There was no telling where – or in some cases when – he might find himself.

For a moment, he thought his body was going to be pulled apart from the ferocious storm of magic swirling through the long, wormlike tunnel. He tumbled head over heels before being expelled out the other end. His feet landed on soft, uneven ground. Unable to keep his balance, he tumbled down the slope. The downward momentum seemed to continue forever before he felt a moment of weightlessness. The next moment he landed with a heavy thud on a path at the bottom. He rolled several times before he came to a stop, his head striking a rock.

Darkness swam before his eyes, the world spun crazily, dizzily around him for a brief second before everything faded to a peaceful black. The last thing that Alexandru remembered before his eyes closed was that he didn't remember there being such a thick, lush forest near Magic, New Mexico. His head dropped down against the cool, damp soil and his body relaxed, blissfully silencing the thundering pounding that had begun to beat at his temple.

~

Ka'ya Stargazer glanced away from the group of young men, all still in their teens, who stood near the fountain. She placed her jug on the wide rim and propped her bow against the side. Their voices faded to silence and she could feel their wary gazes on her. Ignoring them, she picked up her jug and filled it before retrieving her bow.

"Huntress," a voice called out from across the wide road.

Ka'ya turned and watched as two of the tribal Elders approached her. Her lips tightened in annoyance. They never approached her singly. Fear – it had a smell to it with which she was all too familiar. At times, the fear of the tribe threatened to choke her.

"Yes, Elder Mayleaf," Ka'ya greeted with a bow of her head.

"We were told you had returned from the caves. You were successful in killing the beast that attacked the outer farms?" Elder Mayleaf asked.

Ka'ya's mouth tightened and she bit back the words that threatened to escape from her lips. The 'beast' had turned out to be two Cybear cubs whose mother had been killed by a farmer. The cubs were starving and had ventured into the fields looking for food. Ka'ya had spent half a day gathering berries and leading the creatures through a mountain pass to where a large supply of fresh berries, insects, and edible flowers grew. She suspected the mother Cybear had been crossing back to its summer residence after birthing the cubs at a higher elevation.

Ka'ya masked her true opinion of the situation and gave the elder a brief nod, tightening her grip on the jug of water. "Is there anything else, Elders? It is time to break my fast. I have not eaten since yesterday morn."

"Eat if you must, but make it quick. Raiders were spotted on the high trail to the north. We need you to see if they have moved on," Elder Direwolf instructed.

Ka'ya frowned. There had been no raids against the village in almost four years. She had come across a lone raider only a few times since then. There were tales that a new leader had taken control of the Vikar and was making changes. She had seen some of those changes when she visited the city of Perth almost a year ago.

"Huntress, did you hear Elder Direwolf?" Elder Mayleaf asked, breaking into her reverie.

"Yes, Elder. I will leave at first light," Ka'ya replied.

"Why can you not leave before dark?" Elder Mayleaf asked in a trembling voice. "The raiders could come while we sleep."

Ka'ya shook her head. "That is why we have the boundary. The lines are secure. I checked them before I came for water," she said impatiently.

"You will leave tonight," Elder Direwolf ordered.

Ka'ya was about to argue, but bit back her frustrated retort when she saw the expression in Elder Direwolf's eyes. His gaze swept the open area of the village, pausing on a young boy playing with a stick and pebble outside one of the huts. She stepped to the left, cutting off his view of the boy.

"I will leave immediately," she quietly replied with another bow of her head.

Neither Elder spoke again. They simply turned and walked away from her. Ka'ya stared blindly at the ground until she knew they were far enough away that it was safe for her to turn to look at the boy again. Her expression softened when an older woman came out from the small hut to get him. For a fraction of a second, Ka'ya's gaze locked with the woman's – her mother – before her brother said something, pulling her mother's attention away.

"Protect us, Huntress," one of the young men by the fountain mocked, waving his hands in the air while his friends laughed.

"Off into the night with you, Huntress," another teen taunted.

"Be careful how you mock me, peasants. While you cower in your huts, I live as a shadow in the dark," Ka'ya said, turning to give the boys a cold, steady look. "All the lights in your hut cannot brighten the darkest corners. You never know when I might be in one of them, waiting for you to close your eyes."

The boys remained frozen, but she saw the way they shrank back from her, their shoulders raising defensively when she took a step toward them. They parted, watching her with a wariness that spoke of their fear of her when she walked between them. Ka'ya kept her head held high. She had made a promise to herself when she was younger to never let the opinions of the others in her village affect the way she felt about herself. Doubting herself would leave her vulnerable to the jagged spears of animosity.

Her gaze swept to the hut where her mother and young brother had disappeared inside. It was dangerous to approach them too often. It was better if she acted as if she didn't care. The Elders' unspoken threat against her family lurked with malignant intent under every order she was given and she had no desire to give them more incentive to use her mother and brother against her.

Her father had already paid the ultimate price to protect her. They had banished him from the village nearly ten years ago when her brother was but a babe and she was twelve. All because of the mark she was born with – the mark of the Huntress.

The superstitions of the tribe were deeply rooted, and one man, Jorge, the spiritual leader of her people, used those superstitions with the same deadly accuracy as she did her bow or blade. Her mother had told her Jorge had the ear of the old chief and the other Elders long before she was born.

Her mother told her that Jorge was a stranger who appeared a few years before her mother met her father. He had spoken in an unusual tongue, but had been accepted when he saved the life of the village chief from a pack of wolfhounds. Her mother shared how Jorge had come with strange and mysterious things that he said came from the Goddess. The old chief had believed Jorge and proclaimed him their Spiritual Leader.

When the old chief died, Jorge proclaimed that he would guide the village along with the old chief's son. By the time this happened, her father had arrived and tried to warn the son of the old chief of the dangers of allowing Jorge such power. She remembered the expression on her mother's face – the fear – when she quietly told Ka'ya how the new chief and the Elder council had threatened to banish her mother's entire family if her father did not cease his resistance to Jorge.

Ka'ya understood how difficult it must have been for her father. He had still been considered an outsider – much as she was – up until the day he had finally pushed Jorge too far. Shortly after her father's banishment, the new chief mysteriously died and Jorge had rapidly replaced the Elders who stepped down with those in the village who supported his beliefs. Since then, Jorge had ruled the village with a ruthlessness that bordered on insanity. Jorge had become more reclusive in recent years, but he had also become more powerful.

Unfortunately for Ka'ya, Jorge both feared and desired her. It mattered not to him that she was still a child. He believed if he possessed her, it would give him the power of the Huntress.

A smile curved Ka'ya's lips when she remembered her father's response to Jorge's demands that her family hand her over to the Spiritual Leader. Her father believed slicing Jorge's blackened heart out of his chest would be the better alternative. The smile faded when she remembered the price her family had paid for defying Jorge's demands. Days after her father's banishment for threatening to kill the Spiritual Leader, the Elders of the village had dragged her before the cruel, horrid man.

∽

Ten years before:

Ka'ya stiffly stood between the two Elders who had brought her to the spiritual leader's hut. Her nose wrinkled at the foul smell of burning spices. The smoke from it burned her eyes, but she refused to rub them. The woman on her right smothered a cough while the man to her left raised a hand and wiped at the corner of his eye.

She stared at the room with distaste. The dim interior was depressing. It was nothing like the brightly lit interior of her home. The ceiling was covered in soot and made the little light that streamed down through the ceiling look gray and dirty.

The bones of dead animals lay scattered across a long table and on the floor. Bottles of liquids lined several shelves against a wall. Everything looked dirty and unkempt. Ka'ya did not understand how this man could declare himself better than her father. He knew nothing of what it meant to understand the spirit of the land and animals.

"She is here, Spiritual Leader," the woman called.

Ka'ya watched as Jorge appeared from another room. He was a thin man with beady, almost black eyes. Dark shadows under them made the sockets around his eyes appear larger than they were in reality. His alabaster skin was streaked with smudges of soot from his dirty fingers and made him look older than his thirty years. He wore a dirty, off-white tunic over dark brown pants and boots. His hair was thin on top, with just a few strands of fine hair that made a line and was swept to the side.

He silently returned Ka'ya's stare, as if willing her to look away first. Instead, she lifted her chin. Her light green eyes bore into his. She could see the circle of light from the open door surrounding the brown irises of each eye, giving them a malevolent glow. In the center, she could see her reflection. Even when he took a step forward and ran his dirty fingers down along her cheek, she didn't turn away. His eyes narrowed and he gripped her chin hard.

"Do you think to defy me, girl?" he demanded in a reedy voice.

Ka'ya pulled her chin free and glared at him. "Yes," she replied, biting her tongue to keep from saying anything else.

Jorge gazed down at her. She silently returned his stare. She didn't flinch when he raised his hand to strike her. The blow never came – thanks to the sounding of the alarms. Jorge glanced up at the man standing next to her and jerked his head toward the door.

"Find out what is happening," he ordered.

Ka'ya turned slightly when the Elder opened the door. There was a thud that reverberated through her and the Elder stumbled back. In the center of the elder's chest the long shaft of an arrow protruded. The woman at her side screamed when several more arrows flew through the door. Jorge and the woman fell to the ground. Ka'ya took advantage of the open door and bolted.

Emerging outside, she could see more than two dozen Vikar swarming through the village setting fire to carts of hay and slicing through the men who charged them. Her gaze moved to one of the raiders. He was dragging her mother out of their home. Her mother was holding her newborn brother protectively in her arms.

Ka'ya started forward. Her gaze fixed on her mother and brother; she bent near the body of a fallen guard and pulled the bloody sword from his body. The moment her hand wound around the handle, power exploded through her body and a flood of knowledge swept through her mind. It was as if she had lived through thousands of battles, had hunted the greatest beasts, and knew what needed to be done. She gripped the sword with a strength that belied her tender years, twirled, and sliced through one of the attackers as he reached for her.

As she neared her family's hut, the raider who had her mother's arm, lifted the long shaft of his spear to strike her mother dead. Ka'ya pulled her arm back and threw the sword. The blade sank deep in the raider's chest, driving him back against the stone wall of the hut. Racing forward, Ka'ya knelt and helped her mother to her feet.

"Inside," she said in a soft urgent tone.

"Ka'ya," her mother whispered, reaching out to run a trembling hand down her daughter's face.

Ka'ya smiled. "Go inside. I will protect you," she said.

Mayli looked worriedly back at her daughter, but hurried inside. Her brother whimpered, but her mother quickly soothed him. Ka'ya followed her mother into the bright hut. She could feel her mother's gaze on her when she reached for her father's bow and arrows.

"Ka'ya, don't go," Mayli begged when Ka'ya turned back to the door.

Ka'ya glanced at her mother. In the background the sounds of screams and fighting continued. Her face tightened and once again she felt the surge of power rush through her. She knew that if the raiders were not defeated or driven off, there would be nothing left of the village – including her family.

"I have to," Ka'ya replied, turning and drawing back an arrow when the door opened.

She released the arrow. The raider standing in the doorway looked down in surprise before he fell forward. Ka'ya pulled another arrow from her quiver and walked toward the door. Stepping over the body of the dead raider, she released three more arrows in rapid succession before disappearing outside.

Ten arrows – ten raiders dead by her bow. By her sword, she killed another five before the raiders began to target her en masse. Ka'ya knew she was in trouble, but she never gave up. She pulled on the power flowing through her and used the knowledge to strike one deadly blow after another. Ka'ya's desperate need to protect her mother and infant brother gave her the willpower to continue fighting.

Revived by the dwindling number of raiders, the villagers began fighting beside her until the remaining raiders retreated in defeat.

Ka'ya turned in a slow circle as the remaining villagers who had sought to hide slowly emerged from their huts and gathered around her. She could feel their gazes on her and she smiled. Jorge stepped out of his hut where he had been hiding, and she eyed him with contempt. Gripping a bloody sword in her right hand, she reached up with her left and pushed her thin tunic to the side to reveal her shoulder and the mark of the Huntress.

"I am Ka'ya Stargazer. I am the Huntress," she said in a clear voice. Ka'ya could hear the soft gasps of the villagers. Her light green eyes glowed with supernatural fire as she stared Jorge down. She slowly lifted the blood-coated blade in her hand to point it at him. "You will never possess my powers."

The mark that her parents had tried to hide, the one that Jorge had somehow found out about and decided to use for his own purpose, was now clear for all to see. She would not hide any longer. No one would control her.

Chapter 2

Ka'ya brushed the memory of that day aside and focused on the present. Over time, the villagers had grown to fear her. Even Jorge, as powerful as he had grown over the last ten years, kept his distance from her. He sent the other Elders to order her to do his bidding while he hid behind the doors of his hut.

Bitterness rose in Ka'ya's mouth. She would have left the lot of the villagers to their fate if it had not been for her mother and brother. Dru was finally of an age now that she could spirit him and her mother away. She would have to be careful. Jorge kept both under close watch.

"Ka'ya!"

Ka'ya turned to see her mother hurrying after her. Concern swept through Ka'ya when she saw the dark circles under her mother's eyes and the faint lines of tension around her mouth. Glancing around, she scanned for her brother. Her mother was never far from Dru's side.

"Mother, what is wrong? You know that it is dangerous to speak with me. Jorge is still angry from the last time you confronted him," Ka'ya warned in a low voice.

Mayli's mouth tightened in anger. "Day in and day out I watch my daughter from afar unable to do anything about the way you are treated for fear of reprisal. I see the Elders make demands of you and the villagers mock you. If I wish to give you food for your belly so you do not go hungry, I will. They should at least let you rest before sending you out again to search for raiders," she said with a stubborn twist to her mouth.

Ka'ya's gaze softened and she shook her head. "I have plenty of food. I brought this for you and Dru to eat. How is Dru today?" she asked.

"Better. His cough is easier since you brought the herbs from the forest," Mayli replied, looking down at the bag she held. "I worry about him, Ka'ya. Jorge has requested that he become his apprentice. Dru's lungs are too weak to handle the smoke of incense and the filth of Jorge's hut."

"When is he supposed to go?" Ka'ya demanded in a soft voice, her eyes narrowing in anger.

Mayli looked up at Ka'ya. "I told him Dru was sick. Jorge demands that he be turned over to him by the new moon," she replied.

Ka'ya glanced over her mother's shoulder at the dark gray hut. Her mother was right; Dru would not survive long under Jorge. Two boys and a young girl had already perished under his guidance. Jorge insisted they were accidents or natural causes. No one questioned him. Ka'ya suspected the Spiritual Leader was messing with things he did not understand – a dark power that could prove deadly to the entire village. She needed to escape with her mother and brother before the new moon.

"I need a few more days – perhaps a week to finish securing our passage across the Great Water. Gather what you wish to take and make sure to give Dru the medicine to give him the strength for the journey," Ka'ya murmured, reaching for the bag of goods.

"Thank you, Ka'ya," Mayli said, tears shimmering in her eyes.

"I will not let him take Dru and you away from me the way he took Father. At least here, I can see and talk with you," Ka'ya swore.

She gripped the bag and turned away from her mother. She had much to do before the new moon in a fortnight. Picking up speed, she left the path leading across the meadow and disappeared into the forest. She would return to her home, eat, gather the items she would need, and make sure the trail was clear before traveling to the large city of Perth to secure passage across the Great Water.

∼

Alexandru rolled over onto his back and groaned. He started to lift a shaky hand to his brow when he heard a low growl. Opening his eyes, he smothered a loud curse when he saw three large animals slowly approaching him. His brain tried to identify them, but just trying to think caused another shaft of pain to lance through his head.

The animals were the size of a Shetland pony, but that was where the similarities ceased. He had never seen anything like them – at least that he could remember. The rust-and-silver-colored long fur, short ridged snouts, and the four long tusks protruding from their mouths had him warily scooting back across the rock-and-leaf-covered ground.

"Easy," Alexandru said in a hoarse voice. He cleared his throat. "Easy now."

The animal in the front pawed the ground and flashed a set of very long, impressive fangs. Alexandru didn't bother trying to keep the curse that escaped him quiet this time. He flinched, rolling backwards when the two animals on each side leaped toward him.

"Son of a bi…."

Alexandru's curse died when he felt his body rolling over the edge. Tumbling, he grunted when he hit a rotten log and went right through it. Twisting, he tried to turn so he could dig his heels into the loose soil, but the slope was too steep. His eyes widened when he saw he was approaching a drop off. Unable to stop his momentum, he braced for the impending fall and impact. He frantically reached out for a sapling. Above him, he heard the snarls and growls of the animals above him followed by a horrendous howl. His fingers missed the sapling by a fraction of an inch.

Glancing down, he once again tried to dig his heels into the soil. He was about to resign himself to his fate when two arrows flashed by him. One struck a tree to his right while the other struck a tree to his left. Suspended between them was a rope. Alexandru reached up and grabbed the rope as he passed under it. He twisted, and the lower half of his body went over the side of the cliff. His fingers tightened on the rope and he prayed that the arrows and the rope would hold his weight.

Alexandru glanced over his shoulder and swallowed. There was no way he would have survived a fall from this height. Far below him, jagged rocks rose up. Debris from his slide rained down around him before disappearing into the shadows of the dark crevices. Turning his head, he rested his forehead against the damp soil. Whatever in the hell had happened to him, he was having a very bad day, he thought with a wince.

He looked up at the top of the slope from where he had fallen. It was going to be a son-of-a-bitch to climb back up the slope – especially with the way his head was pounding, but he had little choice. He struggled to pull the lower half of his body back up onto solid ground.

Alexandru had just managed to get one knee up onto the edge when a rope landed next to him. Looking up at the top, he couldn't see anything except where it continued over the side. Grateful for the extra help, he released the death grip he had on the rope between the arrows and grasped the new one. Air hissed from his lungs when he suddenly found his body being pulled upward at an incredible speed. He opened his mouth to tell the bastards to slow down whatever in the hell they were using to pull him up, but had to shut it to keep from getting a mouth full of debris when his body rolled and he found himself on his belly.

The speed of his ascent didn't decrease until he was pulled over the edge and back onto the road. He rolled several times before he released the rope. Lying on his back, he stared up at the leafy canopy overhead. Thick branches covered in dark red, orange, and yellow leaves swayed in the breeze. Drawing in a deep breath, he held it when the trees were blocked by another sight – the short muzzle of one of the animals that he had tried to escape just minutes before.

"Oh shit," he cursed.

"*Jo na ta. Nita la bay,*" a low, feminine voice demanded. "*Jo na ta!*"

Alexandru's eyes slowly focused on the figure of a woman as she stepped close to where he lay. It took a moment for his foggy brain to recognize that she was holding a bow in her hand. He blinked several times, his gaze traveling over her face. Her clear, green eyes gazed back at him with a look of suspicion and mistrust. Her hair was blonde with streaks of blue through it. She was wearing a black shirt with a light brown leather vest. His gaze moved down her body, noting the black pants and boots before he raised his gaze to lock with hers.

He opened his mouth to thank her but the words were never uttered. Instead, his head snapped back when she swung the end of her bow and it connected with his chin. The thought that if his head didn't explode it would be a miracle crossed his mind before darkness once again danced across his vision and he lost consciousness once more.

Alexandru's Kiss

DESTIN'S HOLD

Destin Parks will do whatever it takes to rebuild the city he calls home, even if it means working with another alien ambassador. The Councils hope Jersula 'Sula' Ikera's logical mind and calm demeanor will resolve the upheaval caused by the previous ambassador, but no one could have anticipated Sula's reaction to the hardheaded human male she has been assigned to work with. His ability to get under her skin and ignite a flame inside her is quite alarming, mystifying, and leaves her questioning her own sanity.

Together, Destin and Sula must race to stop an alien cartel before anyone is taken off-planet, but the traffickers are not the only ones they will be fighting against – a battle is coming, bigger than anything they've yet seen...

Chapter 1

"No!" a low, tortured hiss escaped Destin as he fought against the paralyzing memories holding him prisoner.

He struggled to free his mind, caught between the realm of nightmares and consciousness, but couldn't break free. After several long seconds that felt like an eternity, he jolted awake with a shudder and drew a deep breath into his starving lungs before slowly releasing it. Pushing up into a sitting position, he noticed he was tangled in the bed sheets.

Destin ran a hand over his sweat-dampened face before reaching to turn on the lamp next to the bed. It was missing. It took him a second to remember where he was and that the lighting system was still alien to him.

With a groan, he fell back against the pillows and drew in a series of deep, calming breaths, holding each one for several seconds before releasing the air in a slow, controlled rhythm. It was a meditation technique he read about years ago. He continued until he felt his pulse settle down to a normal rate.

A glance out the door told him it was still dark. He groaned and laid his arm across his eyes. He was up way too late last night or should he say this morning. Unfortunately, it didn't matter the amount of sleep he got, his body was programmed to wake early.

Destin dropped his arm back to his side and stared up at the ceiling. It was smooth and undamaged. There were no patched places, no cracks, and no bare metal beams. The architects and engineers back home were slowly making progress, but home was nowhere near as nice as Rathon, the Trivator home world.

Throwing aside the twisted sheets, he rolled out of bed. The jogging pants he slept in hung low on his slender hips. He ran a hand over his flat stomach and curled his toes into the soft, plush mat under his feet before he began his daily stretching exercises.

The taut muscles in his neck, back, and shoulders bulged as he tried to work the tension out of them. He might not be as tall as his Trivator brother-in-law, but years of hard work and targeted training had made his body the perfect fighting machine. Scars crisscrossed his flesh, each one a testament to the challenges he had faced over the past seven years.

His arms rose and he stretched, enjoying the cool breeze blowing in from the open doors and caressing his bare back. He could smell the fragrant aroma from the flowers blooming in the garden just outside and the tangy scent of salt from the nearby ocean. The weather here was a balmy seventy degrees if he had to guess.

He turned toward the doors and closed his eyes, blocking out the view of the garden and its high protective walls designed to keep out the wildlife. He tilted his head and listened to the sound of waves crashing against the shore. It was soothing last night, luring him to sleep, but now it felt relentless and violent, an echo of the adrenaline he woke up with.

Destin ran a hand down over his hard, flat abdomen again. His fingers traced a barely visible three-inch scar. It was a new one. He got it when a skittish street urchin fought to return to a building that was slowly collapsing.

Two years ago, he would have died from such a wound. He owed a huge thanks to Patch, the Trivator healer back on Earth. Patch had doctored him up, and after a few weeks of rest, Destin had been ready to travel off the planet.

He shook his head and opened his eyes. His travel through space to a distant world was unimaginable seven years before. It was hard to believe that Earth had received their first contact with aliens almost a decade ago. It was even harder for him to believe he was on an alien planet at the moment – at least until he looked around at the buildings and landscape. Twin moons, thick forests, flying transports, and bizarre creatures made him feel like he woke up in some alternate reality.

Destin turned and quietly made the bed. He grabbed a black T-shirt out of the drawer and pulled it over his head. He didn't bother with shoes; he wouldn't need them where he was going. Within minutes, he silently exited the house that belonged to his sister, Kali, and her *Amate*, Razor.

He crossed through the garden to the far gate. Punching the security code into the panel, Destin waited while the lock disengaged before he quietly slipped through. He made sure the gate was closed and the security system engaged before he turned along the path that led down to the beach. Both Razor and Kali had warned him to stay on the marked paths. He understood why after his arrival. From the air he got a brief glimpse of one of the wild animals that inhabited the planet.

Destin was very glad the paths were secured against creatures like that.

The Trivators believed in living in harmony with the other creatures on the planet. They used only the areas they needed to live and kept large sections of green space. Most of the creatures were fairly harmless, but there were a few that were extremely dangerous – to both the Trivators and their enemies. Invaders would first face the dangers of the forests if they landed outside the protected cities.

The roads and walkways were kept safe by specially placed security markers embedded into the paths. The markers were programmed with the animals' DNA. The embedded sensors detected when an animal approached the marked areas and a shield formed to stop the creatures from entering the path.

Destin didn't understand all the specifics; he just knew that he didn't want to tangle with that creature he had glimpsed from the air. The long tusks, six legs, and massive scaly body were formidable enough from a distance. He really did not want a closer look and was very happy that most travel on the planet was done by air.

The city he saw upon his arrival was magnificent. Large spiraling towers glittered with muted lights while transports moved along the ground and flew through the air. The tower on the far end spilled water from the top of the building in a dazzling waterfall into the Trivator-created reflection pond. Several of the transports disappeared under the reflection pool and reappeared on the other side. The more he saw, the more his excitement grew at the possibilities for Earth.

He paused at the top of the stone steps carved into the side of the cliff and looked out over the vast ocean. The sun wasn't up yet, but there was enough light on the horizon to see the waves break on the outer reef. He stood still, appreciating the beauty and peacefulness of his surroundings.

Destin couldn't remember the last time he had stopped to appreciate the beauty of anything. Death, destruction, fear, and responsibility had been his constant companion for as long as he could remember. He drew in a deep breath and released it.

No longer would that kind of destruction dominate his life. The Trivators' first contact had plunged the Earth into a panicked chaos, but in the past two years, he began to see a change. Progress was being made to heal the wounds. For him, the most important indication that life was getting better was seeing his sister Kali's glowing face and the living proof that there was hope for the future in his beautiful niece.

Originally, he had been reluctant to come, but Kali's quiet plea and Tim's, his second-in-command, assurance that the work Destin had done to restore a new Chicago would be carefully monitored by the team he had built convinced him that he needed the break. That reassurance, combined with his recent brush with death, reminded him of what was important – family. He felt like if he ever wanted a chance to see Kali again, and meet his niece, he had better rearrange his priorities. Until last night, he was convinced he had made the right decision. Now, he wasn't so sure after hearing what happened on another alien world called Dises V.

Destin shook his head at his musings. No, even with what he knew now, he was still glad he came to visit. Seeing Kali again and meeting Ami gave him a renewed purpose to return to Earth and fight for a better life for others.

Focusing on the stone path in front of him, he started down the stairs. He needed a good run to help clear his mind. He might as well enjoy the last few days he had here while he could. Once he returned to Earth, there was a city to rebuild and a lot of fires to put out, among other possible threats.

At the bottom, his feet sunk into the powdered, snow-white sand. He took off at a brisk pace down the long narrow beach beside the looming cliffs. For a brief moment, he was able to lose himself in the enjoyment of his surroundings and replace thoughts of his nightmares with dreams of something better – dreams of rebuilding his city and maybe, just maybe, finding someone to share it with.

∽

An hour later, Destin walked back along the beach. Sweat soaked his shirt and he pulled it off. There was a secluded cove farther down the beach that he discovered on his second day on the planet. He would take a quick swim before heading back to Kali and Razor's house.

If he was lucky, Ami would be awake and waiting for him. His fourteen-month-old niece had taken a shine to him. It might have been all the toys he brought that put the hero worship in her eyes, but Destin didn't care. He had planned a new gift for each day of his stay. Mabel, one of the grandmotherly women that was with the rebellion from the beginning, suggested it.

Destin crossed the empty beach and entered a hole amidst the rocks that had been carved by centuries of wind and water. The narrow gap glistened with natural crystals found in the rocks. Lifting his hand, he ran the tips of his fingers along the rocks. The crystals lit up under his touch. He would love to take some back to Earth with him so he could study them.

His hand fell to his side when he reached the opening leading to the small cove. Out of habit, he glanced around to make sure the area was secure, then walked over to a large boulder protruding from the sand. He tossed his sweat-dampened shirt onto it and pushed his jogging pants down. He stepped out of his pants and shook the loose sand off before he placed them on the boulder next to his shirt. Afraid he might lose the medallion he wore, he slipped it over his head and slid it into the pocket of his pants. His hand ran along the waistband of the jockey shorts he wore, but he kept them on. Life had taught him to never get caught with his pants down. You never knew when you might have to fight, and doing it in the buff could be a little distracting.

Destin walked to the edge of the water and stood looking outward. The gentle waves rolled over his feet and he curled his toes into the wet sand. A smile curved his lips and he slowly walked forward until he was waist deep. Drawing in a deep breath, he dove under the incoming wave, enjoying the refreshing feel of the water as it washed the sweat from his skin and cooled his heated flesh.

His arms swept out in front of him and his legs moved in strong, powerful kicks. The water was crystal clear and he could see the ripples in the white sand along the bottom. He swam as far as he could before his lungs burned and he was forced to surface for a breath of air. He turned onto his back and floated, lost in thought. The peacefulness of the moment, combined with the beauty and freedom of just watching the clouds, pulled the last of the tension he had woken up with out of his body. For a little while, he was alone in the universe with nothing else to worry about.

∽

Jersula Ikera stomped across the soft sand in a foul mood. The thin, dark blue silk cover she wore clung to her lithe body and floated behind her. If anyone saw her from a distance, she would look like she was floating across the powdery white crystals that made up the sandy beach.

Her long white hair was unbound and blew around her. Her icy blue eyes flashed with an uncharacteristic fire and her pale blue lips were pressed into a firm line of irritation. She had come down to the beach to escape for a while, at least until she could find her center and restore the calm mask she relied on to interact with others.

A swift glance up and down the beach showed it was deserted. Jersula – Sula to her family and her few close friends – breathed a sigh of relief. She could mull over the orders she received early this morning in private. They were distressing, but she knew she needed to release some of the anger she was feeling if she wanted to get through the day without making a mistake that could devastate her career.

"Why? Why are they sending me to that horrible place again? Wasn't once enough? Who could I have angered so much that they would send me there again?" she muttered under her breath.

Her mind flashed to the dozens of people that could be responsible. She knew her icy reserve and sometimes blunt attitude had angered certain members of the Usoleum Council, but she was always right in her assessments! It wasn't her fault that most of the political members of the council were sweet, confused people who couldn't think their way out of a wormhole.

Sula glanced back at her transport to see how far she walked along the beach. Not far; it seemed that stomping wasn't the fastest way to travel.

The small transport glinted in the sunlight. It was given to her when she arrived on Rathon six weeks ago. She had hoped to be appointed the new ambassador between her people and the Trivators.

That hope was brutally crushed when her new orders arrived this morning before dawn.

"No, I have to return to that horrible, war-torn excuse for a planet brimming with savages! Those uncultured, hostile, brutal beasts who were ignorant of *any* life forms outside of Earth until a few years ago! They haven't even mastered space travel," she snarled under her breath in frustration before her footsteps slowed and she blinked back tears of annoyance. "That is what they are… ignorant beasts!"

Her anger boiled when she thought of her previous visit. The last time she had been to the primitive planet called Earth, her assignment was to assess the situation left by the previous ambassador who was killed, and it had been impossible to do anything when she received no support from the Trivators or the humans.

At the time, she was forced to wait two weeks before the Trivators would even allow her access to Councilor Badrick's starship. By the time she was finally allowed to board, the previous crew had been recalled, a new crew assigned, and all of Councilor Badrick's reports and personal files had vanished. The only things Sula was left with were a clueless crew, a Trivator named Cutter who had regarded her with suspicion, and a human male who had dismissed her with a look of contempt during their one and only meeting! It wasn't until much later that she unraveled the reasons behind the Trivator and human's animosity. Unable to blink back the tears of frustration this time, she lifted an impatient hand and brushed them away.

Sula had reported her initial findings on Badrick to the Council and her father, and within weeks of arriving on Earth, she was recalled to her home world, Usoleum. Believing she was being groomed to take over the Ambassador's position at the Alliance Headquarters, she had worked day and night on a variety of issues, but it had all been for naught. She had discovered a hidden cache of Badrick's files, and shortly after reporting the discovery, she was reassigned to Rathon. Here, she was to work with the Trivators to wring every bit of information possible from those files and to strengthen Usoleum's relationship with the Trivators after the damage wrought by Badrick's unconscionable behavior – a behavior that had mortified her family.

There were a large number of files to sift through, and in the meantime, she adhered to her assignment to grovel at the Trivators' feet for the past six weeks. It should have shown the Usoleum Council that she would make an excellent Ambassador to the Trivator Council here on their planet. But once again, her hopes were crushed. Sula was the only living Usoleum with experience on Earth, and she was now reassigned there to finish her original task, which is to clean up the mess Badrick left behind – almost two Earth years later! Her only hope for any kind of real success with the humans lay in parsing useful information from those files. To get even the slightest bit of trust and good will on Earth, she needed to be able to answer the question preying on everyone's mind: where were the rest of the missing human women?

Sula still had a couple of days left on Rathon, however, and part of reassuring the Trivators and the Alliance that everything was under control included attending some ceremony between a member of Chancellor Razor's family and a Trivator warrior. It would begin in a couple of hours, and if she was not able to gain control of her emotions before the ceremony, her career would be in even worse shape than it already was.

"This is an insult!" Sula hissed, discarding her maudlin misery in favor of the more empowering anger she felt earlier. "If Father thinks my brothers are so much better at diplomacy than I am, then one of them should be the one to attend the ceremony, not me! When they need a problem solved, they send me in to fix it. Father knows I am more than qualified for the ambassador position. Yet he gives the position to Sirius, the progeny who is least qualified. All Sirius wants to do is chase women that he couldn't do anything with and play at the gaming tables! He isn't even fit to be – to be – to care for the racers in the stables, much less be the Ambassador to the Trivators," Sula muttered with a slashing wave of her hand in the air.

Sula released a long sigh and stepped through the narrow chasm in the rocks. She gazed out at the water protected by the small cove for several seconds before she walked toward it, drawn to the soothing waves. She missed her world. It was mostly water and her people were born within its beautiful seas. They live on land, but the water is where they find solace.

Sula's hand moved to the tie of the gown and she released it. The garment fell to the sand around her feet. Her body was covered in a form-fitting dark blue suit made for the water. She spread her fingers and the fine membranes between them spread like small webs. Stepping forward, she relished the first touch of the water against her skin. Pleasure coursed through her, cooling her fury and soothing her despair.

Her gaze scanned the water. The waves broke against the reef almost two hundred meters offshore. It would be a short swim for her, but she could do it several times before she had to return to her temporary lodging to prepare for the ceremony. Sula slowly walked forward until she was deep enough to sink down below the surface.

The two almost invisible slits along her neck opened and she drew water into her gills. The refreshing liquid filled the second set of lungs with life-giving fluid, extracting the oxygen trapped in the water into her blood when she exhaled. She loved living and working near an ocean. A shudder went through her when she thought of her next assignment. It was so far from the large oceans that covered most of Earth. There was a long, narrow lake, but it wasn't the same. She would have to make periodic trips to the coast to satisfy her body's craving for the salty water.

And I'll need to swim frequently to keep from killing that arrogant human male if he is still there, Sula thought. *Perhaps I will be lucky and he will already be dead, and a more reasonable human will have replaced him.*

Remorse swept through her at her hateful thoughts. It was so unlike her. She hated the idea of hurting anything or anyone. Her six older brothers teased her, saying that was why it was ridiculous that she would even consider becoming a member of the Alliance Council.

Sula pushed the negative thoughts away. She would lose herself in the pleasures of the ocean around her. Pushing off the bottom, her body cut through the crystal-clear liquid like a laser cutter through steel. All around her, colorful fish and plant life flourished in a world few could appreciate.

The cove was protected from the larger marine life that lived on the other side of the reef. She had researched Rathon's oceanographic environment and decided it would be best to stay within the protected barriers that sheltered the coast line. 'Nature's unique fencing' is the way Sula liked to think of it.

She was starting to feel more herself, more collected, but a wave of longing swept through her to just let go, to be wild for a few unadulterated minutes – not the frazzled, bitter release from the beach, but something… untouchable. To hell with her father's belief that she wasn't capable of dealing with the stress of being a leading member of the Usoleum Council or an integral part of the Alliance. She knew she could if she was given the opportunity.

Closing her eyes, she twisted until she was facing upward and allowed her body to slowly sink to the bottom. She relaxed her arms and a serene smile curved her lips. Maybe she would just forget about the ceremony and stay here all day. It wasn't as if it really mattered if she attended. No one, especially the Trivator male and his human mate, would even miss her.

Finally, the peace that Sula was searching for settled over her. Her body floated above the soft white sand. The light from the rising sun created shafts of glittering beams that reflected off the silver threads in her bodysuit and made them sparkle like diamonds. She was unaware of how ethereal she looked against the satin bottom of the ocean, or the fact that she wasn't alone.

Chapter 2

Destin dove beneath the waves and began swimming toward shore. As much as he hated it, he needed to get back to the house. He had promised Ami that he would make her some mouse-shaped pancakes this morning just like he used to do for her mommy.

He swam only a short distance when he caught a glimpse of something sparkling under the water. Surfacing, he glanced around with a frown before he took a deep breath and dove back down. He blinked when he saw the body of a young woman floating along the bottom. His heart thundered in dismay. He had seen enough death in his lifetime. The beautiful woman floating serenely near the bottom was too young to face such a fate.

Kicking downward with hard, powerful strokes, he reached for her.

His eyes burned from the salt water, but he refused to close them. He grabbed her arm and quickly pulled her against his hard length, then changed his grip to hold her more securely around the waist as his feet pushed off the bottom.

Her slender hands clutched his bare shoulders, and her brilliant, light blue eyes snapped open. Destin and the woman locked gazes in mutual shock. Her delicate, pale blue lips parted, and Destin was afraid she would instinctively draw in a mouthful of water. Unsure of what else to do, he covered her lips with his. The moment his lips touched hers, a wave of heat swept through him and he couldn't help but wonder if he had captured a real, live siren.

Destin knew he should release her – or at least her lips – when they surfaced, but the fire that had ignited when he had pressed his lips to hers appeared to have short-circuited that part of his brain. She was not helping his resolve, either. Her hands tightened on his shoulders, but she didn't push him away and her soft lips trembled slightly as her breath mingled with his. It took several seconds before he finally forced his body to obey his command to stop. He reluctantly lifted his head, but still kept her firmly pressed against him.

"Are you okay?" he asked, blinking to clear his eyes of the salt water.

"I… You… Of course, I'm… You!" the woman sputtered before her eyes widened in recognition. "You aren't supposed to be here!"

Destin's lips curved up at the corners. "Where am I supposed to be?" he asked with a raised eyebrow, studying her face with a growing sense of dismay. "I know you…," he started to say.

"You should be back on that horrid, barbaric world," the woman snapped, pushing against his shoulders. "Release me!"

Recognition hit Destin hard. His arms slackened enough that the woman – Jersula Ikera – was able to pull away from him. She pushed at the water to put some space between them, her light blue eyes flashing with fire. This was a much different woman than the one he had briefly met back on Earth. This one was…. The sudden image of a siren flashed through his mind.

Trouble, he thought with a grimace, twisting around and striking out for the shore. The moment he was in shallow enough water to put his feet down, he did. He wanted to put as much distance as possible between him and the Usoleum Councilor he met back on Earth.

He ran the back of his hand across his heated lips. He could still taste her. It was a good thing his back was to her, otherwise she would notice the physical evidence of his reaction to her. It suddenly occurred to him that she would have been aware of it when she was pressed against him.

Damn it! Well, he wasn't going to remind her by giving her a second look. He was sure that would thrill her even more – not.

Destin muttered a string of expletives under his breath as he exited the water. He strode across the beach, passing the film of dark blue material lying against the white sand. He kept his back to her while he grabbed his jogging pants and pulled them on with stiff fingers. He ran his fingers through his soaked hair. The dark brown strands were cut into a short, military style and would dry soon enough.

Destin grabbed his T-shirt off the boulder. It was still damp from his run and he decided it wasn't worth pulling it on. He drew in a deep, calming breath and slowly released it before turning around to make sure Jersula had made it back to shore. He would feel pretty rotten if she drowned while he was trying to hide the major hard-on he had. He could just see himself trying to explain that to Razor and the Trivator council!

A frustrated groan escaped him when he saw her emerge from the water in the form-fitting blue material that left very little to the imagination. Destin's gaze froze on the twin peaks of her nipples pressing against the fabric, and he swallowed hard. They were hard pebbles, perfect for....

"It has been too damn long since I've been with a woman," he muttered under his breath.

He forced his eyes back to her face. His lips quirked up at the corners when he saw her eyes were still shooting indignant sparks. She looked a hell of a lot different than she did when he first met her. He found her fascinating then, too, which hadn't helped his temper during their one and only meeting.

Her long silky white hair, glacier blue eyes, and unusual blue lips had made it difficult to look away. She was an ethereal ice queen. At the time, he was furious with himself for reacting like that to an alien. He had thought she must have been cast in the same mold as Badrick, but the woman angrily snatching up the silky fabric off the sand was anything but icy. He remembered her heated breaths and the softness of her lips.

She clutched the fabric in front of her and her long legs cut across the loose crystals, quickly closing the distance between them. He couldn't help but notice that her hair was the same color as the sparkling sand. Her cheeks were a slightly darker blue than before and matched the deep color of her eyes. He would have to remember that when she was angry, her eyes changed to the color of the ocean back home.

She was breathing heavily by the time she stopped in front of him. His gaze swept over her face, noticing the strand of hair stuck to her cheek. Without thinking, he tenderly brushed it back.

"I'm glad you are alright. When I first saw you floating along the bottom, I feared you were dead," he murmured.

Sula's lips parted in surprise. She swallowed and lifted her hand to touch her cheek, pausing when she felt his hand hovering near it.

"Why… Why did you kiss me?" she asked softly.

Destin dropped his hand to his side and he glanced over her shoulder to the ocean behind her. In his mind, the countless faces of those he had to bury over the years superimposed over her face as she lay so still under the water. He didn't look at her when he replied.

"I thought you had drowned. When I touched you, you opened your eyes and I saw your lips part. I was afraid that you would inhale water and choke. It was the only way I could think of to protect you," he replied with a shrug. "Anyway, I'm glad you are okay. I apologize if I offended you. It wasn't intentional. I've got to go," he said in a stiff tone.

"I…," Sula started to say, but her voice faded when he turned and started to walk away. "Human… Destin!"

Sula's soft voice called out behind him before he had gone more than a few strides. Destin slowed to a stop and partially turned to look back at the alien ice queen who had captured his attention over a year ago. He waited for her to speak again. She swallowed and lifted her chin.

"Thank you," she said. "... for trying to save me, even though it was not necessary."

Destin bowed his head in acknowledgement and turned away. As ghosts from his past rose up to choke him, he knew he needed to put some space between them. Sula was alive, not dead like so many others he had been responsible for. Over the past year, he had worked hard on learning to control the haunting thoughts that often tried to drown him. There were too many would've, could've, should've moments over the last seven years that could never be changed. Dwelling on those memories did nothing but pull him into a deep abyss that threatened to suffocate him.

Sula was in no danger at all and that should be the end of it. There was no reason to keep touching her. It threw him off balance that he had this aching need to feel her lithe body against his again, regardless of whether he had a reason or not.

This reaction was much more intense than the first time he saw her. At that time, he was still reeling from everything that had happened – Colbert's death, Kali being wounded and leaving the planet, the loss of the men who had fought beside him, and the realization that he now had what he wanted – Chicago to rebuild. That, on top of discovering how many women and young girls were kidnapped from Earth for the Usoleum Councilor's greed, made his physical attraction to the new Councilor too much to deal with at the time.

Destin focused on the narrow gap in the rocks in front of him. The moment he was on the other side, he broke into a fast jog. He didn't stop until he reached the back gate to Kali and Razor's home.

∼

When Sula had called out to him, her gaze was focused on the maze of scars across his back. When he half turned, she noticed more on his thick arms and chest, but it was the one on his left cheek that had briefly frozen the words on her lips. Her fingers had ached to trace it. What happened to him back on the planet he called home?

She didn't move until he had disappeared. Glancing down, she shook out the silk cover and slipped it back on. A frown creased her brow when she saw a necklace in the sand near the boulder where Destin Parks had retrieved his clothes.

She walked over to it and picked it up. Her fingers brushed the sand from the small oval disk. Strange symbols, written in the language of the humans, were engraved on the front of it. The medallion appeared to be able to slide apart. Unsure if she should try to see what was inside or not, Sula bit her lip and looked back in the direction Destin had disappeared.

"What harm can it do?" she murmured with a shrug.

It took her a moment to figure out how to work the slide. A tiny catch held it closed. Once the catch was released, the rectangular metal piece slid open. On the side facing her was the image of a young, dark-haired little girl smiling back at her. Frowning, she turned the piece over and saw another image, this one slightly faded. It was of an older woman. She had the same dark hair and shining eyes of the little girl – and of Destin. A series of numbers were etched into the back of the medallion.

Sula knew this must be Destin's family. She carefully closed the piece and pushed the catch back into place. The long, leather cord had a clasp at the end. Destin must have taken it off before he went for a swim.

Her gaze moved back out to the water. For a moment, she could feel his lips against hers and his strong hands on her waist. Her eyelashes fluttered down and a soft moan escaped her when she remembered his body against hers. She had never felt such a reaction to a male before and it shocked her. Especially given who he was and how he had reacted to her when they first met. It was surreal.

Sula lifted the necklace and fastened it around her neck. She had no pockets and didn't want to take a chance of losing it. She would find out where Destin was staying and have a courier deliver it to him. She went through the gap in the rocks and retraced her earlier steps, this time at a slower pace. Her fingers trembled slightly when she lifted them to touch the medallion.

"Well, now I know that Destin Parks did not die back on his planet.

What I would like to know is why he is here on Rathon," she whispered, staring down the long beach. "And will he be staying here or returning to his world?"

A growing sense of urgency filled her the closer she got to her transport. She needed answers. It might take her a while to find them, but she was very tenacious. She wouldn't stop until she found out what she wanted to know about a certain human male.

Destin's Hold

TAKING ON TORY

THIS NOVELLA IS FREE!

What happens when a centuries-old werewolf discovers he isn't the only creature who loves to bite?

"What have you found?" Simon asked as Youssef walked into the elegant office.

"Nothing," Youssef replied in frustration. "There was nothing on the cameras. It was as if they were never there!"

"You said the surveillance system was operational," Simon bit out, turning away from the window to the glare at his friend and chief of security.

Youssef ran his hand over the back of his neck as he frowned. "It is," he muttered. "Every movement along the street was recorded. The time-date stamp showed the exact moment they should have shown up on the camera. Everything is there. Hell, I watched a squirrel play in the damn tree they were standing under and nothing. They weren't there!"

Simon growled dangerously. Two nights until the full moon and the only female the beast inside him wanted was the one he saw yesterday. He would have to be locked up in the special room in the basement if he couldn't find and convince the woman to stay with him. He would lose control of the beast otherwise and that could prove to be deadly to everyone, including Youssef.

He turned back toward the huge set of windows looking out over the long driveway. A white van was pulling in. As it followed the curve in the driveway, he made out the name of the company he had employed to find the exact furnishings he required for his new home.

Alexandru Carson of *Magic Furnishings* had managed to find all of the pieces he had requested so far. Simon wondered if the mysterious entrepreneur could find the woman he had seen yesterday. It appeared to be a task beyond his security chief's ability.

A moment of regret washed through him as he admonished himself for being so hard on his friend. It was not Youssef's fault the camera was defective. His friend had spent years protecting him. In fact, he bore the scars from it across his chest when Simon had lost control one night and almost killed one of the gardeners who had returned after dark when he was running.

"Replace the..." Simon's voice died as the door to the van opened. He watched with disbelief as the woman currently on his mind stepped out of the driver's seat.

"Simon!" Youssef called out in surprise as Simon turned and rushed by him. He glanced back and forth from the window to the open door before he cursed again and turned to follow Simon. "I really do hate it when he does that."

~

Tory carefully folded the papers and slid them back into the envelope. The guards at the front gate were some of the strangest people she had ever met. They acted as if she was trying to steal the furniture instead of delivering it!

She shut the door to the van and looked up at the house. It was beautiful in a huge, I-want-to-bury-a-dead-body-in-it, kind of way. She had seen pictures of houses like this. It reminded her of the houses from the vampire movie she had watched on television a couple months ago.

She rolled her eyes as she walked up the steps to the front door. The actors had been really good, and really hot to look at, but they had gotten the whole vampire thing wrong. Hell, when the little girl had turned to ash, Tory had laughed so hard she had almost wet her pants. Then, there was the other one where they were supposed to be all sparkly in the sun!

"Not unless I took a bath in glitter," she muttered as she raised her hand to knock on the massive door. "Damn, Hugo would love to have a set of these on his house," she muttered as she thought of the gentle giant that lived off of Dust Bowl and Redwood back home.

"Who is Hugo?" The male who opened the door demanded.

"What?" Tory squeaked in surprise. She hadn't heard him walking to the door, so when it opened it had surprised her.

"Who is Hugo?" The male demanded again. "Is he your boyfriend or husband?"

Tory tilted her head and frowned. Great! She came all the way to Charleston to meet... a werewolf! As if she didn't have enough of those running around back home.

She wiggled her nose at the distinctive scent. She refused to admit he smelled a hell of a lot better than Maverick. Still, she didn't want to meet another werewolf! She wanted to meet a cute human man, preferably, one with Type A-positive blood! It was the only one she could safely drink.

"No, Hugo isn't my boyfriend or husband. He's just a g... guy I know. I'm here to deliver some furniture for Mr. Drayton. Can you let him know? I'll need some help carrying it in, as well," she added, folding her arms as the tall male continued to stare at her. "Please."

She decided she better add the last part for good customer service. She didn't really need help moving it. She could shrink the stuff and enlarge it when she got it inside, but she had promised her mom, dad, Nonny, Gramps, Alexandru, and half of the town of Magic that she wouldn't do anything 'different' in front of ANYONE while she was gone.

Tory sighed. *That might mean biting on a Type A-positive neck is a no-no, but I can enjoy a guy's company without biting him.*

"What is your name?" The man demanded.

Tory bit her lip to prevent the word Elvira from popping out. She didn't think he would appreciate her reference to the 1980's Mistress of the Dark. Instead, she slowly looked over the man standing between her and a night out on the town, all on her own. He was tall and handsome with thick blond hair pulled back at his nape. The dark suit he was wearing emphasized the muscles under it. He had a wide chest, narrow waist, and… a blush rose over her cheeks at the bulge in the front.

Okay, eyes to the face, she muttered silently. *Werewolves! I swear they are the horniest creatures in the world!*

She rolled her eyes again. That was why Maverick, Mitch, Hanson, and Jude were never allowed to do track, swimming, or wrestling. Well, they weren't allowed to do track after they chased down Edgar and cornered him.

No, their constant state of arousal, once they hit puberty, made it difficult for them to play certain sports. They were great at football and basketball. Their pack mentality made them great out on the field or court.

"Tory Carson," she said, pursing her lips together. "Are you like the butler or something? Can you give me a hand with the furniture?"

"I'm…" Simon started to say when a low rumble escaped him when the woman in front of him tilted sideways and smiled at Youssef.

"Hi! Are you Mr. Drayton?" she said in a hopeful tone. "I have your furniture."

"I am Youssef," the dark male replied with an amused smile.

"I am Simon Drayton," the blond male said in a deep, gruff voice.

Tory's eyes swiveled back from the dark brown eyes glittering with amusement to the dark blue eyes that were not – glittering with amusement, that is. The smile on her lips curved downward. She hoped she hadn't just blown Alexandru's business with this guy. From what her brother had told her last night, it was an extremely profitable one.

"Uh… Yes… Well… I've got your furniture," Tory said with a bright smile. "I guess since you're not the butler, you wouldn't want to help bring it in, huh?"

Simon's lips twitched at the hopeful look in the young woman's dark brown eyes. He literally wanted to bury his hands in her hair, drag her against him, and see if she tasted as good as she looked. His fingers clenched as he fought the urge.

He had three days! Three days to make her so mindless that all she wanted was to feel him buried inside her. The twitch turned into an easy smile. If she were anything like the other women, she would be eating out of his hand in less than twenty minutes.

He grabbed her hand as she lifted it to push a strand of hair back behind her ear and pulled it to his lips. Pressing a kiss to the back of it, he couldn't resist letting the tip of his tongue caress the soft skin. Pleasure washed through him as he pulled back to give her a look of invitation.

Doubt flashed through him when he saw her nose wiggle and she tugged her hand out of his. She gave him an uncertain, lopsided smile as she rubbed the back of her hand along the leg of her jeans. He straightened when he heard Youssef clear his throat behind him.

"Youssef will see to the furniture," Simon said in a dark voice filled with warning toward his friend. "Follow me."

"Follow... I... Shouldn't I help him? I mean, isn't that what I'm supposed to do?" Tory asked in confusion when Simon Drayton turned and started to walk away. "Isn't that what a delivery person does here? That's what they do back home."

Youssef gave Tory a reassuring smile. "I will arrange for the furniture to be brought in, Miss Carson," he said with a bow.

Tory glanced toward Simon, who was standing stiffly, watching her with a frown. She bit her lip. If she had a choice between going with a sour-faced werewolf or staying with a... she sniffed. She almost groaned when her mouth watered.

"What blood type are you?" she asked suddenly, looking at Youssef with wide eyes.

Taking on Tory

ADDITIONAL BOOKS AND INFORMATION

If you loved this story by me (S.E. Smith) please leave a review! You can also take a look at additional books and sign up for my newsletter to hear about my latest releases at:

http://sesmithfl.com
http://sesmithya.com

or keep in touch using the following links:

http://sesmithfl.com/?s=newsletter
https://www.facebook.com/se.smith.5
https://twitter.com/sesmithfl
http://www.pinterest.com/sesmithfl/
http://sesmithfl.com/blog/
http://www.sesmithromance.com/forum/

The Full Booklist

Science Fiction / Romance

Cosmos' Gateway Series
Tilly Gets Her Man (Prequel)
Tink's Neverland (Book 1)
Hannah's Warrior (Book 2)
Tansy's Titan (Book 3)
Cosmos' Promise (Book 4)
Merrick's Maiden (Book 5)
Core's Attack (Book 6)
Saving Runt (Book 7)

Curizan Warrior Series
Ha'ven's Song (Book 1)

Dragon Lords of Valdier Series
Abducting Abby (Book 1)
Capturing Cara (Book 2)
Tracking Trisha (Book 3)
Dragon Lords of Valdier Boxset Books 1-3
Ambushing Ariel (Book 4)
For the Love of Tia Novella (Book 4.1)
Cornering Carmen (Book 5)
Paul's Pursuit (Book 6)
Twin Dragons (Book 7)
Jaguin's Love (Book 8)
The Old Dragon of the Mountain's Christmas (Book 9)
Pearl's Dragon Novella (Book 10)
Twin Dragons' Destiny (Book 11)

Marastin Dow Warriors Series
A Warrior's Heart Novella

Dragonlings of Valdier Novellas
A Dragonling's Easter
A Dragonling's Haunted Halloween
A Dragonling's Magical Christmas
Night of the Demented Symbiots (Halloween 2)

The Dragonlings' Very Special Valentine

Lords of Kassis Series
River's Run (Book 1)
Star's Storm (Book 2)
Jo's Journey (Book 3)
Rescuing Mattie Novella (Book 3.1)
Ristéard's Unwilling Empress (Book 4)

Sarafin Warriors Series
Choosing Riley (Book 1)
Viper's Defiant Mate (Book 2)

The Alliance Series
Hunter's Claim (Book 1)
Razor's Traitorous Heart (Book 2)
Dagger's Hope (Book 3)
The Alliance Boxset Books 1-3
Challenging Saber (Book 4)
Destin's Hold (Book 5)
Edge of Insanity (Book 6)

Zion Warriors Series
Gracie's Touch (Book 1)
Krac's Firebrand (Book 2)

Magic, New Mexico Series
Touch of Frost (Book 1)

Paranormal / Fantasy / Romance

Magic, New Mexico Series
Taking on Tory (Book 2)
Alexandru's Kiss (Book 3)

Spirit Pass Series

Indiana Wild (Book 1)
Spirit Warrior (Book 2)

Second Chance Series
Lily's Cowboys (Book 1)
Touching Rune (Book 2)

More Than Human Series
Ella and the Beast (Book 1)

The Seven Kingdoms
The Dragon's Treasure (Book 1)
The Sea King's Lady (Book 2)
A Witch's Touch (Book 3)

The Fairy Tale Series
The Beast Prince Novella
*Free Audiobook of The Beast Prince is available: https://soundcloud.com/sesmithfl/sets/the-beast-prince-the-fairy-tale-series

Epic Science Fiction / Action Adventure

Project Gliese 581G Series
Command Decision (Book 1)
First Awakenings (Book 2)
Survival Skills (Book 3)

New Adult

Breaking Free Series
Capture of the Defiance (Book 2)

Young Adult

Breaking Free Series

Voyage of the Defiance (Book 1)

The Dust Series
Dust: Before and After (Book 1)
Dust: A New World Order (Book 2)

Recommended Reading Order Lists:

http://sesmithfl.com/reading-list-by-events/
http://sesmithfl.com/reading-list-by-series/

ABOUT THE AUTHOR

S.E. Smith is an ***Internationally Acclaimed, Award-Winning, New York Times and USA TODAY Bestselling*** author of science fiction, romance, fantasy, paranormal, and contemporary works for adults, young adults, and children. She enjoys writing a wide variety of genres that pull her readers into worlds that take them away.

Printed in Great Britain
by Amazon